Spirals of Destiny

Book One:

RIDER

Elizabeth,
Always strive to be your best!
I hope you enjoy.
R. B.
11/11/2013

Jim Bernheim

Gryphonwood

Also by Jim Bernheimer:

Horror, Humor, and Heroes

Dead Eye: Pennies for the Ferryman

Gryphonwood Press

Published by Gryphonwood Press
www.gryphonwoodpress.com

Cover art by Fiona Hsieh
http://chaoslavawolf.deviantart.com

ISBN: 0-9825087-6-X
ISBN 13:   978-0-9825087-6-3
Printed in the United States of America
First printing: May, 2010

Dedication

First, I'd like to thank my wife and daughters for their patience during the writing of this book. I love you three so much.

Next comes my publisher, David Wood and my cover artist, Fiona Hsieh. A great story won't reach the bookshelves without a publisher that believes in the plot and few will bother looking at it without exceptional cover art. Thank you both.

Now comes my chance to thank all those who donated their time by reading the rough drafts and providing me valuable feedback. The members of the Pendulum writing group on the Permuted Press forums (Bobbie Metevier, Matthew Baugh, Frank Farrar, John Oliver, John Harper, Rakie Keig, and Zombie Zak) lead the pack with their front to back critiques of Rider. I look forward to seeing each and every one of you in print.

Then there are the "usual suspects" consisting of Ted Vinzani, Matthew and Lindsey Schocke, Brian Albright, Dave Bagini, Sean Melton, Chris Gibson, Moses, Noel Lacaillade, Benny, and Chuck all pitched in. Special thanks to Heather Sinclair, Anne Walsh, and Holly Root-Gutteridge for helping me with the teenaged female mindset. A special nod goes to a real life Kayleigh (Wright not Reese, but close enough) for her assistance.

I'd also like to thank all my readers. You're the people who've brought me this far.

Chapter 1 – The Cracked Horn

A jolt of energy coursed through Majherri's body, nearly sending the unicorn down onto the sand. Staggering, he felt the ocean water cresting over his hooves. The human girl, who had touched him, had collapsed in a heap into the water and was shaking her head. She was likely trying to understand what just happened and she wasn't alone.

It was the Bondspark, something Majherri thought he'd never experience again! No unicorn before him had ever survived losing their rider. Somehow, Majherri had and now his life had meaning again. Part of him rejoiced at making a connection with another human. At the same time, he felt an ominous sense of fear building deep in his soul.

The clatter of his hooves, the sound of wheels turning, and the ever-present chatter of humans: Majherri preferred the noise. Silence invariably allowed the echoes of Danella's final screams to invade his mind. She commanded him to run to safety and warn everyone. The words were still there, but the images were lost.

Ahead lay yet another small town, filled with hands wanting to caress him. Those hands were attached to young girls praying for a connection to him and the chance to become a battle maiden. If he could make those noises humans use to speak, he'd tell them to be careful what they wished for.

Not that they'd listen. The younglings, the other riderless unicorns, were just as foolish. They stared at the missing tip of his horn, the crack running down it, and the mysterious scars on his left side. Then, they would ignore anything he said. Deep down, he knew they thought that his fate couldn't happen to them. Majherri's greatest problem was that he couldn't even tell them what occurred.

Within days, he stopped conversing with the younglings.

Along the road, some of the locals, children with a few adult minders, followed the caravan's progress. They pointed at him and his brethren, and threw flowers to the selectees from the previous towns.

"They're so beautiful! Mother, can I try and pet them now?" One of the girls shrieked and tugged at her mother's arm.

The mother chided her daughter. "Laura, you have to wait until the battle maidens bring the procession into town. The candidates go first and then you'll have to wait your turn in line with the other children."

"But I don't want to wait in line!"

"Perhaps you should have thought of that before you insisted that we come out here."

Majherri listened to the young girl whine about the unfairness of it all. In days past, he would have run over and let her stroke him briefly, basking in the attention. T'rsa, his sister, teased him about being such a prideful and rebellious member of the herd.

She hadn't done that in almost a year.

His apathy bothered her, but Majherri couldn't work up the interest to care. Most in this expedition and the others back at the Sacred Isle avoided close contact with him. He was a pariah, an oddity, and an example of something to be avoided at all costs. His was a fate worse than death!

Summoning a bit of his old courage, Majherri made his way to the surprised humans and presented himself. The one called Laura immediately reached out and touched his face. Majherri felt no magical connection and did his best to tolerate the rough caress. Even the mother reached over and rested her hand on his side.

"Look at the scars, Mother!"

"Laura, you shouldn't say that!"

Majherri snorted and backed away from the pair. Flipping his mane and tail in anger, he trotted to catch up to the rest of the caravan.

Typical! I try and grant a child her wish and that is my reward.

The group came to a halt in the center of the town amid cheers. Even in his state, the festive atmosphere nearly got to him. For a moment, he felt like prancing, but the moment, like so many others, passed without action on his part.

T'rsa's rider, Meghan Lynch, gracefully slid from the saddle. Tall and lithe, she was one of the school's instructors and recruiters. Fine, lightweight armor protected the brown-haired woman. She removed her open-faced helm and carried it in the crook of her arm.

Majherri watched the town elders greet and fawn over Captain Lynch. Not only was she T'rsa's rider, but also Danella's twin sister. Other than the darker hair coloring, they were identical! Every time he looked at her, he felt ashamed that he'd outlived his rider. There was little doubt in her words and her actions that she blamed Majherri for Danella's death.

The bitter resentment ran deep on both sides. He no longer cared for Captain Meghan Lynch. His sister could have chosen better! If Danella had accepted the commission and become a teacher, Meghan and T'rsa would still be scouts and Danella would likely be alive.

Lynch addressed the crowd of humans as the wagon drivers and guards set up the bales of hay and practice targets for the demonstration. His eyes lingered on a breastplate scarred by flame. It was a bittersweet reminder of his past. The Captain spoke of the benefits of becoming a battle maiden and joining the High-King's elite unicorn cavalry; the strongest force in the land. The humans lapped it up as a feline would milk from a cow. She explained how any girl selected would learn to tap into the magical energy stored inside the bonded unicorn and be able to perform magic from one of the four elements.

Naturally, the sounds from the crowd grew in intensity when the shiny coins were mentioned. The family of any girl chosen would receive a substantial amount of these. Majherri often wondered about the fascination with these small circles of gold and silver that most humans seemed obsessed with.

Danella tried to explain it to him once, but he kept blowing his breath onto her neck to tickle her until she gave up, laughing at his silliness. A poignant stab of pain accompanied that otherwise happy memory.

Feigning interest in the demonstration that followed, he was sorely tempted to trot over to the line of young girls separated from the crowd with the floral wreathes around their heads and let them touch him. It was the same one performed in place after place. Instead, the unicorn gazed at the clouds above and looked for any positive signs in the blue sky.

Time passed and a voice interrupted his searching. "Majherri, go and take your place. Don't upset Meghan any more than she already is." The voice belonged to an earth maiden, an officer named Lindsey Sheppard. She rode Pasha, a whimsical female that seemed to be paying an unusual amount of attention to him as of late. A few strides away, Captain Lynch scowled at him as the riderless younglings were already in a line.

The performance is over. Time, once more, to shatter the dreams of female humans.

Hanging his head in shame, Majherri walked toward the three younger unicorns and stood at the end of the line. T'rsa snorted and kicked some dirt on him with one of her hind legs, expressing her displeasure.

The first candidate approached. She was a hesitant blonde. She caressed Lycenae's mane for three or four strokes before the young male unicorn stepped back and away from her. She stepped to Sage, but the female too rejected the young human. Majherri scolded himself for not stepping into the first spot in line; this one was going to be a crier. He could tell by the way the girl's lips trembled. Drucene rejected her too and he spotted the first signs of tears starting.

As the girl reached out for him, Majherri closed his eyes and searched his feelings for any reaction from his dormant magic. There was nothing, not even the faintest stirring. He opened his eyes and looked at the hopeful girl still petting him and shook his head, pushing her away.

It was painful to watch the barely teenaged girl sobbing into the arms of her father, who offered meaningless words of comfort. Danella told him that they always focused on the ones that are selected and rarely was any consideration given to those found wanting. Majherri considered how crushing it must be to a young female's pride. The three excited younglings next to him had no idea the damage they were inflicting on these emotionally volatile young women.

His new found sympathy was a direct result of losing his own rider.

More hands tried to touch him and were led away. Two bore the rejection stoically, but the third was another crier. Drucene made a connection with a fair haired girl and pranced around her happily as the humans roared in applause. There was always a sense of pride in the towns and villages when one of their own was selected.

Six more females tried to join their comrade before Lycenae chose his rider, who turned to her parents and smiled. "I knew it! Didn't I tell you that I'd be chosen?"

Oblivious to the ceremony, the parents rushed forward and fawned over their offspring, a girl named Rebekah. Again, Majherri wished he had been at the front of the line, just to reject her out of principle. As he well knew, too much pride and arrogance was a bad thing. Majherri didn't particularly care for Lycenae, so he decided the pair deserved each other.

There were five more candidates, but none managed to garner any reaction from Sage or Majherri. Still, the town was overjoyed to have two selections. T'rsa continued to ignore him and Rheyssurah shot him a look of pity and mistrust, moving closer to his sister to comfort her. Rheyssurah never sought his approval, not that Majherri would have given it. It was one of the few things that still could penetrate the numbness in his soul.

Majherri considered expressing his disapproval, right then and there, but opted to leave. He once had status, but now had none. The maidens invited females of all ages to come get a brief touch of the unicorns.

I already tried that once today, and was not satisfied with the results. I've had my fill of this!

In defiance, he walked off. Lynch barked at him, but he swished his tail at her dismissively. Lieutenant Sheppard interceded and sent Pasha after him. He could easily lose her. Pasha served in a combat brigade and wasn't a scout, but he tolerated her presence and headed toward the ocean. The heady smell of the sea enticed him. Before being promoted to Lead Senior Scout and transferred to the Western Battalion, much of his and Danella's time was spent along the southern coast. His rider loved watching the relaxed might of nature as the waves pounding the shoreline.

Slowly, he wandered through the empty streets, looking for anything that interested him in the windows of the human shops and for an access to the ocean. After about ten minutes of searching, he spotted the path to the beach and made his way down it. All the while, he felt close to Danella and wondered if she was smiling down on him from the great pastures in the sky.

Part of him wished he had never staggered out of that western desert bearing wounds both physical and emotional. He'd warned the Greater Herd and scouts scoured the area, looking for signs, but the steppes were massive, and the shifting sands left no traces. If only he could remember what happened. With no bond, Danella was declared dead and they waited for Majherri to die from the wasting.

When he did not, they had the human oracle examine him. She said to send him out to search for a new rider.

Pushing his hooves into the sand, he tried to enjoy the feeling and stave off the bitterness. Danella wouldn't want to see him like this! Majherri noticed a sound that was almost hidden beneath the noise of the waves. It was the sound of a human female crying.

For once, could I go somewhere without these crying humans plaguing me?

Danella was made of sterner stuff. Rather than wait for a water maiden to come along with healing tears, she simply ripped an arrow out of her flesh, applied her flame to cauterize the wound, and rejoined the battle. Unlike her sister, Danella didn't mind the scars and boasted that they proved she was alive.

Majherri now bore several scars of his own. He felt anything but alive. The unicorn debated the options available to him, but the human already was staring in his direction. He could just trot away. The girl was older than the candidates with blondish hair that looked like the harsh sunlight made it lighter than it should be. The garments she wore were nice by human standards. She seemed to be conscious of her grooming. It was a good trait, at least the unicorn supposed.

The girl isn't one of my would-be suitors. At least I'm not the cause of her tears.

He somehow felt better with that knowledge as she wiped her eyes and addressed him.

"It's beautiful, isn't it?" she said. "I come here and just watch the waves when I'm sad."

Majherri nodded and turned to gaze into the horizon and watch the gulls circling in the distance.

"I'll leave if you want to be alone," the human put forward. The sniffle in her voice said otherwise, but since she was trying to be courteous, he looked back and moved his head sideways in a noncommittal gesture. If she kept talking, he might take her up on that offer.

A blissful minute of silence followed before the human spoke once more, "I watched the demonstration, but couldn't bear to watch the selection. I heard the crowd cheer twice. I suppose it's too much to ask that Rebekah Morganstern wasn't chosen. She's such a spiteful brat."

The human is a fair judge of character. He regarded her and tried to figure out how best to break the news. Unicorns understood the human language, but it didn't work the other way.

"She was, wasn't she?"

He nodded.

The young woman's face flushed. Majherri guessed in anger. "She had the nerve to say that I shouldn't be allowed to attend the festival and called me impure of all things! Oh, I'm sorry! You didn't come here to listen to my problems."

He nodded again. His hopes that she'd still her tongue were dashed as she took this as a sign that she should talk about him.

"You've been in a serious scrap haven't you? I knew unicorns were tough! I bet your rider must be proud. What? What did I say? I'm sorry! Don't go!"

She'd been standing on his right side and hadn't noticed the scars, as he circled behind her, she saw his left side and gasped, "Oh no! You didn't win that fight."

Majherri couldn't summon the strength to lie and avoided her gaze. Pathetically, he glanced out at the ocean and partly wished for a giant wave to come and drag him out to sea, finishing him. At that moment, he'd have welcomed the release. The noise he made was unnatural for a unicorn. It was a primal cry of pain. The human responded to it and threw her arms around his neck.

That's when the magic inside him stirred. His bond to Danella had been a rising surge of magic. This was a violent release of pent up heat and energy; something restrained that finally snapped and broke free. To say he was both shocked and worried was an understatement.

Chapter 2 – The Girl in Poor Standing

"People of Helden, I bring you greetings from High-King Barris. Today, we are here to see if any of your young maidens can bond with our remaining unicorns. They will judge you and if you are deemed worthy, you will be asked to join our elite ranks. If you are selected, your family will be paid two hundred gold coins for their permission to take you with us."

Kayleigh Reese, packed into the crowd of people, watched in awe. There were so many unicorns all in one spot! Every few months, a scout would pass through Helden on patrol, and perhaps even stay the night at the inn. They were mesmerizing! Mother, lost in her latest sculpture, couldn't be bothered to come see them and gave Kayleigh the impression that she shouldn't be wasting her time either, but she'd never seen a demonstration before.

The lead battle maiden continued, "Even should you be selected, you will want to think long and hard on your decision. Becoming a battle maiden is not a choice one makes lightly. Some that are chosen will not be able to endure the rigors of training. The bond can break, never fully forming. It is painful for the girl and the unicorn. I can promise you the training will be hard, because I am one of the instructors. This is not for the faint of heart. Years of grueling physical and mental education will push you beyond your limits, but if you truly have an affinity for your unicorn, you will persevere, for yourself, your steed, and the magic that connects you!"

The warrior mounted her unicorn and readied an arrow on her bow. The target was an empty shell of scorched armor with a damaged shield placed in front of it. A brief moment of serenity crossed the woman's face as she loosed an arrow. Kayleigh, along with every other set of eyes in the village square, followed the projectile. Just as it was about to hit the shield, it shimmered and splattered on the metal as if the contents of a bucket were tossed at it. The stream of water wrapped around the shield and solidified, burying the arrow deep into the breastplate.

Over the sounds of the cheers, the battle maiden announced the next demonstration. An earth maiden rode in front of the crowd demonstrating something called "Thunderhooves." The ground shook violently like a full column of knights was rushing by. Many of the targets fell, but the woman rode by one of the few that still stood and smashed it with a mace leaving a massive dent in the helm.

Kayleigh clapped and shouted as an air maiden darted back and forth at unbelievable speeds and then hurled a spear from an impossible distance. It overshot the target, when it should have never gotten near it in the first place. The most remarkable thing was the air maiden didn't appear to be a hulking bundle of muscles like the previous rider. She was tiny and waif-like. The leader explained that all battle maidens can draw physical strength from their mounts as well as the elemental magic and that any one of them was the equal of two men.

To drive that point home, the water maiden asked for two volunteers in the audience to come lift a barrel filled with grain. Kayleigh scowled recognizing one of them was Morgan Jacobs. Her expression changed to a grin as he strained and failed to lift the item higher than his waist. The second man, Helden's blacksmith, lifted it with considerable effort, but raised it triumphantly to his shoulder to the applause of the townsfolk.

Captain Lynch gestured to the youngest of the command and introduced her as Rider Annabeth Welsh, a fire maiden. She couldn't be more than twenty – a scant four years older than Kayleigh! The brown haired woman walked to the blacksmith and asked him to give her the barrel. Old Gregory scoffed, but the warrior insisted. She smiled and easily put the heavy load onto one shoulder and switched it to the other effortlessly.

Kayleigh was speechless and could only clap as the woman dropped the heavy barrel and vaulted onto her mount. She drew a bent sword and trailed flames behind it, making short work of the few remaining targets. Circling back in front of the audience, the unicorn reared and his front hooves became encased in flames and it kicked outward several times, dazzling everyone. Those flames disappeared the moment the hooves smacked down on the ground.

The leader addressed the appreciative crowd saying, "I have talked at length of the benefits of joining our ranks. Now, let me remind you of the hazards. We are warriors. There is a reason that the High-King turns to us when there is trouble in the realm. When we fight, it is not some immobile target or hay-stuffed dummy that suffers our wrath. Sometimes, we mourn our lifelong friends when we bury our fallen."

Whisking hair from her face, she finished, gradually beginning to smile. "That I say for you parents, brothers, and sisters of the candidates. It will be up to you to speak to them, should they be selected. One look at them tells me that nothing I can say would dissuade them. I see a warrior's spirit in each of these young ladies before me and hope that one or more of them will join our sisterhood."

Gesturing to the two wagons and the dozen or so young women standing next to their unicorns, Captain Lynch said, "Over there, you see those already chosen from the settlements south of here. I have four unicorns that have yet to select a rider. I hope that in a few hours, I will have none. Good luck to you all!"

Kayleigh considered staying, but her gaze strayed to Rebekah Morganstern and her friends standing up and waving to the crowd.

A little over an hour before, she'd encountered Rebekah and some of the other candidates.

"That's a lovely dress, Reese," Rebekah had said with a less than pleasant smile.

"Thank you, Rebekah. Your dress is very pretty as well." Kayleigh waited for the insult from the wealthy merchant's daughter. She was not disappointed.

The short brunette with her hair plaited down her back put a finger to her own chin. "It reminds me of something. Oh yes, I know what it is. We use something like it as a tarp on one of father's wagons."

The pair with her laughed. Kayleigh simply continued walking, refusing to let the biting words get to her.

"Why Kayleigh, I would think you'd be the last person to want to see the unicorns."

"Should I care what you think, Rebekah?"

"Unicorns are symbols of beauty and purity. Since you are neither, why don't you avoid the town square today, lest your presence spoil someone else's chance? Perhaps you should wait down by the docks for some fishermen to get back from setting the crab pots and see if you can earn some coins, whore!"

"I'm not a whore!" Kayleigh screamed.

"From what I hear, like mother, like daughter," Rebekah answered bluntly.

"Morgan Jacobs is a liar and my mother is an artist!" The boy had offered Kayleigh coins. When she slapped him and ran off, he boasted that she had taken his money and gave him something in return.

"Who only ever has men for clients, why is that?" Morganstern was clearly enjoying herself at Kayleigh's expense.

"That's not true and you know it," Kayleigh fired back. Her mother had female clients at times, though a majority of them were men. She could have countered Rebekah's words with comments about the girl's father being one of her mother's clients, but it felt useless to even try. Everything felt so useless!

Rebekah sneered and delivered her final blow, "In that case, answer this one question and I'll apologize for everything I've ever said about you. Who is your father?"

That was enough to make Kayleigh flee to the cruel laughter that dogged her steps. She hid in an alley and cried before regaining her composure and making her way to the demonstration. Morganstern be dammed! She wanted to see unicorns.

With the demonstration over, Kayleigh quickly walked away and headed for the beach. Everyone would be at the festival planned for after the selection. The beach would be all hers.

Looking back up at the unicorn that was every bit as startled as she was, Kayleigh said, "What just happened?"

She stood and squirmed in her now wet cotton dress. It was dyed a deep blue, a simple affair, made for warm weather. The slight chill in the air was already getting through the damp material. She wouldn't be able to wear it much longer, but it was something she and her mother made.

This makes no sense! I was tested when we lived in Laurent. I tried every feather, clump of fur, and even a few things I didn't want to touch. Not a blasted thing happened. How could this happen now?

"Are you okay?" She asked, while scolding herself. *If he wasn't okay, what exactly would I be able to do about it?*

If a unicorn could look confused, this one certainly did. He backed away from her slowly, staring at Kayleigh like she was a threat. A second unicorn, this one a saddled female, trotted over and Kayleigh watched as the two shared what must have been a meaningful nonverbal conversation. The newcomer kept motioning with her head towards Kayleigh and seemed very excited. The male was suddenly skittish. Kayleigh stood brushing the sand off of her skirt and felt very self-conscious. She was used to people ignoring her in a conversation and saying things about her as if she wasn't there, but this was the first time the participants were not human.

The female goaded the male to approach again. Kayleigh held her hand out to him and he brushed his head against it. The jolt was still there, but with both expecting it this time there was no repeat of the prior awkwardness. His coat was coarser than she'd imagined.

A sensation of warmth replaced the power of the jolt. It

was much like what Captain Deros once described to her class. The old fisherman had brought in his albatross familiar and discussed how the two would use the weak magic they could generate to sense where the fishing was good. The old man always had full nets and traps when his ship returned.

As she continued to stroke the side of the unicorn's face, Kayleigh wondered about the irony of magic. Most humans had none. A small few could tap into the magic of a familiar, should they actually locate one that suited them. Still, they were reliant on the strength of the creature, with the unicorn ranking among the strongest in the land. A very select group could actually command magic on their own. They were Sorcerers and Grand Viziers, coveted by those in power. Many became Kings and Queens in their own right.

So consumed in her thoughts and the feel of the unicorn's coat beneath her hand, she barely noticed the female unicorn bolting back up the path to town. Kayleigh was left there with the equally perplexed male.

I should say something.

"I wish I knew your name," she said. "I'm Kayleigh, Kayleigh Reese. This is strange. I thought that riders were chosen when they were thirteen. I'm sixteen already."

She was babbling, but there was nothing else she could think to do. Trying to recall the sea captain's lecture, Kayleigh closed her eyes. He said that if he concentrated, he could sense the general state of his familiar. She guessed she should just relax and try. She focused on her hand touching the beautiful creature. A feeling of nervousness and anxiety washed over her. It was very potent and she worried for her unicorn. That realization shocked her. This unicorn had chosen her! What would everyone say? What would they think? It triggered a wave of insecurity in her fed by whatever was bothering the magical steed next to her.

Trailing the finger from her other hand along the horn, she marveled at the intricate spirals. She stopped at the broken piece and traced the length of the crack that ran down it. Sadness and a sense of loss washed over her and Kayleigh's eyes sprouted fresh tears. Anger bubbled to the surface. Someone had hurt him.

Ruefully, she eyed the unicorn and said, "I suppose this is a poor time to tell you that I've never ridden before in my life. I'm also no good with animals. My mother never let me have any. Won't she be surprised."

Sarcasm had always been a defense mechanism for her. It was easier to have a cold and acerbic wit than put up with the whispering, pointing, and stares from the others in her age group. Amidst the trepidation, she felt there was a hint of mirth coming from the unicorn.

Well, if anyone would understand me, I guess it would be him.

Together, they stood for quite some time. Not knowing what else to do, she moved closer and rested her head on him. Her long, sad day had taken a most unusual twist to say the least!

Suddenly, her new friend tensed. She looked up the path and saw two unicorns and their dismounted riders at the other end. They were making their way down. Kayleigh couldn't tell who was more nervous between the two of them. She stood, scrambling to brush the matted sand clinging to her dress and make herself presentable.

The battle maiden leader, Captain Lynch, approached her. The look on her face was not the pleasant one Kayleigh saw during the demonstration. "You there! Who are you?"

"Kayleigh Reese." Her hand rested on his mane, if the hairs on his coat were coarser than she'd imagined, these were by far the softest things she'd ever felt.

"Majherri is letting you touch him voluntarily?"

She knew his name now. That was good and the name seemed to fit the unicorn. She answered the woman, "Yes."

"And you feel the Bondspark?" The woman sounded slightly irritated which confused Kayleigh.

"Yes."

"Are you certain?"

Now it was Kayleigh's turn to get perturbed. "Would he still be letting me touch him if I didn't?"

"Do not take that tone with me, girl!"

The other rider intervened saying, "Captain Lynch, Meghan, why don't you let me speak with the candidate?"

"Candidate? Look at her!" The one named Meghan scoffed. "Does she look thirteen to you? What game are you playing at Majherri?"

Kayleigh looked at Majherri and she got the impression this Meghan didn't like her unicorn, and obviously, the feeling was mutual.

Summoning her courage Kayleigh said, "Leave him alone. He was just as surprised as I was!"

"When I speak to you girl, you will know it. I am speaking to Majherri right now! Majherri, come here this instant!"

Kayleigh actually felt scared. This wasn't enduring the taunts of a hurtful teenager. The woman was a trained warrior and obviously a formidable fighter. The unicorn snorted and shook his head in defiance.

"Meghan! No!" The other reached for her as she started forward. The arm was brushed aside as she stalked towarda Kayleigh.

"I will not tolerate any more defiance from you, Majherri." The woman grasped at the circle of leather around the unicorn's neck to pull him along and roughly pushed Kayleigh away.

She wanted to cry out that Meghan had no right to take Majherri from her. She hoped that the other rider would do something.

Someone did, but it wasn't who Kayleigh expected.

Majherri reared out of the woman's grip and kicked her hard with his forelegs. Meghan tumbled to the sand and quickly rose to her knees. She spun around on the unicorn with her hand on her sword pommel only to find the horn less than six inches from her face.

A tense standoff ensued. One of the unicorns circled

Majherri and looked like it was going to attack. The other battle maiden shouted for order and looked at Kayleigh. "You! Calm him down! Now!"

"What do I do?"

"Walk over to him, speak to him, and lead him back."

She hesitantly stepped to his side and patted him. Anger, resentment, and even hatred welled up inside of her and she knew it was coming from Majherri. Swallowing hard, she thrust her hand into his soft mane and tried to speak in a soothing tone. "Relax Majherri. This isn't a way to settle things. That's it. Why don't we just take a few steps backward and sort this out."

He resisted at first, but he allowed her to lead him back six feet. She could sense a great deal of nonverbal communication between the three unicorns going on. It was impossible to figure out, so she turned her attention to the pair of warriors.

Meghan snarled, "What is he thinking?"

The other woman responded, "I believe he was reminding you, Captain, that he is not your unicorn and doesn't have to take orders from you. Furthermore, I think Majherri isn't the only one that needs to rein in their temper."

"That's quite enough Lindsey. I'm in charge of this expedition."

"Then act like it!" Turning toward Kayleigh, Lindsey adopted a more formal tone. "Kayleigh, walk Majherri back up the path and wait for us. *Captain* Lynch and I will have a brief discussion and then we will join you. Finally, let me be the first to say congratulations, candidate, on being chosen by your unicorn."

The one female unicorn, which still looked to attack, turned and kicked a small cloud of sand on Majherri as they walked by. Kayleigh coughed a bit, but wanted to be anywhere other than this beach right then. At the top of the path she glanced down and saw the two armored women in a very heated argument.

She dusted the sand off of his coat and wished she had a

brush or something to distract him from this anger. "I don't know exactly why you hate her, but I'm sure you've got your reasons. We'll get through this...I hope."

Chapter 3 – The Doubts of Others

The slow walk back to Kayleigh's house was filled with a heavy and awkward silence. The sound of his hooves clattering on worn cobblestones echoed off the buildings and through the narrow streets. The sea helped cleanse the air of the human city's stench. A sad consequence of being a creature of battle was that Majherri's sense of smell was keen and humans were unclean by nature. Cities under siege were cesspools of foul odors, so by comparison, this wasn't bad.

He watched the other humans leaving the festivities. Many stopped and stared. The unicorn was used to it. Majherri also noticed some whispering and pointing directed at his new rider. He sensed Kayleigh was uncomfortable being the center of attention.

His sister was angry with him for threatening Meghan. T'rsa's constantly swishing tail left no room for doubt there. Let her pout; Meghan was not his rider and Majherri did not need to heed her! His actions were justified by the female going for her blade.

She wanted him to get a new rider and now she's angry that it happened. He snorted. The world was full of temperamental females – ones that stood on both four and two legs.

Kayleigh, his new rider, walked next to him. Tiny sensations of power coursed through both their bodies whenever her hand brushed against his coat. It made absolutely no sense. His bond with Danella had been true! His rider had mastered powerful fire spells, magic that would not have been possible without a workable bond.

Turning his head slightly, he saw that the other female unicorn was eyeing him. Pasha remained an enigma. It was far too early for mating season. Perhaps she was like those first unicorns when he returned from the desert, viewing him as an oddity and wanting to test him in some way. The journey back across the continent would be long and arduous. He would have ample time to sort out Pasha's game.

The group stopped and Majherri heard Kayleigh say, "This is my house."

Lindsey answered, "Why don't you go in and ask your mother to come out? Sometimes these things go best when a person is surrounded by the most beautiful creatures in the realm."

Kayleigh appeared skittish, almost as if she feared that, when she went inside, the group would simply ride away, like some kind of cruel human joke. Majherri stared at the young female and tried to reassure her. She mustered her courage and went inside.

"What do you propose we do with a sixteen year old recruit?" Meghan immediately growled at Lindsey.

The black haired woman shifted in Pasha's saddle. "I believe we will train her, test her, and perhaps fight alongside her. But I am newly returned to The Academy and this is my first season teaching, Captain Lynch. What problems do you expect from having a sixteen year old first year recruit?"

"Think about the difference between yourself at thirteen and sixteen. She'll either start as lead rider or be thrown in over her head with the third years. Either way, she will upset the balance of the class she is in. Then someone gets to escort her back here as a failure."

"Much of your argument is based on the girl being a failure. She's been selected for all of fifteen minutes and you're already preparing for the day that her bond is broken and she returns here in disgrace. What if she does not, Captain?"

"Let's hope you are right then, Lieutenant Sheppard."

Majherri snorted reminding them that he was here and could understand what they are saying.

Lindsey pivoted Pasha to face her superior. She reared Pasha's forelegs and smacked them down on the street. A release of magic from the earth maiden sent a small tremor through the ground and rattled the windows of the surrounding houses. "I think Majherri believes he can train this young girl. Even if he can't, he'll try harder – just to spite you. Every one of us here, humans and unicorns, knows the problem is between the two of you. This girl, through no fault of her own, is now caught up in your feud."

"You will mind your place, Lieutenant!" Meghan said sharply.

"As long as you do as well, Captain."

Majherri glared at Meghan Lynch and the woman stared back with accusing eyes that blamed him for the way things were going as well.

The tense atmosphere was broken by Kayleigh leading an older woman out the front of the door.

"I still don't see how this is possible, dear. We had you tested on your twelfth birthday in Laurent. You didn't react to anything, whatsoever."

Lindsey spoke, "Good evening, Madame. I am Lieutenant Lindsey Sheppard and this is Captain Meghan Lynch. We were quite surprised when your daughter made a connection with this unicorn. I assure you my mount was there and she sensed the Bondspark."

Majherri assessed the human female. She was slim and wore nice clothing. Her hands were spotted, not by signs of age, but rather that watery substance humans drew pictures with. Kayleigh's mother was obviously an artist. Occasionally, these artists came to the academy to attempt to preserve images forever in canvas or stone.

"Greetings, noble riders and steeds, I bid you welcome. My name is Brenda Reese. When Kayleigh was tested, the acolyte conducting it said she was very inert and had no affinity towards any magic at all."

Meghan said, "The testing procedure is not always accurate. Sometimes oversights happen. Mistakes can occur."

"Of course, but may I see proof? Not that I doubt your word or that of your unicorns, but my daughter is all I have."

Meghan nodded. His future rider approached and rested the back of her hand on his cheek. Fortunately, the spark that connected them was still there. Majherri felt her apprehension and she, doubtless, felt his left over hostility towards T'rsa's rider.

"If there was no semblance of a bond, he would have shied away from her by now and on the beach, your daughter was able to lead him up the slope with hardly any trouble at all."

"But I thought this was only for thirteen year olds. That is the custom. This is all very peculiar."

Majherri watched the other humans debate this. It was strange to observe. Some humans actually rejected the bonds and turned their back on his brethren. It seemed so ... wrong. Kayleigh kept her hand on him throughout. This was a good sign. Unicorns that fail to find a rider age quickly and die. When he first returned from the wastelands after losing Danella, the other humans and even the herd thought he would as well. If he were to be honest with himself, Majherri had been waiting for the chance to die – until now.

"No, I don't think this is a good idea. You get squeamish when you gut a fish, dear. It's not the life you want." Turning to the humans, Brenda nodded and said, "Thank you for the opportunity, but we are not interested."

Majherri felt a swell of resentment from Kayleigh. He may have even fanned the flames as she exclaimed, "What kind of life do I want? I think that's the first time you've ever taken that into consideration."

"And what do you mean by that!" The mother exclaimed.

"We've never stayed in one place more than three years in my life! Every time I make friends and start to settle in, you move us again. You've been hinting that we've been here too long, already. I want to feel like I belong to something ... anything."

The mother looked stunned at the daughter's rebellion. "After all I've done for you! You treat me like ... this? How dare you?"

Majherri felt Kayleigh's remorse instantly, but he had found a rider again and this was as much about him as it was Kayleigh.

Captain Lynch broke the tension. "If the parent refuses, we don't take runaways. Am I to understand that you do not give your permission, Madame?"

"No, forgive me Kayleigh, but the High-King's city is no place for a girl like you."

The unicorn felt tremors of panic coursing through his body. He couldn't even tell if they were coming from him or her. Meghan dismounted and started to move toward them. She was going to forcibly separate him from Kayleigh.

I'll fight for her, human.

"But I'm sixteen, not thirteen," Kayleigh said in a hushed tone. Majherri sensed that she'd stand by him as well. Raw determination beat back the fear and panic.

"The young woman does have a point." Lindsey said brushing a strand of hair away with a gauntleted hand. "She is within her rights to claim her independence."

"You would renounce me!" The thin mother growled in anger, swelling beyond the petite size of her frame.

Tears flowed freely down the rider's cheeks and Majherri felt a sharp twinge of betrayal. "What would you do with me, mother? Am I supposed to be your assistant for all time, wandering from one town to the next? I could marry one of the boys on the docks. I've always wanted to be a fisherman's wife. Isn't there a saying, 'Only fools turn their backs on the chance to do magic?' Is that what you want me to be, a fool? Even more mocked than I am already?"

An angry staring match began – a battle of wills. Without the connection, Majherri wasn't certain of Kayleigh's resolve, but fortunately, she still clung to him. Her hand reversed and was firmly on the back of his neck, slightly painful, but he savored the pain as something that made his life meaningful again. He wanted this. He needed this.

Slowly, Brenda Reese, a rigid personification of fury spoke, challenging her daughter, "Go ahead then, renounce me. We don't even need to go to the elders. These warriors are able to bear witness."

"I don't want to, Mama, but I will."

Lynch intervened. "Before you do this, girl, take your hand off the unicorn. If this is to be your decision, it shall be of your own volition and not influenced by your fledgling bond with that one."

Anger, guilt, and apprehension swirled between the two of them and Kayleigh let go. She stared at him, confused and perhaps wary.

Lindsey dismounted and took Kayleigh's hand. "We'll walk up the street for a minute and let this young lady clear her head. She has a very important decision to make."

Majherri watched fearfully as his rider was led away.

Meghan turned to the angry mother and pointed an accusing finger at him and said, "This one wants your daughter as his rider. He is strong-willed and could easily have been feeding her emotions. He understands how the bond works. She does not."

Long minutes passed and the mother glared at him. Meghan glared at him. The two female unicorns glared at him. He simply turned and looked at the two shadowy figures walking along the darkening street. The rest of them did not matter – only his rider. His fate belonged to someone else now. It was out of his control.

He raised his head and looked at the stars as they began to appear in the fading light of the day. Some sought predictions, or made wishes to them. Majherri didn't believe in any of that, but even so, the tiny lights in the sky were fascinating.

Pasha moved alongside and looked up at the sky as well. He wasn't certain if she was mocking him, or simply interested in what he was doing. He knew she was easily six years younger and entering the stage of life where she'd be looking for her first mate.

That idea suddenly piqued his interest. Unicorn relationships were much less complicated than those of their riders. Danella would often vent her frustrations in that area with Majherri. The same skills that made her a terror on the battlefield tended to intimidate those interested in her. He'd pretend to be sympathetic, but it actually had been rather humorous. Danella understood this and entertained him anyway.

Was he betraying her memory? Did he even deserve another rider? He was torn. The bond, once fully realized, wasn't something that could just be broken and rebuilt. He'd seen many of his kind wither and die without their riders. That was always the way it had been.

Except for now … now, everything was different.

Chapter 4 – A Parting of the Ways

"You need to calm down and find your emotional center." Kayleigh listened to the woman's voice. She had long jet-black hair and probing blue eyes that looked at her intently. They were nearly the same height at five foot seven inches, but the battle maiden was a powerfully built bundle of muscles, the likes of which Kayleigh had never seen.

"What just happened? I've never been that upset with my mother before." *Then again, she's never told me I can't have a unicorn.*

The woman walked easily in her armor, barely making any noise and said, "The bond can be powerful, sometimes even overwhelming for both parties involved. It's like suddenly gaining a sister or a brother. You might have noticed at the selection ceremony that the candidates ride in a wagon. Through most of the first year, we limit the amount of time a rider spends with her unicorn on purpose, since the early teenage years are already difficult enough."

"I didn't stay for the ceremony." Kayleigh admitted while looking down at the street.

"Is that so?" Lindsey asked, making her feel even more uncomfortable.

Kayleigh decided to change the subject. "What can you tell me about Majherri?"

"I do not know everything, but he survived the loss of his first rider – a fire maiden named Danella. That has never happened before and has many of us confused. If that shatters your image of us as all-knowing protectors of the realm, I'm sorry, but that is the truth."

"And why does Majherri hate Meghan?"

"First off, if you do intend to leave this town with us, her name is Captain Lynch and I am Lieutenant Sheppard. The easiest way to explain the rift between them is to tell you that

Danella's last name was also Lynch. They were twin sisters selected by a pair of sibling unicorns – again, a most unusual oc-
currence. T'rsa, Captain Lynch's partner is Majherri's sister."

Kayleigh's thoughts swirled trying to digest all of this.
"Thank you. That explains a lot."

They walked in silence as Lindsey led her down a side
street toward an area where they could overlook the ocean. In
the faltering light, the waves were hard to see. The reassuring
crash of the water hitting the rocky shore created a steady tone
that the townsfolk referred to as the "heartbeat" of Helden.

"I grew up in the northern kingdom of Geron. We have
lots of lakes, but no oceans. Do you dislike living here?"

"It's just a place," Kayleigh replied. "We move every few
years. Mama is always looking for new inspirations for her
paintings and sculptures."

"Are you an artist as well?"

"I dabble. I don't quite have the eye for it. I could paint
this landscape and it would probably be technically perfect, but
bland and boring at the same time."

"Perhaps you are being smothered by your mother's crea-
tivity and need to find your own inspirations?"

"I don't think I'll ever be as good as her."

"Maybe not with canvas or stone, but riding a creature
that shares an emotional bond with you is something of an art.
If you're both afraid and angry, the bond will feed it and
double the effect. You will spend a lot of time in your first year
meditating and learning how to accept the bond."

"Do you think I should come with you? What happens to
Majherri if I don't?"

"It's not important what I think. I made my choice long
ago. As for Majherri, I don't know. He shouldn't have survived
the loss of his first rider. If he doesn't have a rider when we
return, he returns to the pasture, a great field where the herd
roams. You'll become well acquainted with those riderless unicorns. Part of your duties will be taking care of them as well."

"I don't know anything about taking care of horses, much

less unicorns."

"You'll learn," Lindsey answered with a reassuring tone. "One of the problems you'll have is because of your age."

"What do you mean?" Kayleigh looked at the moon peeking out from behind the cloud cover.

"You're three years older than the others in your class. Traditionally, the oldest is made lead rider for their class. The position makes you the recruit in charge of the others. After the first few months, the other recruits will be allowed to challenge you in a jousting match or hand to hand combat to see if they can unseat you. In a class full of girls the same age, this allows the most competitive and capable to rise to the top. You will make this more difficult, because you have a natural advantage over them, but it would be grossly unfair to thrust you into third year training. Where you are placed is a decision for people higher in rank than even Captain Lynch."

Kayleigh kicked a stone with her shoes. Her tone was somewhat dejected as she said, "You're saying that I'll be something of an outsider there as well."

"Perhaps, perhaps not. Your future really depends on what you make of it. I would heartily recommend a positive attitude. Plus, you have another advantage. Majherri is already a battle tested mount and a fighter. The new unicorns are just as much a question as their chosen riders. Graduate from The Academy and you'll never have to worry about belonging somewhere again. You'll be a battle maiden and part of an elite warrior caste. People will cheer your arrival. Enemies will fear your presence."

She listened to the battle maiden carefully and tried to picture herself riding Majherri in full armor. Her heartbeat quickened, and she liked what she saw in her mind's eye.

But to have this, I must renounce my mother to her face. If I don't have the courage to do this, I probably don't belong on Majherri in the first place! Why can't she be more supportive? Why does it have to be like this?

Taking a deep breath she said, "Let's go back. I know what I must do."

Lieutenant Sheppard nodded and didn't ask for her answer. As Kayleigh walked, she became more aware of Helden than she ever had before. Almost like a painting, she saw the sharp details in the growing darkness. True, she was leaving this place, but it was where destiny found her and made an offer that she'd be a fool to refuse. She wanted to remember this place. It was where her life made an abrupt change. Kayleigh steeled herself in preparation for what was to come. It would be the hardest thing she'd ever done, but she knew that there were much harder things ahead of her.

The small group was still there. A few of the neighbors were outside as well, drawn to the majestic presence of the unicorns. Her heart leapt at the sight of Majherri. He stood away from the rest, keeping his own council. From what she just learned about him, he was an outsider as well. That suited her. They could be outsiders together.

Her leaping heart met the pit of her stomach upon seeing her mother's angry face. She'd never seen that look before. It tested her will to continue. It demanded she be an obedient daughter and follow her mother's orders. Kayleigh forced her legs forward.

If this is my first fight as a battle maiden, let it be my first victory!

"Well?" Brenda Reese demanded. Kayleigh instinctively trembled at the harsh tone.

"I'm going with them. Majherri found me, even when I wasn't at the ceremony. My decision affects him as well. If I don't go, I'll be a painter, a basket weaver, or who knows what. If I go and fail, I can still be any of those things, but I might just have a greater destiny ahead of me and I have to try. If I don't, I'll always be looking over my shoulder and wondering what if? Give me your blessing, Mother. Don't make me do this. Please!"

"You want to run off and become a warrior and you want me to approve! I will do no such thing! Are you in that much of a hurry to die?"

"Mama …" Kayleigh started, but was cut off by her

mother pointing an accusing finger and shouting at Lieutenant Sheppard.

"You! Tell her how many of your ilk died in the last civil war. The southern nations rose up and tried to free themselves from the High-King's rule. Don't bother. I'll say it for you – hundreds died, nearly one in five of your riders. Besides them, tens of thousands died. Entire cities were put to the torch. It cost me her father!"

Lieutenant Sheppard nodded. "You are correct. It was a very costly war almost two decades ago."

"War is not the answer! War is blind obedience! I did not raise you to be a murderer! I saw that war with my own eyes and know that no matter what anyone says – war is evil. It is never, ever justifiable and if you ever had one shred of respect for me, you will not do this."

There was a pause after Brenda's eruption. Kayleigh knew her mother hated violence, but she'd never vented so. It was so raw and painful. Mama never talked about her wanderings before Kayleigh was born. Now, she had an idea why. She never spoke about Kayleigh's father, but now she knew that he died in that war.

Bracing herself, the young woman said, "Goodbye Mama, I'll go get my things."

"You have no things in this house! Its doors are closed to you evermore!" Brenda Reese spun and entered the house, slamming the door, and leaving Kayleigh fighting a battle against her tears. One she lost in catastrophic fashion seconds later, collapsing to the unforgiving cobblestone street. There were so many things in that house that held great meaning to her. Now, they and the memories they held were gone. Kayleigh immediately thought of her sketchbooks and poetry.

Lieutenant Sheppard lifted her up and Kayleigh saw the faces peering out the windows and the crowd that had gathered. "Be brave, young rider," the woman whispered. "The first steps into the unknown are always the most difficult."

With that, she motioned for Majherri to come closer and

guided Kayleigh's hand to the unicorn. Kayleigh immediately felt gratitude and relief pouring into her to push back against the sadness.

The lieutenant tried to calm her, "We'll get you some things to travel. We can use the money that would have gone to your family."

"No, we will not." Captain Lynch answered. "That money is for the families and not for the recruits."

"Which every family gives a portion back to the selectee."

"That is the family's choice Lieutenant, not ours," Captain Lynch shot back. "The woman here indicated she wanted no money, and since this rider was not chosen at a ceremony, I see no reason to make any payment."

"Captain Lynch?"

"Yes, that is my title and name. Thank you for remembering who is in charge of this expedition and this is my decision. You seem to have a vested interest in this recruit, Lieutenant. I place her in your care." Before Lieutenant Sheppard could reply, Captain Lynch mounted Majherri's sister and galloped off into the darkness.

"Very well, ma'am," Lieutenant Sheppard answered the disappearing rider. Turning to Kayleigh, she offered a small smile and a pat on the back. "Come along recruit. You'll be traveling a bit light for awhile, but we'll get you sorted out soon enough."

That woman hates me! What have I gotten myself into? I have nothing but the clothes on my back. How will I … what will I…

The anxiety was met with a spike of reassurance coming from Majherri. His firm gaze implored her to trust that he would always take care of her, protect her, and fight beside her.

Kayleigh's resolve firmed. *I might just have this dress, but I've got a unicorn. And right now, he's worth more than anything to me.*

"I don't suppose you have any extra clothes I can borrow?" Kayleigh asked forcing some dry humor that she didn't feel into her voice.

"We might be about the same height, but we're not exactly built the same, recruit. I can probably spare a couple of things that might fit you. However, your fellow recruits will likely be willing to part with a few items and if they are not, Captain Lynch cannot tell me how to spend my gold coins."

"What do you teach at The Academy?"

"I'll be your year's physical trainer and I'll be the most hated instructor in your class. You'll stare at the calluses on your hand and soak in a tub cursing my name, just like I cursed my instructor. Some days, I will work you so hard that you'll be barely able to walk. If you're lead rider, those are the days you'll have to get up anyway and prove yourself. Just remember that I'm preparing you for the rigors of combat. The strength and reflexes I drill into you may one day save your life."

"I won't let you down." Kayleigh said firmly.

The woman scoffed at her. "Yes, you will. I guarantee you'll fail, often in fact. But as long as you keep trying, you'll never let yourself down."

"Okay, I understand."

Sheppard's soft features hardened. "Here's our first lesson. 'Okay' is not the correct answer. The correct answer is 'Yes, ma'am' or 'Yes, Lieutenant.' Normally, that'd earn you a lap on the Trail of Pain. Do you like running, climbing rocks, rope ladders, and crawling through a field of mud? Actually, it doesn't matter. You're going to anyway, so get used to it."

"Understood, ma'am."

"That's better. Now let's get you some food and see if we can scrounge up some of the basics you'll need. Follow me."

As they walked, Kayleigh could still feel the eyes of the neighbors on her. By tomorrow, the news would be all over Helden, but then the knowledge dawned that she wouldn't be here to hear it. A futile glance back at the cottage she once called home showed no one in the windows. Part of her longed to run back there and beg for her mother's forgiveness, but she kept her feet moving forward.

Mama always encouraged me to try new things. She said I could be extraordinary. Now when something truly extraordinary happens, she becomes crazed. Why is she acting like this? Does she really hate war that much? Why can't she be happy for me?

Since no answers were forthcoming, Kayleigh followed Lieutenant Sheppard to the edge of town where the group of wagons camped. A man was giving orders to several others around a bonfire. As they approached, the man walked to meet them. He moved with assurance and pride. He was a young man, in his early twenties, clean-shaven, tall, and he wore a thick leather glove on his right hand that ran to the elbow.

"Good evening, Lieutenant. What have we here?"

"Our latest rider."

"I thought there were only two in this town."

"Good fortune has sent us a third, Sir Aeric. This is Kayleigh Reese, she is Majherri's chosen. Kayleigh, this is the honorable Aeric Tomas, Knight of the High-King's guard, oldest son of Duke Desmond Tomas and Duchess Alanna Tomas. He is in charge of the men and the wagons and is our most excellent guide through these countries. He is Captain Lynch's equal and you will treat him as such."

The man rubbed his chin thoughtfully as Kayleigh gave a respectful curtsy, determined to get off on a good foot with this man. "Majherri chose a rider? Very interesting indeed. Welcome to the expedition, young lady. I'll have some men get your baggage stowed and take you to the other riders."

"I'm afraid she has no baggage, Sir Aeric."

Kayleigh listened to Lieutenant Sheppard briefly recount her situation. She was grateful for the darkness that masked her embarrassment. Now, she was depending on the kindness of strangers – a veritable beggar among royalty.

The man looked her over, and she felt uncomfortable under his assessment. "Well young lady, you're here now. I'll take you to meet some of your fellow riders. The other two selected from this town are supposed to be joining us at dawn's first light. Good evening to you, Lieutenant."

"And to you as well, Sir Aeric."

The man motioned for Kayleigh and Majherri to follow.

They stopped at the large bonfire first, and the knight sent a few of the wagon drivers looking for whatever they might have on hand. Minutes later, she had a bedroll, two towels, a riding cloak, two tunics, one pair of breeches, and a pair of boots that needed mending, but might fit.

As he led her to a smaller fire where several teenage girls sat around the circle, she asked, "Sir Aeric, I was wondering about your glove. Are you a bird handler?"

He smiled and pointed to the sky. The shape of a predatory bird came briefly into view as he replied, "Funny you should ask. Sometimes I wonder if she is handling me. I do happen to have a magical familiar of my own. A hawk may not be as impressive as your unicorn, but my Rain is excellent at gathering information. When she lands on me, I see everything that she has just seen. She helps me find the best trails, streams and ponds where we can make camp. More than once, she has spotted a potential ambush on this trip."

Still new to all this, Kayleigh was in awe of any magical creature. She stammered, "Helden has a fishing captain. He has an albatross that helps him find the best places to fish and warns him about dangerous storms."

"Yes, I had hoped to meet him, but things didn't quite work out and I was too busy managing the camp to seek him out."

From the corner of her eye, she noticed several of the girls discreetly straightening their appearances and smoothing their dresses as they neared. Only then, did she realize that Sir Aeric was rather handsome. She'd been too preoccupied with her own troubles to truly notice.

"Good evening, recruits. This one is joining your ranks. Make her welcome. The other two will be here in the morning."

Naturally, this started a couple of them murmuring and a few pointed at Majherri standing close by. It was as if a collective, "Oh" passed through them.

Sir Aeric continued, "I must be off. It was a pleasure making your acquaintance, Miss Reese."

She curtsied as best she could with the bedroll and her newly acquired goods in her arms as the knight walked off oblivious to the enthralled stares of almost twenty teenagers.

Kayleigh was wary. Their faces held no immediate judgments, only curiosity. Hoping this was a turn for the better; she smiled back at them and said, "Hello, I'm Kayleigh Reese."

Chapter 5 – The Road to Miros

"What is *she* doing here?" Majherri watched the one called Rebekah say with a haughty tone. The wagon drivers were looking for places to stow the luggage, but stopped to see the spectacle. This Rebekah annoyed him. He was sorely tempted to wander over and destroy her luggage and solve the drivers' problems.

"I was chosen by Majherri." His rider answered. He felt some pride in the way she said the words.

"You're not thirteen!"

"Apparently, that doesn't matter, Rebekah." Majherri detected a hint of anger.

"You don't belong here!" The younger girl's sounded petulant.

"I have a unicorn that disagrees with you."

"Does it know that you're not pure and that you're a dirty, stinking whore?" A few of the other females gasped at the accusation.

His rider stepped closer to the younger girl. "In a few minutes, we'll be riding out of Helden. We'll be away from your rich father, your uncles, and everyone else that makes you believe you can say anything to anyone and get away with it, Morganstern. Say those lies aloud again, and see what happens."

Majherri no longer was interested in trampling the girl's luggage, he considered trampling the girl, but it was more interesting to watch Kayleigh in action. She had the temperament of a fighter, which was good. He couldn't help but picture how violently Danella would have responded, but a furious Kayleigh was showing considerable promise. Already, the younger rider was backing away; cowed by the angry stance of his chosen one.

Lycenae, the young male who had chosen this petty female, huffed and looked like he was thinking about intervening. Majherri snorted and drew his attention. He lowered his horn at Lycenae and clawed at the dirt with his front left hoof letting him know that any action on his part would be met with swift retaliation. They locked gazes for a moment and he could see Lycenae thinking over his options.

So typical of a young one, Majherri thought. *All posturing and no willingness to act.*

He lurched forward only about a foot or two, but it was enough to make Lycenae jump backwards and show his fear. The standoff was broken and Majherri was the clear victor. Part of him relished exerting his reclaimed status over the foolish youth. This was a long way from the great pasture and Majherri was in no mood for the silly games of wobbly-legged children barely weaned of the teets of their mothers. Even among the four unicorns bonded to the Battle Maidens, he probably had the most combat experience. If the scars on his side and the cracked tip of his horn made him some kind of grotesque freak that they feared, so be it.

The humans took note of his actions. They were untrained in unicorn ways and probably didn't understand the subtleties of the conversations unicorns have. Instead of the heavy reliance on spoken sounds, his race used body language, such as swishing the tail, the positioning of one's head and horn, and flaring nostrils to convey their conversations. Yes, noises were used, but Majherri, like most others in the herd, long ago realized that if all humans had to communicate with was their body language – they'd be completely lost as a species. It was something of a running joke among his kind.

"You stay away from me!" Rebekah growled. "And keep your unicorn away from mine!"

"I wasn't the one running over here looking for a fight, Morganstern," Kayleigh said pointing to the nearest wagon. "I'm riding in this one. Perhaps you should choose another."

Majherri snorted as the spoiled girl and her equally spoiled unicorn walked away. The dark-skinned girl from one of the earliest stops in the Southern nations approached Kayleigh.

"I take it she isn't your friend." The girl said in a heavily accented voice.

His rider exhaled, trying to release her pent-up aggression. "Not hardly, I'm sorry I'm awful with names and I've forgotten yours already."

"Alicia Santiago. I was the first girl selected and have been part of this expedition from the beginning. Lieutenant Sheppard asked me to explain what we call 'The Rules of the Road' to you."

"And what are those?"

"We all pull our own weight around here – part of your training starts today. I'll show you where we keep Majherri's brushes. Tonight, when we stop to make camp, I'll show you how to brush your unicorn. Hopefully, you'll have better luck with Majherri than we had."

"Why's that?"

"He doesn't like to be touched for very long. If he doesn't like what you're doing he'll give you a little kick and leave a bruise. That one, he has a temper!"

Majherri raised his head. The young girl's admonitions were a point of honor with him. He'd behave for Kayleigh. She was his. The rest of them weren't his. It was really that simple.

"What other things do I need to know?"

"We gather the firewood for the campfires. We clean up after meals and we take our turns cooking. The soldiers and the drivers have their jobs to do. Unless you have permission, you are not allowed to ride your unicorn. You only spend time with your unicorn when the maidens give permission. When Lieutenant Sheppard orders us outside the wagons, we get out and we walk alongside. Last one out has to carry 'the bag.' It's heavy and filled with sand. You don't want to be last out."

"I'll keep that in mind."

"Can you read and write?"

"Yes." His rider answered.

"Good. There are a few who can't. During the ride, we study, we learn, and we help each other. The classes at the Academy will be more difficult on those without the basic skills."

"This whole thing has been somewhat unexpected. I have no idea what classes we take." Majherri moved up to Kayleigh and began bumping her arm with his snout. "What do you want, Majherri?"

"Paragor does that when he wants an apple. There's a barrel in the wagon."

Kayleigh scrambled up into to get one. Majherri had sustained himself on grass and flowers, refusing anything else from the other chosen riders. He felt a twinge of guilt that he had previously been so surly to them. Admittedly, those were not his proudest moments. Still, now that he had a rider, there was absolutely no reason he should continue to deny himself a delicious treat. It wasn't his very favorite, but after losing Danella, he could never eat another peach.

He munched on the apple as Alicia told Kayleigh about the classes at the Academy. Danella had not been the most attentive of students. She only excelled at the courses that held her attention. He wondered how much different Kayleigh would be.

"There's a lot of physical training, ranged weapons, riding, meditation, lectures on how to provide for your unicorn, and general studies to get everyone on a level field for the classes that come later. There are also classes in subjects like history and etiquette when dealing with the noble class."

Majherri almost choked on the apple recalling how much Danella hated the etiquette class. To be perfectly honest, Majherri never quite understood how to differentiate between a regular human and one of these nobles. Without the trappings of fine clothes and heraldic symbols, they didn't look much different than the others. It was all rather silly to him. Danella's comment when Meghan was promoted to Captain was, "She's always been better at being a kiss ass than I was. I'll take scout missions in the field any day over teaching kids!"

Eventually, the full wagons started moving northward toward the human village of Miros. He could sense that his rider was troubled. She'd scanned the crowds of well wishers looking for the presence of her mother, who was nowhere to be found. It didn't take a physical bond to see that she was distressed. As soon as Pasha's rider ordered the chosen ones out of the wagon for physical training, he trotted up next to her, though she was shouldering the heavy bag and seemed angry with herself.

His sensitive ears picked up her muttering, "Didn't realize everyone would jump out of the wagon like it was on fire!"

For a human, his rider was in good shape, even if her sandals were ill-suited for this task. Kayleigh did seem quite used to walking. Given her admission that she'd never ridden a horse before, it made sense that she was good on her feet, although the words sense and human didn't always go together all that well.

"Recruit, you're not authorized to have contact with your mount at this time." The fire maiden riding Rheysurrah came alongside them.

"He came up to me!"

"Be that as it may, you need to send him back with the rest. There will be time to spend with them this afternoon."

"Yes, ma'am. Majherri, you need to go back with the other unicorns."

He'd spent this entire trip with the young ones. Their foolishness stopped amusing him over a month ago and he had no desire to move among them. This simply proved his point about how the words humans and sense didn't necessarily belong together.

As a result, Majherri remained exactly where he was, a few feet to the side of his rider.

"Recruit!"

"Yes, ma'am."

"You're unicorn is not listening to you."

"Yes, ma'am. Majherri, please…" His rider pleaded with him. This seemed to amuse the other human riders greatly and Majherri figured that he was now causing his rider trouble.

Still, he was uninterested in what the rest of his kin were up to, but he didn't wish to embarrass Kayleigh further. The only sensible thing to do was to trot to the front of the wagon train. He slowed when he reached the front wagon and the trio of mounted men there. They would be pleasant enough company for the moment.

"What are you doing up here? Get back with the others!" Meghan rode up quickly on T'rsa and scolded him.

Majherri turned his head slightly eyeing the human captain and his sister with contempt. He sped up in front of the trio of horse riders and moved to the left side of the trail. Slowing, he allowed the men to close with him. This placed the trio of men between him and T'rsa and plainly told all present that he wasn't interested in Captain Lynch's opinion.

This seemed to cause the men as much humor as it caused Captain Lynch irritation. She attempted to order Majherri to the rear and he ignored her, all the while enjoying himself immensely. It took a few minutes, but the woman left.

The male leader, the one with the hawk addressed him, "Ever the rebel, Majherri?"

The unicorn snorted and raised his head in pride.

"I guess they should be careful what they wish for. Before you chose a new rider, they were angry that you wouldn't do anything without being forced to. Now, you do as you please and won't listen to them. Well played indeed. I thank you for the entertainment."

The two riders with the knight laughed heartily as they moved through the overcast morning. Rain clouds were coming in and Majherri knew that they would be here by midday.

When the hawk returned, the knight ordered the wagon train to divert from the trail a half a mile to a running stream and allow the horses and the unicorns to rest. Alicia brought Paragor next to him and proceeded to show Kayleigh how to properly brush Majherri.

Kayleigh was too timid, not putting any real force behind the brush, voicing concern about his scars. On one hoof, it was nice to be brushed again by someone that instinctively didn't annoy him. On the other, was it too much to ask that she do it correctly? He bit back the urge to be frustrated with her. She was trying to learn and he knew he was being impatient. He'd already gone through all this before.

From the way Paragor's coat was so easily brushed, Majherri suspected that Alicia was already aligning with air magic. Often, the unicorns could tell what direction a rider was headed long before the placement ceremony, thirty days after arriving at the Academy. Bits of the trail would cling and linger around the legs of an earth maiden's unicorn. Some referred to their mounts as "Dirt Kickers" or "Dust Catchers." The briefest hint of soot would follow a unicorn with a fire maiden for a rider and they were affectionately called "Smokies." Danella had nicknamed him "Brimstone" at one point. Water maiden and air maiden mounts were always the cleanest, with the windswept look of a "Cloud" easier to distinguish than shiny appearance of a "Misty."

Paragor nodded respectfully to him, observing Kayleigh's struggles and wisely not commenting on them. Majherri was grateful for this. Their riders had developed a fledgling kinship and he suspected that he would be seeing much of Paragor in the coming year. He had spent so much time coveting the roll of an outsider that he wasn't certain how to fit in amongst a group so much younger than he was.

And his rider thought she had a difficult task. He was at least fifteen years older than any of these younglings. Fitting in with them wasn't going to be easy.

Chapter 6 – Blood and Magic

Kayleigh wasn't sure what to make of Majherri's antics during the first two days of their trip. He seemed to enjoy being a thorn in Captain Lynch's side every step of the way. She worried that this would ultimately come back to her. Many of the other recruits were careful to avoid speaking with her when the Captain was near.

What do they expect from me? I'm still trying to figure out how he likes to be brushed! He's going to do what he's going to do regardless.

So far, traveling was a mixed blessing. The wagon was bumpy, but having moved around throughout much of her youth, Kayleigh easily acclimated to the nature of this trip. One of the girls, a shy brunette named Francine, was from Laurent and it gave her someone else to talk to besides Alicia. They even had a few shared acquaintances. Kayleigh's travelling nature meant she "knew" a lot of people, but didn't have many friends to show for it.

Morganstern continued to make snide remarks whenever no one in authority was around to hear. On the first night around the recruit fire, while Kayleigh took her turn stirring a pot of stew, Rebekah said, "My pants got caught on a splinter of wood getting out this evening. I wonder – should I mend the hole or just give them to our resident pauper?"

The other girl from Helden was one of Rebekah's friends and also seemed to delight in Kayleigh's situation. Fortunately, many of the other girls paid them little heed. Some were still struggling with reading and writing. Even more had been poor where they came from and understood poverty in ways Morganstern could never begin to. For every one that joined in laughter, there was another who rolled their eyes and went back to doing what they were previously occupied with. It was annoying, but for the chance to become a battle maiden, she could tolerate the sneering looks.

Kayleigh also found herself wondering what the duties and responsibilities of lead rider would be. It occurred to her that there could be several ways that she might be able to repay Rebekah for all her *kind* words.

"You read a lot," Alicia commented while the wagon bounced along.

"My mother always encouraged me to read literature and poetry, but never much about history. What I know is based on growing up and moving around. It doesn't come from books. So, I've got some ground to make up. I can't keep it up for long. Eventually, my head starts to hurt, or Lieutenant Sheppard decides that we need to stretch our legs."

"Don't you like carrying the bag? You seem quite good at it."

Most of the others snickered and tapped on the wooden sides of the wagon to ward against the earth maiden calling them out for another walk.

Kayleigh smiled and said, "Actually, I need to get my strength up and carrying 'the bag' is good practice. I don't mind it so much. I get the feeling from the way she described the Trail of Pain that we're going to be missing a few miles with a satchel of sand on our back."

"Do you really think so?" Francine asked.

"We're going to learn to fight with sword, mace, and ax, while carrying a shield. Those things get heavy after awhile."

"Maybe we should take turns carrying the bag?" A blonde farm girl named Ellen said, already wary that she wasn't a good reader and not wanting to give up an advantage of being one of the stronger girls in this wagon. Several others murmured in agreement.

Suddenly, everyone was eager to carry the bag. Fifteen minutes later, the recruits were ordered out to exercise. Instead of scurrying out, Kayleigh's wagon was pretty orderly and since it was her idea, Ellen took the first turn with the bag. Walking alongside the wagon, the driver, an old man named Ben, caught Kayleigh's eye and winked at her having heard the entire conversation. The man smiled a near toothless grin and threw his head back in laughter.

Perhaps she was wrong to convince the others that this really added to their physical conditioning. It might actually help. Either way, Kayleigh was just happy that she didn't have to out maneuver a bunch of overly spry thirteen year olds or carry the bag for a change.

Things settled into a routine over the next few days. She got better at brushing Majherri – or he was lowering his standards. Kayleigh worked with Ellen and Francine to improve their reading skills, Most importantly, only every sixth time Lieutenant Sheppard called them out did she have to worry about shouldering the bag of sand and walking for a few miles. The five other girls in her wagon might be chosen for one of the greatest honors in the land, but for the moment, they were still young teenagers and much of their behavior, at least to Kayleigh, was somewhat predictable. There were silly jokes and stories from home. Kayleigh managed to tell a few of them without dwelling on her mother's recent actions.

During the evenings, she had scrounged some parchment and a piece of drawing charcoal and occupied her time doing sketches. First of Majherri, but when the others noticed her talent, she drew the other recruits and their unicorns. It was an easy way to make friends.

Rider Welsh interrupted her latest piece of artwork by calling all the girls around the fire.

"It's time for a brief refresher for some and an introduction for the others. What is the smallest unit a battle maiden and her unicorn will operate from? You there, what's your answer?"

She was pointing at Rebekah, "It's the squad, which is anywhere from four to eight riders."

"Do you agree with her?" Welsh pointed a finger at the other girl chosen from Helden, who nodded.

"Okay, how about you?" The accusing finger was now directed at Kayleigh. She didn't want to agree with Rebekah on principle and the way Rider Welsh asked the other girl implied that it wasn't the answer.

She thought about seeing the scout a few months ago. "One rider and one unicorn."

"Correct. A scout or a message courier will often operate by themselves or in pairs. The basic field unit is the squad, which is commanded by what?"

"A Senior Rider." The answer came too quick for Kayleigh to spot the speaker.

"Good! What formation is next?"

Kayleigh didn't know the answer and was glad someone else said, "Section made up of three to six squads and commanded by a Lead Rider, or a Lead Senior Rider."

"Almost, you forgot a Lieutenant," Rider Welsh said and adopted a grin, "We have to have something for our officers to do."

That drew a glare from Lindsey Sheppard, who was brushing her mount's coat nearby.

Kayleigh followed as more information was given to her. Sections might be responsible for patrolling a Duchy or a medium-sized city. Two to four sections were a company that would be led by at least a Captain. Three or four companies were a battalion commanded by a General and there were five battalions on the Blessed Continent – one for each the north, south, east, and west. The final battalion was stationed at the High-King's capital city. Rider Welsh was a member of that battalion, on loan for the recruiting trip. The lesson continued for a time before they were dismissed for the evening meal.

In about two hours, they would be in Miros. Kayleigh could sit and watch the choosing ceremony and the warrior demonstration she'd been denied back in Helden. She looked forward to it. The maidens that were here weren't prone to showing off. The most Kayleigh saw was when Lieutenant Sheppard used

Thunderhooves to encourage the recruits to get out more quickly.

The wagon train halted in the middle of the road shortly after Sir Aeric's hawk returned.

"I wonder if we're making a quick trip to a stream." Ellen stated.

"Seems kind of silly if we're within ten miles of Miros. We can get fresh water there – along with another banquet." Francine replied. "It's kind of chilly this far north. Isn't it still supposed to be summer?"

Speculation ran rampant when one of the mounted soldiers told Ben to come up front. He looked back at the girls and told Kayleigh to come up and sit in his spot. He handed her the reins and told her to make sure the horse team didn't go anywhere. The other girls started asking her if she could hear anything.

Like ten whole feet makes a world of difference!

Majherri came alongside of the wagon and looked at her in what she could only describe as amusement. She pointed up towards the group gathering at the front wagon and gestured with her head. He must have guessed what she wanted him to do and the unicorn made his way to the front.

She watched him casually trot next to the wagon behind the group. He paused to nibble on some grass.

He's pretty good at eavesdropping. I'll have to remember that!

Less than a minute passed and Majherri's head snapped up and looked at the talking group. He immediately started back to Kayleigh.

"Hey Ellen, toss me an apple. Majherri knows what's going on."

"You don't have permission to touch your unicorn, Kayleigh," Francine warned in her mouse like way.

She smiled back and said, "I'm just going to give him an apple. He looks hungry. I certainly won't be trying to touch him, though he might touch me. Where's the harm in that?"

Majherri came for the apple she held out to him. He deliberately missed it and rested his head against the back of her hand. She felt tension, concern, and a sense of danger emanating from him. Nodding, she pulled her hand back and held the apple out a second time. He took it from her and headed back toward the other unicorns.

"Well?" several of her wagon mates asked in unison.

"There's some kind of trouble ahead."

"I wonder if it's another ambush?"

Kayleigh looked back at Alicia. She heard Sir Aeric mention an ambush, but didn't know any of the details. Brushing some of her hair out of the way, she said, "It might be the Yar."

"The what?"

"They are a tribe of nomads and raiders who live in the mountains to the north. Every few years they come down and raid Miros and some of the other towns. It's one of the reasons Miros and Helden have walls."

Kayleigh's fears were confirmed when Ben came back a few minutes later. "It looks like there's fighting going on in Miros. We're going to move off the trail and behind that hill. Half the guards are going to stay with us and the rest along with the battle maidens are riding there to see if they can help."

It took a few minutes to move back behind the hill. Kayleigh and the others watched as Ben and several of the drivers went back to the road to cover the tracks of the wagons. They were accompanied by a pair of the remaining guards.

"Where's Majherri?" Kayleigh asked, suddenly realizing that her unicorn wasn't with the others. She fought back a momentary panic and took a deep breath.

Ellen was the one to spot him. "There, he's on top of the hill next to those trees. If you close your eyes and concentrate, you can usually find your unicorn."

Kayleigh nodded her thanks, exhaled, and watched him. Everyone else was milling around, but Majherri was on the top of the hill overseeing the road. It made her wonder who was really in charge. Clearly it wasn't the ones who thought they were. She started to go to him.

"Hold it right there, Miss. Stay with the group." One of the guards cautioned her.

"My unicorn is up there."

"Well if it sees something, it'll come back down here. It doesn't have a saddle, so you'd only slow it down. But if you want to be useful, come with me."

Kayleigh obediently followed the man in chainmail to the pair of the wagons that contained the props for the demonstration. "We've got some spare weapons stored in here. You go ahead and get the rest of your girls armed. Find out which ones are any good with a crossbow. I can load them if the draw is too difficult."

"Uh, yes, sir." She replied processing what was happening.

"Sir?" he laughed. "Sweetheart, I work for a living. Now get to it."

Knowing she should be acting like some kind of a leader, Kayleigh gathered the rest of the chosen riders and handed out the smaller and lighter weapons. Only Ellen and a girl named Lacey had ever used a crossbow before, so she gave them knives and sent them over to the guards. For herself, she took a beaten up old sword that had obviously seen better days. After a moment, she decided it was too heavy and picked up a small hatchet instead. She'd used hatchets before to make kindling and hammers, roughly the same size, with chisels to shape stone. Of course, the wood and rocks never had the ability to fight back. The tattered and worn leather wrap around the wooden handle felt uncomfortable and crude in her comparatively delicate hands. She gulped nervously.

This is just a precaution. We'll be fine as soon as the drivers get back from covering the tracks. As long as Majherri isn't worried, there's nothing wrong.

The moment she uttered that in her mind, her unicorn at the top of the hill let out a loud whinny and started racing back down the hill. He was moving fast – faster than she'd ever seen something move. Letting out several snorts, directed at the other unicorns he galloped to her side and lowered himself down.

"Are you sure that's a good idea, Majherri? Our first time riding together didn't go over that well." Kayleigh referred to the awkward mess that was yesterday.

He responded with a look and a snort that left no room for doubt. It couldn't have been any clearer if he had actually said, "Get on, now!"

Needless to say, he didn't have a saddle. Kayleigh handed her hatchet to Francine and struggled to climb on. He was probably unhappy that she used part of his mane as something to grip onto, but she made it onto his back. Once mounted, she felt the bond coursing through her body. It seemed both strange and natural at the same time. Kayleigh noticed that the other unicorns had moved much closer to their riders, almost protectively.

"You're not supposed to be on your unicorn!" Alicia said.

"It's not my idea!"

"Well if you're going to do it, at least try to stay up. Follow me! You'll need something to hold on to." Alicia ran to one of the wagons and grabbed a length of rope. Majherri opened his mouth and bit down on the center of it. Alicia handed her both ends and she held them tightly in her left hand for some stability.

The first screams and sounds of battle came while she was trying to get used to holding the rope and balancing bareback on Majherri.

Her unicorn darted back to Francine who held the ax out to Kayleigh like it was going to bite her.

"Recruit! You're going to get yourself killed! Get down right now!" The guardsman she'd obeyed earlier commanded. Majherri snorted at him and charged off.

Kayleigh was scared as hell. Majherri fought back with confidence. She could tell that he knew what he was doing. He was begging her to trust him. She wanted to, but the pounding in her chest betrayed her true feelings as they rounded the hill.

She saw at least five or six men, swathed in dark cloaks and furs – the Yar. They carried spears, nets, axes, and vicious looking short stabbing swords. The two guards were surrounded and were back to back, trying to protect each other. The three wagon drivers were on the ground and likely dead. Bile fought its way up into her throat as Majherri went to a full sprint. His eagerness for battle brushed aside her terror as his tail would a group of flies.

The raiders were stopped by the sight of a charging unicorn coming at them. It allowed the two guardsmen to wound a pair of Yar warriors and improve their odds.

One with a spear and another with a net and sword moved quickly trying to force Majherri between them. It might have worked with a regular cavalry rider and his or her horse, but Majherri shifted directions so fast that Kayleigh had to hold on for her life. Seconds later, she felt the same feeling that he was going to turn sharply.

This must be how unicorns tell their rider what to do! She thought as Majherri pivoted hard again charging right at the one with the net. The raider tried to throw the net, but Majherri leapt to the right and plowed the man under. Kayleigh tried to block out the sickening cracks as the legs of her unicorn drove into the screaming man. Majherri paused just outside the spearman's reach and lowered his horn to parry the thrusts. They circled each other in some kind of deadly dance amidst the fighting of the guardsmen.

A jolt of raw anger shook Kayleigh out of her stupor. Majherri needed her to do something! She realized that somehow, she was still holding the hatchet. Not knowing what else to do, she pulled it back and threw it as hard as she could. The man ducked it, but Majherri pounced driving his horn into the man's chest and lifting him off the ground. Kayleigh batted the raider's hands away, but he grabbed her shoulder and her throat.

Heat, like a sudden fever, swelled from her connection with Majherri up through her body as she fought to breathe.

Her hand smacked at the masked man in a futile gesture at first, but then, she saw flames and realized her hands were on fire and so were the wrappings on the man's head.

The grip on her neck eased and Majherri unceremoniously dumped the man to the ground. Fire still danced around her right hand as another raider wielding a large ax charged toward them. Kayleigh pushed her hand at him and a gout of flame leapt from her palm. The Yar warrior tried to shield himself against the magical flame, but he stumbled, falling to the ground. Majherri reared, with his front hooves on fire, and brought his full weight down on him.

Kayleigh couldn't hold on and slipped off hitting the ground hard. She was momentarily knocked senseless. A few seconds, or perhaps a minute later, the face of one of the guardsmen filled her vision.

"Are you okay, girl?"

"What?" She croaked – her throat still raw from the attack.

"You must have hit your head pretty hard. Easy, sit up. That's it. It's all over now."

Still shaking off the effects of the fall, she heard a scream. It was the other wounded guardsman using his sword to finish off the Yar that Majherri initially trampled. Kayleigh looked for Majherri. He was about twenty feet from her. The hair on his head and neck was matted with blood, like a horrific vision of death. Her eyes drifted down to her clothes and she saw the blood stains on them as well.

"The remaining two tried to run for it, but your unicorn ran the savages down. We were pretty much done for, so thank you for saving our lives. C'mon, let's get you back on your feet."

He offered his hand to help her up. When she took it, she screamed in pain. The flesh on the palm of her hand was burnt and blistering welts dotted the reddened skin. She sagged back to the ground clutching it to her chest.

Majherri was at her side instantly as the guard wrapped

her hand in damp strips of cloth.

"Walk back to camp and have someone put salve on your hand. Tell Lloyd to send a few more guards up here. We've got to bury our dead."

Kayleigh stood up, walking slowly. Her good hand firmly gripped Majherri. She could feel reassurance coming from him, but those emotional jolts crashed on the shores of her aching numbness. Kayleigh stopped and vomited at the sight of Ben, her wagon driver. His eyes were open in silent terror. People always said that when someone died that they were at peace. The look on his face told a different story. Even with Majherri as a physical and emotional crutch, the walk back to camp was on trembling legs and with tears streaming down her cheeks.

Chapter 7 – Harsh Truths

"Are you that eager to kill another rider? Do you expect the hand of fate will provide you with a third?" Meghan half asked and half accused Majherri. The unicorns and the majority of humans pretended like they weren't listening. Lynch had a reputation for coolness, except when it came to Majherri.

The unicorn snorted and dismissed her. *Go ahead, human. Get your angry tantrum out of the way.*

"I hope you're proud of yourself. You dragged an untrained girl out onto the battlefield, who can barely even stay on you, for what? The chance to do battle? Is that it? You could have easily killed her!"

He turned away in contempt as the woman continued berating him and gazed at the onlookers. There were no looks of support from the other maiden warriors or their mounts, just returned from the battle at Miros. Naturally, the two human guardsmen seemed reluctant to defend him.

You'd think they'd be more grateful that I saved their lives.

He lifted his head. She wasn't here during the battle. His rider was never in any serious danger. A pitiful group of raiders was not exactly the same thing as going into battle against an ogre.

Majherri kept within a few steps of Kayleigh as the fire maiden, Annabeth, surveyed the damage to Kayleigh's hand. He simply tuned Captain Lynch out and focused on the more interesting conversation.

The small, waif-like fire maiden whispered to his rider, "You need to learn control, if you're going to be throwing heat like that around. The way we teach is to put gloves over our hands. The flame is always conjured on the outside of the glove like a barrier. Eventually, we take away the glove, but maintain the barrier in our mind. Even after you master this, burns will still happen when you're not focused on what you're doing or rushing the conjuration."

"Am I going to be okay?"

"It's pretty nasty and we used up our supply of healing tears to tend to the wounded in Miros. You'll have to use the salve, until we can get some more." Annabeth glanced up at Majherri and then at the water maiden like she was measuring the odds of that happening. "Anyway, I'll start working with you on the basics of fire magic. Burns are an occupational hazard, but we don't want this to become a habit. Welcome to the sisterhood of the eternal flame, fellow fire maiden."

Kayleigh smiled weakly as her hand was rebandaged. "Will you be teaching me at the Academy, ma'am?"

"No, just here on the road. I'm on loan from the High-King's battalion to do demonstrations. Your instructor is probably leading a recruiting team that went north and west."

"Thank you."

"You're welcome. If you want to really thank me, put a good word in for Rhey with Majherri."

"I don't understand, ma'am."

Annabeth chuckled looking directly into Majherri's eyes. "My unicorn seems taken with Captain Lynch's T'rsa. He's courting her, but her brother here seems to be a bit of a stick in the mud."

He's resorting to having his rider beg mine for help? How unworthy of Rheysurrah. I thought my opinion of him couldn't get any worse.

"I'll do what I can," Kayleigh said. Majherri overlooked this display of treachery from his rider. She was still very young and trying to please the rest of the humans. He'd put up with this from her.

Turning his head back to Captain Lynch, he could see she was livid that he wasn't paying any real attention to her *righteous* fury. The armored woman angrily marched up to his rider. "Get up. You and I are going for a walk."

"Yes, ma'am," Kayleigh said with a note of hesitancy in her voice.

Majherri followed to see what Meghan intended to say to his rider. T'rsa fell into step next to him. Her body language quickly told him that she was of the same opinion as her rider.

I did what I had to do and I'd do it again. The human has spent too much time teaching and not enough time doing. I choose where I fight and when I fight. You either battle on your terms or someone else's.

Humility wasn't one of his strong suits. Outright defiance was. He and Danella had perfected it into an art form, which was why she was such a good independent scout.

The foursome walked back to the road and the scene of the battle. As soon as they were out of the earshot of the camp, Lynch said in a stern tone, "I want you to understand this, Reese. My anger is directed at Majherri and not you."

"Yes, ma'am. I understand." His rider responded.

"No, I don't think you do. He knows how the bond works. Each recruit and the unicorn spend years sorting each other out like when a couple gets married. All the other recruits and their unicorns are discovering it for the first time … except you and him. There's no way you wanted to charge into battle on his back. He made you do it!"

"But we saved those guards' lives. Well, mostly it was him."

"Yes, the two of you did just that. It's the upside in all this, but here's what I'm looking at Reese. Majherri is a strong willed unicorn. He will run roughshod over you if you let him. If it were just the two of you, I wouldn't be as interested. Trust me, there're plenty of maidens out in the battalions that are 'horn whipped' and allow themselves to be led around by their steed. But you, you're going to likely be lead rider for this new class. Every one of these recruits in this year is going to look to you for guidance … especially after this. Fair or not, you're going to be a role model to all these girls."

"Your rider's being a bit overbearing, sister." He flared his nostrils at T'rsa.

She responded that the truth must be a hard thing for him to hear and that this is entirely his fault.

He pawed the ground with his hoof. *"Oh, I brought a bunch of human raiders into the area. Maybe I should make certain that young male sniffing your backside most every second of the day knows what a fool you really are!"*

"What are you asking me to do?" His rider stated, oblivious to the spat Majherri was having with his sister.

"You've got a tough road ahead of you, Reese. I'm going to ride you hard and not take any of this wishy-washy rubbish from you. I'm responsible for the whole class – every rider. If you can't stand up for yourself, the others won't either and everyone suffers. I'm telling you now so we're perfectly clear on this. If you start becoming a burden to the class, you're going to get promoted to the second year or even the third year and be completely lost in your training. You'll be Captain Anella's or Sycroft's problem then."

"You'd do that?"

The woman fixed her gaze on his rider. "In a heartbeat, recruit. You and I know that I hate him. He hates me. I will do my level best to separate my feelings about you from what I think of him. That's why I'm telling you this up front. You deserve a chance to succeed, just like every other recruit. You're not going to wash out, if that's what you're worried about. There's never been a recruit who was able to manifest elemental magic that's washed out of The Academy before. That's a strong bond after only a few days. And I know Majherri won't let you fail, you're his only chance at redemption. So let me offer early congratulations. The years ahead are a formality for you. But what I'm concerned about is what kind of fire maiden you will be at the end of your training? Will you be Majherri's equal partner, or his tool? That's what we don't know yet."

They stopped. Three small piles of earth on the otherwise flat grassland marked the passing of the wagon drivers. The bodies of the Yar raiders were left to rot in the open. In the faint light, the two that were charred could still be seen. Captain Lynch rolled the most badly burnt of the two over and surveyed it looking for something. She reached onto his belt and retrieved a knife made completely from bone. It was straight and designed for throwing. She held it, testing the balance and nodded.

"You're blooded now, Reese. Our tradition is to take a weapon from our first kill and make it our own. Eventually, you'll be able to store some magic inside of it and call on it even when you're not in contact with your unicorn. Search around for a sheath or get one in Miros tomorrow."

Lynch reversed her grip and extended it to his rider, who took it by the handle and stared at it as the Captain continued, "Blooding usually doesn't happen until the fourth or fifth year of training. Many recruits make it to the battalions without ever being blooded. Part of your training is supposed to prepare you for this eventuality. Taking a life is never easy – it should never be. Be afraid if it ever does become that way for you. Fortunately, this was cut and dry. These were raiders and they needed to be killed. They deserved to be killed. You did help save two men under my command and it is more than should have been asked of you."

"I'll be okay … ma'am." The pronouncement lacked conviction, but his rider said it anyway.

"I expect nothing less, Reese. I doubt you will ever seek me out, but if you need to clear your mind, Lieutenant Sheppard or Rider Welsh will be available for you to speak with in private."

"Thank you."

"You are welcome. After we leave Miros, I'll need a day or two to recover before I can use my healing magic on your hand. There are still too many there who require my help. I don't want you to think that I am needlessly cruel. In the meantime, the pain you feel will be a reminder that you need to prepare like no other recruit before you, because there has never been another recruit like you before."

There was a pause and Lynch signaled for T'rsa to come close, sliding into the saddle in one fluid movement. "I am going for a ride to clear my head, recruit. Make your way back to camp and think about what we discussed this evening. "

Seconds later, they were alone and staring at each other. It was somewhat uncomfortable. He stepped closer and she hesitated before sticking the knife in the length of rope she used as a belt, and placing her uninjured hand on the side of his neck. He vehemently denied what Lynch was implying about him. Kayleigh's eyes showed that she didn't entirely believe his denials.

"She has a point. I didn't leave my home just so you could be the next controlling force in my life. I wasn't ready to fight." She said quietly.

It was easy to use hate to justify his decisions with Lynch, but less so with Kayleigh confronting him.

"If you're expecting me to be Danella, you're in for a letdown. I can't be her. You just heard her. They're going to hold me to some unreachable standard. It's not fair! I just want to be a battle maiden, not the second coming of General Jyslin!"

Her words were tinged with her fear and insecurities. Majherri knew how much Kayleigh worried about fitting in with the others. Young human females tended to concern themselves with things like that. He sent her a feeling of camaraderie.

"That's what we're supposed to be – a team. I can do that, but you need to meet me part of the way. I've got enough on my hands without being a part of what you and Captain Lynch have going on."

Another awkward silence ensued. Even among beings that can communicate raw emotion to each other, sometimes there was nothing else to say. "Come on, let's get back to camp. I need some rest. We probably both have a lot to sleep on."

Majherri kept his head held up, but it was much more of an effort than before. He paced his rider back to the wagons and after she climbed into her sleeping roll, he made his way back to a clear area to watch the stars. Pasha found him there.

"You angered your rider, my rider…actually just about every rider in camp," Pasha commented without any accusation in her tone.

"Better the two human warriors died without injuring any of the barbarians and then the whole group descended on a camp filled with children and unicorns that know not their horn from their tail. That would have gone well."

"True, but did you really need your rider at this time?"

He thought the female's question over. Majherri had been separated from Danella in battle before and thought nothing about waging war on his own. He knew why this was different. Perhaps giving the answer its own voice would help rid him of the demons plaguing his steps.

"I had ... doubts of my own ability. I lack the confidence of my earlier years. My last battle, I did not win. I don't even know what really happened, other than my rider was killed. I may never know. Could I have done more? Could it happen again? That failure haunts me, Pasha. There! I've said it. Does that make you happy? Both you and T'rsa have been looking for a confession this entire trip."

The younger female maneuvered around to look at him from his scarred side and where the crack in his horn was most prominent.

"None of us could come out of a fight with the scars you carry without giving our all. It's obvious you fought to the best of your ability."

"And it wasn't enough!" He reared and pounded his hooves in frustration. It was strong enough to make her flinch.

Pasha approached him again, closer this time and rested her head against his own. *"No, it wasn't. But for the first time this trip, you've shown how much it hurt you. You're starting to live again. T'rsa feeds off her rider's anger, but deep down she wants you to heal."*

"And what do you want, Pasha?"

She twisted her head in amusement. *"What I want, you're not ready for right now – maybe someday soon though."*

Chapter 8 – A Fragile Tether

"Abasa won't let me touch him!" Francine exclaimed with a strangled cry.

Kayleigh looked up from where she was changing the bandage on her hand. The girl seemed like she was panicking and her smallish unicorn kept moving away from her. The rain from last night had broken and only a few clouds dotted the morning sky.

Captain Lynch approached, "What is the matter, recruit."

"My unicorn ... there's something wrong!"

The water maiden looked even more stern than usual. "Do you still feel the bond?"

When Francine didn't respond immediately, Captain Lynch shook her by the shoulders. "Answer me! The bond? Is it there or not?"

"I don't feel it!" The young girl screamed.

Annabeth, the fire maiden moved over quickly and ushered some of the other recruits back. Kayleigh gathered that this was somewhat serious based on the tone. The scene in front of her was much easier to process than last night's battle. She'd barely slept at all and hadn't eaten more than an apple and a hunk of bread for breakfast.

Part of her wanted to join the onlookers, but common sense won out. She stayed where she was and watched as Majherri wandered over to her. Reaching into her bag, she pulled out the coarse brush and began working on him.

"Are they going to be alright?" she asked Majherri running her hand across his coat.

She found herself staring into the dark orbs of Majherri's eyes and a feeling of loss and sadness passed through her being. Her unicorn didn't think Francine and Abasa were going to get through this. Together, they watched Lieutenant Sheppard and Captain Lynch roughly handle Abasa into a submissive position, helped by their mounts, while Rider Welsh forced Francine's hand on the unicorn.

The young unicorn was clearly frightened and letting loose fearful wails.

"Welsh, get her on Abasa," Captain Lynch ordered. "We'll lash the two of them together and hope that forces the bond to reconnect! Rope! I need rope, right now!"

Kayleigh watched Alicia turn and sprint in her direction. Using her undamaged hand, Kayleigh reached into the bed of the wagon and pulled out a coil of rope. She tossed it underhanded to Alicia, who spared her a grateful smile before heading back to the disturbance.

Abasa managed to free himself, throwing the two Battle Maidens restraining him to the ground. T'rsa and Pasha immediately moved in and pinned the young unicorn back against a tree. Lieutenant Sheppard was the first one back on her feet. She grabbed Pasha's mane and gestured at the ground beneath Abasa. The area blurred slightly and Kayleigh could see Abasa beginning to sink into the suddenly giving surface.

He tried to get out of the muck, but the ground solidified, locking three of Abasa's four legs and effectively immobilizing him. Lynch and Sheppard worked quickly, maneuvering Francine onto the back of her steed. Welsh started binding the two of them together.

A short time later, Sheppard released the duo with Captain Lynch tying the other end of the rope to T'rsa. Abasa pulled and tugged, but T'rsa was easily a match for the much younger unicorn. This thrashing continued for easily five minutes before Abasa stopped bucking and seemed to accept his current state.

Captain Lynch looked around and clearly did not like all the gawking. She said, "The rest of you are supposed to be breaking camp! There's plenty of work to be done in Miros, so get moving!"

Kayleigh finished brushing Majherri and loaded her bag

and bedroll into the wagon. She helped Ellen with her gear and the two of them started packing Francine's items.

"Ellen, can you handle the wagon?"

"Huh?" The blonde asked, momentarily confused before recalling what happened to their driver last night. "I can handle a wagon."

"Good, I'll have one of the others sit with you and you can show them how to do it. I'd do it, but..." Kayleigh trailed off looking at her injured hand.

"What was using magic like?"

"I was so scared, I didn't even notice," Kayleigh tried to dismiss it, not wanting to really discuss the matter. What happened was really beyond her description and she couldn't find the words to do it justice. With whatever Francine was facing, it wasn't the proper setting to speak about something like this.

"I hope I'm a fire maiden like you. Most of us won't find out until the testing, a full month after we reach The Academy."

Casting a glance around, Kayleigh loaded the last of Francine's things into a rucksack and replied, "I think we need to worry about getting there first."

Kayleigh was thankful that she'd gotten Ellen to take the reins. The other wagon missing a driver had to be told to do this. Part of her upbringing with her mother was to be the practical one. By the time she was eight; Kayleigh made meals or reminded her mother of things that needed to be done. Her mother often got lost in her current project and would overlook mundane things like eating.

I hope she'll be okay without me. What am I thinking? She's the one who all but threw me out into the street with nothing! I need to focus and stay grounded. If I do that, then maybe I won't completely fail at this lead rider thing after all.

She spent the miles in quiet contemplation. Ellen and Alicia were driving the wagon and the rest were reading quietly. Kayleigh just stared at the tree line and wondered what was on the road ahead.

"You don't look well, Reese. How's your hand?" Lieutenant Sheppard asked as she brought Pasha alongside the wagon.

"I'm okay, ma'am. How's Francine?" She replied, glancing up at the front of the wagon train where the unicorn with rider firmly attached was being led by Captain Lynch.

Sheppard surveyed all the expectant faces and said, "Abasa is the youngest unicorn in the herd. The bond might not retake. Every bond is different. Some are exceedingly strong and run deep. Others are a fragile tether until they are fully realized. The mental state of both the rider and the unicorn also come into play. The attack last night might have been too much, too soon for both involved. All of you need to be aware of this over the next few days as you spend time with your mounts. If you feel something isn't right, tell one of us – immediately!"

Kayleigh recalled Francine's actions last night, holding the ax out to her and scared witless. To her mind, the bond was like a pair of ropes knotted together.

"What happens if it doesn't retake?" Alicia asked.

"We'll try to force the bond for a few days, but if it doesn't reappear, we'll send her back home."

The idea of going home struck everyone like a slap in the face.

"What happens to Abassa, if that happens?"

The Earth Maiden took a moment to compose her answer. "He would return to the herd and come back out next year looking for a new rider."

"But what about their bond?" Ellen asked.

"The bondspark is a connection, not a guarantee. Unless you were selected early, odds are that well over a thousand hands have touched your unicorns. There may be someone better suited for your unicorn. Whether it's fate, destiny, or just plain old dumb luck, you made a strong enough connection to be chosen as a rider. You got there first. The bond is something to be nurtured. Only when you reach the point where you can call upon the unicorn's magic can you relax and stop worrying."

"Does that mean Kayleigh can stop worrying?"

A slight smile spread across the stocky woman's face. "I think recruit Reese has several other things to worry about, but this isn't one of them. Now for a change of subject, Miros will be substantially different from our other stops. There isn't going to be a celebration. These people just lost friends and family to raiders. We'll try to do some good work while we're there. All of you are expected to do your part. We'll leave most of our supplies behind and take only enough food to get us to our next destination."

As the lieutenant made her way to the wagon following them, the whispering began. Kayleigh tried not to pay much attention to it, but one thing stood out.

"I guess it's why we have to take a seven year vow of chastity," one of the others said.

"What exactly do you mean by that?" Alicia asked, turning around.

"Well, if what she said about the bond is true, that might be why they have us take a vow of chastity. Having a male suitor might interfere with the bond."

"I wonder why it's seven and not five? Why doesn't it just go to graduation? What do you think, Kayleigh?"

"Um … this is all still new to me," she said while scrunching her nose in thought, "I didn't even know about a chastity vow up until you just mentioned it. If I have to guess it is probably that the first two years after you graduate, they keep you too busy for romance."

Alicia nodded and said, "That sounds correct. Rider Welsh told me that even after you leave The Academy, you still have plenty to learn."

Kayleigh stayed a part of the conversation just for the sake of being involved. As the wagon moved on, she could only wonder what other little surprises about this new life were waiting for her. Being nervous seemed like a perpetual state for her.

Miros looked much different from Kayleigh's previous visits. Even the bright late summer day could not mask the dreadful appearance of the small town. It had only half the population of Helden … less now. Her eyes were drawn to the parts of the wall that had been breached and partially collapsed. From what she heard, the attack came just before sunrise, probably after the sentries had spent the entire night awake and were looking forward to the end of their shift. This season, she had taken her turns on Helden's walls and knew, all too well, how fatigue could set in after eight hours of looking out into the darkness from the elevated towers.

One of those towers was blackened and had seen better days. It was occupied by a stern looking man with a crossbow as they passed. The only one who seemed to look more frustrated than him was poor Francine, who had been taken off of Abasa within the last mile. She sulked in the corner of the wagon and rejected any attempts at conversation. They would try again once they left this place.

Inside the walls, things weren't much better. Some buildings were burnt down to their frames. The stench of death and decay was in the air. In the square were the remains of individual funeral pyres and one large pile where the townsfolk had flung the bodies of the ten raiders who were killed.

Still, the people of Miros mustered up their hospitality and welcomed them officially to the town. The elders thanked Captain Lynch for their timely arrival. The four magic wielding battle maidens immediately turned the tide on the Yar and scattered the looters. Most of the women and children fled offshore on the boats of the fisherman and waited for the nightmare to end. Kayleigh tried hard not to imagine what it must have felt like.

She saw Sir Aeric, who had stayed overnight in the town along with his guards. The man appeared tired, but carried himself with both dignity and determination.

The group that stumbled onto the camp must have been

looking to scout out Helden for a possible raid. It made Kayleigh feel better knowing that the threat to her former town was eliminated. When the wagons stopped, they climbed out. Captain Lynch and the other maidens, except for Lieutenant Sheppard brought the remaining unicorn forward for the choosing ceremony.

"Alright," Sheppard addressed the girls, "work with the drivers and consolidate the supplies into that wagon over there. The rest, we are going to give to the town."

Aside from the small chest of gold, the gesture of two wagonloads of dry goods was mostly symbolic, but the crowd appreciated it nonetheless. When the gift of two hundred gold coins was announced, Kayleigh looked at Lieutenant Sheppard and the earth maiden shrugged her shoulders. It was the chest that should have been hers. Knowing that it was going to help people took some of the sting out of it, but, even so, Kayleigh returned to her work with an angry expression on her face.

From the corner of her eye, she saw Majherri standing very close to Abasa. Her unicorn was obviously giving Francine's a stern talking to. It included butting and tapping horns against each other. Kayleigh had no real idea how to interpret unicorn conversations, but she got the impression that Majherri was throwing his weight around.

"They're gonna send me home, I just know it!" Francine muttered passing her a sack of flour.

"You shouldn't worry about that now," Kayleigh replied.

"…says a girl who can already do magic with her unicorn. Thanks for the advice, Kayleigh. I'll keep it in mind."

"I'm just trying to help!" Kayleigh said.

The harsh reply came back, "This isn't like teaching me to read. This is losing my unicorn!"

Maybe it was the pain from the burn on her hand, or the queasiness from not eating, the fact that this could have been Helden, or even seeing Majherri doing what he could to help, but Kayleigh eyed the smaller brunette and hissed, "Look around! These people have real problems. This isn't the time or place for whining. You've still got a chance to reconnect with Abasa. The villagers here have to rebuild there homes and say farewell to their dead."

Several of the surrounding girls stopped what they were doing, this being the first time they'd heard her utter an unkind word at anyone other than Morganstern. Kayleigh had gone out of her way to be pleasant, but this problem wouldn't be solved with sugar. Instead, it needed some salt.

"What did you say?"

"Put things in perspective. Even if you can't reconnect, you still get to go home and live your life."

"But how am I supposed to reconnect with him?" Francine pleaded, drawing some looks from the nearby villagers.

Kayleigh paused and tried to think it through and not sound callous. "Look at what changed. You're scared from the battle last night. We all were. But you've got to put it behind you."

"She's right, you know." The pair turned to see Lieutenant Sheppard behind them. The earth maiden continued, "Recruit Reese, let her hold your knife."

Kayleigh did as instructed and handed the bone knife to the nervous teenager. The girl held it like it was going to bite her at any second.

"What is it?"

"Huh?"

"That is not the correct answer, Recruit Andover. I'll ask again. What do you have in your hand?"

"A knife."

"Is it a knife for cutting food, recruit?"

"No."

"That's right," Sheppard said. "It's a weapon. It's meant to kill something. Accept it. It's what you're going to be trained for. Your fear is intruding on your bond. It threatens to undo it, permanently."

"It is not!" Francine replied a little too loudly.

"Oh really? Which one of you was more affected by the

battle and the deaths? Abasa, or you? Were I to guess, Abasa is eager to prove himself and was impressed by what Majherri did."

Francine stood there refusing to meet the lieutenant's eyes. To Kayleigh, it appeared that the younger girl was withering under the stern gaze of the officer.

"We are warriors. You might have accepted that in your head, but you must accept it in your heart. Hasn't Captain Lynch already told you something similar?"

Francine lowered her head further, "Yes, ma'am."

"That's why we don't let you away from school until the end of your third year at The Academy. You need to have those fantasies you've built up erased and the reality put in its place. If you can't truly accept it, your bond with Abasa won't come back no matter how long we tie the two of you together. Now, give Reese back her knife and both of you get back to work. I'm going to see if I can use my magic to help repair the damage to their walls."

Defeated, Francine offered the knife back to Kayleigh and stared in helplessness. The younger girl wanted to rage that it wasn't true, but everyone knew it was.

After the wagon was unloaded, they watched the end of the ceremony. The final rider was selected, she was a small and skinny redhead named Helena. Understandably, there was little excitement in her expression. Kayleigh was close enough to hear the girl's mother say that her father and brother would have been proud.

Kayleigh choked back a few tears, knowing all too well what that meant. When Captain Lynch called for the other unicorns to come forward, Kayleigh looked at Majherri. As expected, he refused to move. She marched over to him.

"Majherri, go be nice for awhile," she scolded him. "They've suffered a great deal and anything we can do to help, we should."

She stared into his eyes and there was a struggle of will and pride. Deciding to try and exert some authority, she said,

"I followed you into battle without question. The least you can do is something simple in return."

Moments passed while the unicorn weighed her request. Eventually, Majherri agreed, giving the impression that it was against his wishes, but he would do it for her ... this time.

She breathed a sigh of relief as the stubborn creature trotted over to where the villagers of Miros stood in awe of being close to living, breathing sources of powerful magic. Even without their bond, she could see his discomfort, but she knew it was his way of offering to work with her as a team.

Chapter 9 – A Touch of Magic

The lightened wagons and favorable weather made for a quick trip to the next town. It took a trio of apples and two brushings, but Majherri forgave Kayleigh's demands that he prostrate himself and allow those unclean, unwashed, and unworthy hands to paw him like a piece of meat. His rider was happy to be able to purchase some of the necessities that she'd been denied.

Danella certainly would have never asked that from him!

In some ways, his new rider was like the young male, Abasa, skittish, easily upset, and uncertain of her place. Just as he had scolded the unicorn with the broken bond, Pasha scolded him for being needlessly rough when breaking in his new rider.

As if Captain Lynch, or all the doubters will be easy on my rider! Kayleigh needs to be prepared for the seasons ahead.

His flawless argument was rebutted by the female in a series of body movements and tail swishing. *"Be mindful that you're not trying to remake your old rider. Hooves down that path will leave you both wallowing in misery. If you really want to help your rider, I suggest you start by making peace with your sister."*

He lowered his cracked horn in defiance. *"She should be the one making peace with me!"*

The tip of her horn traced the circles up to the break. Tiny flickers of magic appeared where the two met. Why he allowed this when he was angry, he wasn't certain. Pasha had an infuriating effect on him, and she knew it!

"Both you and T'rsa are cut from the same cloth, stubborn and prideful. If you are so eager to quarrel with the human Lynch, make allies with your sister and the earth is soft on your journey, or in your case, the heat warms and strengthens you. T'rsa's ties to her rider mean that she won't make the first move. You must be the one to raise your horn in compromise."

Majherri moved away from her horn, but only a tiny bit, to not insult her. He blinked and blew a long, resigned breath. *"I will consider your advice."*

"That is the most intelligent thing you've said in some time. There's hope for you yet." The younger female seemed pleased and turned away from him swishing her tail attractively.

He snorted, mostly to himself, and wondered if he'd be able to attract the attention of a different female before mating season began.

"Majherri, would you come here, please?" His rider's voice interrupted his thoughts concerning the mysteries of the female unicorn.

Kayleigh stood by the fire maiden and her obnoxious mount, Rheysurrah in a fairly open area away from the others and with at least a short trot to the nearest tree. Obviously Kayleigh was about to get a lesson in channeling magic and they were establishing a safety zone. Majherri thought back to the night of the battle. He managed to set his hooves alight, which said something for the potential of his rider.

Moving alongside her, he nuzzled her hand in greeting as she listened to Rider Welsh speak. "First, we'll just focus on a slight touch with the finger tips. You're going to concentrate and feel the heat in your connection. Even in combat, you'll want to draw on the magic through one hand and release it with the other."

"Why?"

Welsh laughed, "Well, it's the biggest drawback to being a fire maiden. The energy flows from your unicorn through a connection. If you're not using a hand to connect, it comes from you legs when you're riding. The heat can burn a big hole in your pants and the rashes are no fun either, trust me on that one! So, you can spend a lot of time sewing and a lot of money on salves, or you can learn to keep a hand on your 'corn when drawing fire magic out of it. If it's any consolation, water maidens get a similar speech, because most of them get off their 'corns and look like they've wet themselves."

Majherri reasoned that Rider Welsh was one of those overly cheerful types that annoyed Danella. He paused, picturing his former rider and briefly worried that there'd be a day when he couldn't remember what she looked like. He didn't like the direction this series of thoughts led. Kayleigh was his rider now. She deserved his loyalty and attention.

"Alright," Annabeth said, "let's start with something simple. Place your hand at the base of Majherri's neck, just like I'm doing. Close your eyes and concentrate. Can you feel the magic there below the surface?"

Majherri lifted his head upwards as he sensed Kayleigh trying to connect with the power inside him.

"Yes."

"Good. Now here's the way I think about it, picture a soup ladle in your mind. You're going to dip it in and pull some of that power up your arm and into you. Does that make sense?"

"I think so."

"If that doesn't work, you're from the beach areas, so picture it like pushing your hand into the sand and the power is all the grains that are clinging on your skin."

"Which one's better?" Kayleigh asked.

"My instructor liked the sand thing. Soup ladle works for me. You'll eventually find the visual that helps you the most. Meanwhile, keep feeling the power and watch me. I'm going to snap my fingers on my other hand and make a little spark … just like so. Be careful, that hand is recently healed, so let's not burn it again."

Swishing his tail with undisguised irritation, Majherri realized that this was going to be a very tedious process. He felt a slight pull on the energy within him. It was negligible at best. Nothing happened at first, but on the third attempt, Kayleigh managed to make a tiny flame floating between her thumb and forefinger. Pure excitement rushed through the bond from his rider. He tried to recall how it had felt the first time Danella performed fire magic, but couldn't quite remember the scene.

"Well done!"

Majherri glanced at Rheysurrah, who rolled his eyes for both of them. It was amusing how humans could be so impressed with little things. Now, if she had triggered a full Fireshade, where Majherri and his rider were enveloped in a majestic blanket of blazing spellfire, that would've been impressive.

Danella had managed the Fireshade in battle three times … that he knew of. Just as a group of earth maidens using Thunderhooves could break a formation, a single fire maiden using Fireshade could scatter opponents by becoming a charging fireball. The terror it inspired was legendary and only one in perhaps twenty fire maidens ever managed the feat. A look at Welsh and Majherri doubted such magic was meant for her.

"I do not like the way you are looking at my rider!" Rheysurrah warned tossing his mane and lifting his head, so that he could stare down at Majherri.

"Fortunately, your permission is not required for how I look and what I think."

"Be careful Majherri, the humans have a saying. I believe it is pride comes before the fall. You've already fallen once. I would think that you would be less full of yourself with this second chance."

"What are they doing?" Kayleigh asked.

"They're posturing. Our unicorns don't like each other that much."

"I get the sense that Majherri's not that popular."

"Lieutenant Sheppard's mount seems to like him as well as Andover's 'corn. That's probably from the work you two did to help that one reconnect with Recruit Andover. Now let's practice this basic fire conjuration a few more times until you've got it. The thing is, keep the fire between your fingers and not burn them."

Majherri sensed pride from Kayleigh at being recognized for achievement. *She tries too hard to fit in and perhaps I try too hard to stand out. We are an oddly matched pair.*

Rheysurrah snorted and conveyed his anger. *"Do you think what I said is funny!"*

"No. I was reacting to my rider. Surprisingly, my sun does not rise and set with what you have to say. What is funny is that your rider asked mine to permit you to pursue my sister. Actually, I take that back. It is sad that you have brought your rider into a matter that is most certainly not her business."

"T'rsa says it is none of your business either!"

Majherri was puzzled by this declaration. Every time T'rsa had mated and he was present on the sacred island, she forced the males come to her for his approval. There was a jolt of anger and he felt Kayleigh's grip tighten as she reacted to it.

"Poor, poor Majherri, you may have a rider, but you still have no status. That must keep you awake at night, does it not?"

It was a pathetic taunt from an inferior. Still, it required a response. *"In that case Rheysurrah, I give you my blessing. She has clearly become a fool to the human that rides her and has lost the ability to draw the attentions of the better unicorns in the herd. You will have to do. Pursue her to your heart's content. It gives me one less place to avoid if both of you are in the same pasture."*

"Whoa! Whoa! Rhey, calm down! Kayleigh, why don't we break for the night? We'll get together tomorrow."

Majherri let out a sound of amusement and triumph as Rheysurrah's rider led him away. That human gave him several angry looks.

"You did that didn't you?" Kayleigh asked the obvious question.

He gave her pride and assurance in return. *I will do it again and as many times as necessary.*

His rider removed her hand and broke the connection between them. She rubbed her forehead and swept the blonde hair out of her eyes. "Could you at least wait until I've had my lesson to anger her unicorn?"

Tolerance was not something Majherri was accustomed to. What his rider asked of him would require an effort on his part, but he would try.

Before thirty of the human minutes passed, Pasha found him. She usually was able to sneak up on him, much to Majherri's dismay, but he was ready for her this time.

"What did you say to Rheysurrah that has him wanting to challenge you?"

"That is amusing! He is considering challenging me when he chided me for having no status. Does he covet my position? I was just doing what you said I should. I made a gesture to my sister and gave my blessing for him to pursue her."

Pasha gave off an air of being bemused. *"I'm certain you used that same tone with Rheysurrah. He is clearly overreacting. Although, I know he and T'rsa have spoken. She seems displeased with your kind gesture."*

Majherri mused that one positive thing this female had was a sense of humor. *"That is a shame. My words and their meaning were sincere."*

Pasha made humorous noises. *"Obviously. Do you wish to know what your sister said when I announced my intention to pursue you?"*

"You're being rather bold now. Perhaps, I will be less of an outcast when we return to the pastures surrounding the school. You may have competition."

She snorted, ignoring his comment. *"T'rsa asked why I was set on punishing myself?"*

He chortled at the idea of Pasha asking T'rsa for her permission. *"And how did you answer my sibling?"*

"You are more interesting than irritating, at least for the moment. Try to keep it that way. I also know that despite your current behavior, none of your previous mates spat when your name was mentioned. A few even indicated that they might consider you again, so you must have some redeeming qualities. I'm sure I'll discover them at some point."

Majherri openly laughed at her. *"You didn't speak to the right ones, then! But they are correct, you could do a lot worse. The males in the herd are becoming less impressive with each season."*

It was then that he noticed how much he was enjoying the banter. He could still feel the emptiness where Danella used to be, but Kayleigh was his new rider. It was time to begin anew, even if that meant spending so much time with these foolish younglings.

Things became more relaxed as the caravan moved away from the northeastern coast of the continent. The threat of raiders and bandits receded when they travelled the inland roads toward the more densely populated kingdoms. In all his years, Majherri never quite understood why the powers above and below allowed the humans to occupy the highest place on this world.

At least all the wars and fighting gave him something to do.

Chapter 10 – A Sliver of White

"It's like nothing I'd ever dreamed of," Kayleigh said staring at the great city before her, the words dribbling from her gaping mouth. It seemed that each city had gotten progressively larger. But Talcosa dwarfed them all.

Talcosa, seat of the High-King and the Council of Kings, home to the Great Library, said to have a copy of every tome ever printed, and the largest city in the world. Kayleigh felt like she needed to refocus her eyes to see it all rising above the walls that surrounded the city.

Because of her mother's wanderlust, she'd seen a great deal of the south and the east, but it was always the small villages and rarely the cities. Kayleigh mused that every village she ever lived in could be fit into a tiny corner of this monstrosity. It made her think of watching the tiny ant hills and all the creatures that scurried around them.

Their caravan had joined with others, a constant stream of wagons on roads made smooth by the unending number of travelers upon them. Every wagon was piled high with goods to feed the marketplaces. Mixed in amongst the merchants were fancy carriages, decorated with heraldic symbols from lands she'd only read about. These were filled with nobles of all ranks, each looking to make their mark on the greatest society.

Columns of soldiers rode in various directions, proudly with banners held high. Those that passed dipped their colors upon noticing the unicorn riders. There was a nervous energy in the air amongst the recruits. The wagon drivers and the soldiers were anxious to get home, Sir Aeric back to his estate, and the battle maidens back to The Academy.

Hardly anyone slept last night. Excitement was in the air as one journey was almost complete and the next one about to begin. Several times, Lieutenant Sheppard had them out walking alongside the wagons, but weeks of this had strengthened the recruits to the point where they could easily pace the slow moving wagons on the clogged roadway.

"I see it! I think I see it!" Ellen exclaimed pointing off to the left. The great city butted up to a massive lake that fed the sea of humanity that surrounded it. They could see the tiny dark specs of the numerous fishing boats out gathering the lake's bounty.

Further toward the center of the great lake was an island of modest size. While the city encroached on the edge of the lake and threatened to explode, the island had only a few buildings on it and the land was obviously well kept, but undeveloped. It was The Academy and Kayleigh knew it was about to become her home, the first home she had chosen and not simply been brought to.

Compared to the towers and ziggurats of the High-King's city the castle on that island was not terribly imposing, but everyone knew that the amount of magical energy on that isolated strip of land was staggering.

"I'm not looking forward to the boat ride," Francine said.

"That lake's as smooth as glass," Rebekah Morganstern answered. "You don't have anything to worry about." Her father owned many of the fishing boats in Helden and though Kayleigh doubted the girl had ever been out on one during a squall, it didn't stop Rebekah from talking like she had.

"Do you know how to swim?" Kayleigh asked.

Francine's sheepish look was all the reply needed.

"Guess you're not water maiden material."

Kayleigh eyed Rebekah and said, "Do you always have to be so mean?"

Morganstern replied with a look of mock innocence. "I don't know what you're talking about, Reese."

"She's just jealous because you're going to be lead rider," Ellen said with a scowl on her face. Rebekah had been just as critical of Ellen's farm girl background.

The girl laughed it off and tossed her hair over her shoulder. "Jealous? Of her? Hardly. No, I plan to enjoy watching Reese run herself ragged trying to prove that she belongs."

"Here I thought you were going to challenge me as soon as you could."

The false sincerity was practically oozing from the younger teen. "Goodness no. That would be a waste of time. You'll fail long before anyone challenges you. If they don't pick me as your replacement, I'll just have to see if the next person deserves the spot."

Kayleigh took a calming breath. Rebekah was goading her into an argument and trying to humiliate her. "I won't fail. Get used to taking orders from me for the next five years, Rebekah."

"I doubt it. From what Rider Welsh says, lead riders rarely hold the position for the full term, much less for multiple years. My father loved to make wagers, perhaps we'll get all the students to place bets on the day you get replaced. The person closest will win the prize. What do you think about that?"

She was about to respond, but saw that Captain Lynch was approaching. One thing she had to admit was that Rebekah always seemed to know when to end a conversation and get the last word. It usually left Kayleigh seething.

"Recruits! We need to prepare to enter the city. In a few moments you will be given your ceremonial white robes. You will walk beside your unicorns, ahead of the wagons. You will look straight ahead. You will not engage in trivial conversations. In fact, you will not speak at all. You will follow us down to the docks, where we will board the ferry that takes us to The Academy. Do you understand me?"

"Yes, ma'am," the voices chanted as one.

"Good. Until you are inside The Academy, those are the last words I want to hear from any of you. Now, line up and go to that wagon. Rider Welsh will give you your robe. Place it over top of your garments and then lead your unicorn to the front."

Kayleigh accepted the robe from the fire maiden. She had

worried that it would look out of place on her older frame, but it adjusted to her size. She realized that the robes were enchanted! The lining was soft and pliable. The fabric flowed with her movements. To all appearances, she glided across the ground.

The color was amazing. It wasn't just a plain white garment. It was glossy and had depth to it – like polished ivory. Even if she hadn't been told to be silent, there were no words she could use to describe the splendor of the robe she was wearing.

Majherri gave her an appraising glance and she could tell he was happy for her … even if he acted like this whole ceremony annoyed him. Kayleigh knew that much about her steed already. He butted her gently in a futile effort to get her to relax.

She was positioned at the front, directly behind Captain Lynch. Lieutenant Sheppard quickly rode up and down the forming line and arranged the recruits and their unicorns.

"Eyes forward, Reese," Lynch said, not even looking at her.

After a few more moments, the traffic into the main gate was halted for this procession. Naturally, Kayleigh felt uncomfortable with all the attention on her. She simply did her best to fix her gaze squarely on the Captain's back.

Once inside the gates, the massiveness of the city seemed to press down on them. Even with the spacious streets, twice as wide as Helden, they were a sliver of white in a sea of humanity. From the corners of her eyes, she could see the faces of the onlookers. They stopped what they were doing and turned to watch the young maidens and their unicorns.

Streets went off in what seemed like every direction. Talcosa was a maze unto itself. Back in Helden, Kayleigh often stared out into the ocean and allowed the great expanse a chance to kindly remind her that she was small and there were things that were larger than she would ever be. Talcosa was unapologetic and overbearing. Buildings loomed, larger than anything she'd ever seen. Order mingled with chaos and everything swirled in constant motion.

Kayleigh knew this place intimidated her. How could it not? But still, she moved forward in the wake created by Captain Lynch and Majherri's sister. Winding their way through the streets, the buildings abruptly receded into open expanse of the Great Market. It was rumored that anything and everything could be bought and sold in this area filled with small buildings, carts, tents, and wagons. Kayleigh overheard men arguing over a small patch of earth and who was allowed to sell there. They paused as the group passed, but immediately resumed. As they moved closer to the docks, the temperament of the crowd changed. They were less inclined to stop and stare, less interested in anything but their own business. It even felt a little hostile.

At an intersection, Captain Lynch halted the column and they waited for a series of wagons filled to the brim with goods to pass. People tried to scamper through and get to whatever destinations were ahead of them, but Lynch maneuvered T'rsa into the wake left by the wagons and her words rose above the chaotic din.

"Make way! Make way!"

The crowd, like a living entity, momentarily held its ground, but the warrior refused to stop moving forward. On the long ride here, Kayleigh had been told time and time again that one of the greatest strengths of the magic between rider and mount was the ability to project an aura of authority that bordered on fear. That magic multiplied by a full formation of riders was what broke enemy lines and chased off opposing cavalry. It was part of what made them the most feared fighters in the land.

From her position right behind Captain Lynch, Kayleigh felt that authority for the first time and saw the swirling crowd bend, forcing itself painfully out of their way.

Part of Kayleigh relished the idea of wielding that kind of power, just as another feared it. Regardless of her insecurities, the column pushed forward until she could see the water and the docks. Boats lined every pier and there was constant movement as ships were both loaded and unloaded at the same time. At the center of this bustle was a single pier with no activity whatsoever. Six armored warriors stood at the closed gate. Only when Captain Lynch approached did one remove a key from around his neck and unlock the gate, swinging it open.

The man saluted and spoke to Captain Lynch, "On behalf of my sovereign liege, I welcome you back to Talcosa and bid you a final safe journey to your isle. The ferry captain is waiting for you."

"Thank you, Sergeant of the Guard. It is good to be back."

Getting onto the wide pier was a relief. Much to Kayleigh's surprise, it did not creak from the weight of the unicorns like the piers of Helden complained under the stress of supporting the ocean's bounty. This was solid. This was eternal. This was everlasting.

"Continue walking your unicorn to the gangway, Recruit Reese. Stop when you get to it and wait for me to formally request permission to board."

Kayleigh started to open her mouth to reply, but fought back the words. No answer was needed and she had been told to remain silent until they reached The Academy.

Once they stopped, Captain Lynch dismounted and an older man dressed in finery walked down the gangway. His hair and beard were black and spotted with gray, but he carried himself with strength and a relaxed power. As Captain Lynch went down to one knee before him, Kayleigh recalled seeing paintings of the man before.

The "ferry captain" was High-King Barris himself.

"Rise brave warrior, and be welcomed back to my city."

"Thank you, my liege."

He smiled and gestured for her to rise, scanning the assembled recruits. "The rest of the new class? A most promising group indeed! I see the seeds of greatness before me. You are the pride and joy of all the land, ready to learn how to become the greatest protectors of all. Your journey truly begins here and now. It is my great honor to take you to your new home."

Kayleigh could barely meet the man's eyes and she knew her face was flushed with embarrassment, just as she knew every other recruit was in a similar state of disarray.

"Permission to board?" Captain Lynch asked.

"Permission granted." The High-King answered.

He stood there, smiling as Kayleigh passed by and led Majherri onto the ferry. Despite her best efforts, his gaze met hers and she felt like he was staring right into her soul. Majherri nudged her, breaking the connection and Kayleigh moved forward. She peered back as the other recruits experienced their own struggles. When Ellen looked like she was about to faint, the man caught her and said something about working on her "sea legs." High-King Barris was one of the most accomplished mages in the land, and Kayleigh knew there was more going on. Whatever he was doing was subtle, but she felt it.

With all the unicorns onboard, the High-King signaled to a man in robes. A wave of his hands caused the ropes to loosen from their moorings and the gangway to simply disappear. A gesture from the High-King's hands immediately started the ferry moving forward.

The ferry picked up speed and almost seemed to glide across the surface of the lake. The Academy grew closer and in the distance, Kayleigh saw dots of white on the grass near the pier, hundreds of them. Each one was a unicorn with a rider in the same white robes.

They were her sisters, and after all this wandering, Kayleigh was finally home. She vowed to keep that feeling with her for all time, no matter what.

Chapter 11 – Extra Duty

Those moments of awe his rider experienced upon arrival were rapidly replaced with the drudgery of life at The Academy. He had watched them go from one building, wearing their nicest dresses to this etiquette class and leave looking like a defeated pack of rabble. The unicorn found it ironic that they were trying to remake these young women into the finest warriors in a world dominated by the males of their species, only to confuse them by giving classes in proper social behavior, dance, and serving leaves in hot water. Every unicorn knew that water free of any impurities was the best water of all!

After their lesson on how to be a proper human female, they rushed back to their barracks to change into tunics to tackle the obstacle course. The course was ever changing. As soon as the human recruits became comfortable with the pitfalls, more would be added. Today was such a day. The rope swings were replaced with a rope net that the females had to climb up and over. Less than half were able to achieve this and all were disheartened by the performance. Currently, they were in the stables and his rider and another were becoming better acquainted with a pitchfork.

"I'm beginning to wonder if this was one colossal mistake," Kayleigh muttered quietly dumping straw and manure into a wheelbarrow.

Majherri snorted. It was his way of reminding her of his superior hearing. His rider was working off what the humans called "demerits" and he didn't require physical contact to sense her frustration.

"You know I'm not talking about you," she replied in a whisper. "We both know what *she's* doing isn't fair."

Captain Lynch had decided to set the tone early for her class and she was a strict disciplinarian. This extended to Kayleigh's role as lead rider for the newly formed class. Regardless of her personal performance, for every five demerits the class earned as a whole, Kayleigh received one hour of extra duty. In a class of over forty new recruits, from various educational, personal, and emotional backgrounds, all trying to conform to life at The Academy, those demerits came at a full gallop.

The male unicorn knew that this rule usually wasn't enforced on a lead rider until the first season ended. It was blatantly obvious why it was already in effect. The fairness, T'rsa's rider promised Kayleigh never quite materialized.

She set the pitchfork down and rolled her sore right shoulder in a slow circular motion.

The strange movements of humans never cease to amaze me.

"You're making fun of me, aren't you?"

"Are you talking to me?" Ellen asked from the next stall.

"No, Majherri is keeping me company," Kayleigh replied.

"Oh, sorry about all this … I didn't mean to get caught skylarking during Etiquette class. When I was selected, I only thought about learning to use a bow and a sword. Proper posture wasn't a consideration. 'Sides, cleaning out a stall is the same whether it's a horse or a unicorn. At least it's something I'm good at."

"Don't worry. It wasn't just you. Four people also failed the personal inspection this morning. Either way, you've got a leg up on most when it comes to the bow and sword. You'll get etiquette soon enough. It just requires practice and attention to detail."

There was an audible sigh from the stall next to Majherri as Ellen declared, "I used to make fun of all the town girls, trying to be perfect little ladies. Now, I am one!"

"Ah, but none of them have a unicorn right? Try not to get down on yourself, Ellen; do you want some extra help?"

"Maybe, you seem to pick it up easy enough."

His rider shrugged and said, "My mother … she usually painted or sculpted nobles or the merchant class. Good manners and the like were things I picked up along the way. I may be a little too busy right now, but there are several riders from noble families. I'll see what I can arrange, but in return you might have to help one of the others with riding or something similar."

"Sure," the other girl answered from her stall while filling her wheelbarrow with another load of blackened hay.

Kayleigh grabbed a rag and used one side of it to wipe her hands somewhat clean and the other to get the sweat from her brow. She patted him and he could feel her calluses already developing. With a smile she said, "I know you're the most beautiful creatures in all the known lands, but you can make an awful stink!"

Majherri flipped his mane in humor and regarded her comment ironic considering what human cities smelled like. There wasn't enough hay in all the land for that.

"Awful stink, you say?" An unseen party asked before stepping into the waning light.

The unicorn looked at the male. He was young, but carried himself well. The fanciful decorations on his tunic marked him as one of the upper class humans. It was the same as the man who possessed the magical bird on their recruiting trip.

The male bowed, "Brian Tomas, at your service. Well, if we are being correct, I am the stable master for this building, so technically you two are at my service."

"Greetings. Are you, by chance, related to Sir Aeric?" his rider asked, laughing politely at his joke.

"He is my older brother and part of the reason I've been absent until today. His lot in life is to be a knight of the realm, fight in battles, spending months without a comfortable bed. Mine is helping my uncle manage the stables and be surrounded by young maidens and unicorns. I'm fairly certain I have it better. Now, you were saying something about smell?"

The one called Ellen proffered her pitchfork and Majherri watched as the nobleman selected a chunk and held it to his tiny nostrils before crushing it and considering the texture. His rider contorted her face and tried, in vain, to suppress a choking noise.

"Yes, this does rather smell and it's a bit compacted. The unicorns in this group are getting too many fruits and not enough grass. This happens a lot when a new group takes over the feeding duties. I'll speak to the new class's lead rider and caution her about overfeeding."

"That's her right there," Ellen said gesturing with her tool. Naturally, some of the loose material splattered on his rider's cheek.

"Ellen!"

"Oh, sorry!" The younger girl exclaimed while Kayleigh tried to hide her embarrassment and wipe it off with the rag.

"Well, I always say, if you don't get any on you, you're not doing it right." The male's statement seemed to take the edge of the situation.

Humans are generally more entertaining in small numbers. Sadly, in large numbers, they mostly try to kill each other.

"So, you are Majherri's new rider. My brother spoke of you."

"He did?" Kayleigh replied looking somewhat uncomfortable.

The stable master waved his hand dismissively and said, "Oh, nothing but good things, I assure you. Now, I don't know if your unicorn remembers me, but I was just starting int the stable when he was last here."

Majherri shuffled forward to get a better look at the human and found that he did recall him. The "boy" grew into his lanky frame in the time since Majherri last saw him. His shoulders were broad and he possessed an air of dignity. There were many similarities to Sir Aeric.

"Well, it is good to be back on the Sacred Island. Father insisted I attend welcoming festivities for Aeric, which lasted a full week. Next mother's birthday was only a few days after that and I didn't dare be rude. After a time, I was beginning to believe they were trying to keep me there and began to plot my escape. But enough about me, the two of you seem to have a bit of extra duty this evening. How many more stalls do you have to clean out?"

Kayleigh replied, "Six. It's easier than trying to groom the younglings, who don't have a rider. They don't let me touch them for very long."

"Well, that is their nature, but you have much work to do. I'd offer to help, but since it is extra duty, it isn't permitted. Although, I suppose I could be a gracious host and fetch the two of you some fresh water and perhaps a bucket for Majherri."

"We're fine. No need to bother." His rider answered. Majherri spotted the signs of a blush on Kayleigh.

"Oh, but I insist. I thought my stables were going to be in a terrible state when I arrived and this is so much better than I hoped. It's the least I can do."

His rider and the other made a show of trying to refuse him, but Majherri noted how susceptible the pair of females was to the male's charm and "good" nature. After the noble left for the well, Ellen commented on his good looks and his rider seemed dismayed at her overall appearance. Watching humans interact always amused him. Still, even after all these years, he was no real judge of what constituted mating stock among humans.

Sadly, neither was Danella. Even so, his rider and all the others will swear a vow of chastity soon that lasts for many seasons. Life must be difficult for this Brian — so many potential mates and none actually available. Of course, humans have no set mating season to begin with, which is why they are the strangest of all animals.

Such thoughts led Majherri to think of Pasha and he stopped listening to the humans tittering like birds. He'd seen her out when the recruits were stumbling, in their two-legged way, about the long obstacle course. Rain pelted the trainees without mercy. Pasha's rider would constantly dismount and berate any of the trainees that the human did not think were working hard enough, or complaining too much.

She was doing so often that Majherri wondered why she

even bothered returning to the saddle.

The rest of the first season herd did not care to watch the humans exercising in clear skies, let alone bad weather. They usually grazed in the pastures and waited for their humans to come to them for riding lessons. Considering Majherri barely tolerated any of the younger ones, this made for the perfect place to escape from their collective foolishness, even if watching humans climbing ropes and crawling through mud was just as silly, but he was interested in his rider's progress. The opportunity to converse with Pasha was a definite bonus. He walked closer, swishing his tail in greetings.

"Your rider is a good specimen, Majherri, even compared to those that are actually her age. The rest of them leave much to be desired. My rider will have a difficult time with this herd of humans."

"They do seem to fall a lot, part of the problem with only having two legs and a poor sense of balance."

Pasha pawed the ground with one of her forelegs, indicating humor. *"You are gaining a reputation for avoiding the herd and following your rider around."*

Majherri snorted and answered her. *"The unicorns saying these things are no more a proper herd than the humans wallowing in the muck like pigs over there are trained warriors!"*

"I see this is a subject that brings out your temper. I meant it in jest."

He fought to relax. This wasn't going the way he hoped it would. *"I need to apologize. The younglings are irritating. Once my first rider graduated, we only returned to the Sacred Isle for mating season. Now, it will be twelve full seasons before I can leave this place again. I already feel confined."*

"This is a pleasant change! I'm surprised and flattered."

That was better. He felt foolish and off balance because of his outburst. Shifting uncertainly on his hooves, he replied, *"The fault is not with you, but me. I've missed your company. Your rider keeps you busy and the others are a poor substitute for your wit."*

"You look very much like a unicorn that I know, but you act nothing like him."

"I am becoming more comfortable with once again having a rider. When I put my mind to it, I can be rather charming."

Wide-eyed, she regarded him. *"Is this your way of courting me?"*

"I suppose it is," he answered in the affirmative and tried to gauge her reaction.

"What happened to you looking at other options?"

"Did I mention how irritating the younger ones are?"

She scoffed at his answer. *"So I am less irritating than the younglings who won't be mating this season. Is this your idea of charming? Perhaps you should try again."*

The female was toying with him. Of this, he was certain. He would try a more direct route. Drawing himself up into a rigid stance, he replied, *"To my knowledge, there are three females on the island that I have previously mated with. I haven't bothered to see if any of them are already paired off. I will ask only one this season."*

"Well that seemed rather heartfelt. I'll have to keep you in mind as mating season approaches. At this moment, you seem up to the challenge, but you attitude changes with the breeze." Her body language betrayed, ever so slightly, the aloof tone she tried to affect.

"You plan to make this difficult, Pasha. I've missed mating season before, because of where my rider was ordered to serve. Be careful. This little game you play could easily backfire."

She moved alongside him for a moment and he enjoyed having her that close. Last mating season, he'd just lost Danella and neither wanted nor received any offers to sire any children.

"It's not really a game, Majherri. I just think I am worthy of more effort on your part. This is a good opening gesture, but I will not settle for anything less than your best."

He noticed Pasha's rider returning from instructing the other humans. Lieutenant Sheppard smiled, misunderstanding what was transpiring.

"I wish it was that simple for me. Unfortunately, I have to interrupt and ride back to see how the stragglers are faring. You're welcome to come along."

He glanced at his rider and considered the offer. Kayleigh

was climbing a rope net up to a platform. Her hair was matted to her head by both rain and mud. Her eyes were not tired and could see that she was determined to finish strongly.

She's doing well. I will see her later. Let us see what other gestures this prideful female has in mind.

Majherri fell in stride behind Pasha, enjoying the view. Though he'd hoped it would be a simple arrangement, the challenge of winning Pasha over gave him something interesting to do. Just because he could miss mating season, didn't mean he wanted to. He had a second chance and he should make the most of it.

Chapter 12 – Magical Selection

"Reese, wake up. Francine said that you wanted to get up thirty minutes early. The inspection is in an hour." Kayleigh wiped the sleep out of her eyes and thanked Helena, while wishing that there was more time to rest. The other girl nodded curtly and walked back to her guard position ten feet from the door.

She didn't want to get out of bed, but Captain Lynch was inspecting today and there was no telling how many demerits were going to be handed out. Alicia mentioned there was even a betting pool.

Kayleigh vowed to show no fear. She was getting good at cleaning out stables. Either way, she wouldn't give the Captain the satisfaction of declaring her unsatisfactory. Stepping onto the wooden floor, she started making her bed. She centered the worn mattress square in the wooden frame. The pillow was positioned at the head of the bed and the blanket folded correctly and placed at the foot. Two drawers under her bed and a footlocker at the end contained her possessions. The contents were neatly arranged, even though this was not usually something that was inspected. Against the wall, behind the bed, Kayleigh saw her desk and quickly checked to make certain it was organized.

She glanced down the dimly lit aisle at all the identical beds where the rest of the recruits slumbered. The barracks were all stone walls with wooden floors, but the first year barracks was dull and plain. Earth maidens from each year were responsible for decorating the outside and as such, each year was progressively more elaborate. The fifth year barracks resembled a miniature castle that rivaled the splendor of the main buildings. At times like this, she wished she could have been an earth maiden. Sculpting was something she dearly enjoyed and earth magic would speed the process along.

Of course, I don't exactly have time to do any! Oh well, next year we are allowed to have privacy curtains. Something to look forward to, I guess. The fifth years supposedly get semi-private rooms.

She headed to the bathroom. One of the things that did impress Kayleigh was the barracks had an indoor bathroom, instead of an outhouse. Tanks of water were filled every night by water maidens from the upper classes, though there were at least two instances where that task was 'forgotten' as a form of hazing.

Running water was something even the prim and proper Rebekah Morganstern wasn't used to.

Opening the small valve, she filled a basin and used a washcloth and some lye soap to freshen herself and the rest of the water to rinse her hair. The row of empty bathtubs beckoned, but she ignored her sore muscles. Even if there was time to heat the water, once in, she doubted she'd be willing to get out.

After the selection ceremony, I'll find the time for a good soaking. There isn't any extra duty allowed tonight.

Kayleigh finished making promises to her tired body and changed from her nightshirt into a fresh work tunic and pants. One of the nice things about the island was how quickly she was able to go to the quartermaster's office and 'shop.' All Kayleigh need do was say what she wanted and the man would tell her the price. The goods arrived within two days. She'd resisted the urge to buy a new dress for Etiquette class. Her blue one would do for now and she still had an attachment to it. Stopping before lacing her boots, Kayleigh regarded the image in the mirror.

If I cut my hair, I won't need to spend as much time on it in the mornings.

Unbidden, memories of her mother came. She could almost hear her say, "You have such beautiful hair. Why ever would you want to cut it and look like a boy?"

With squinted eyes, she beat back the tears that threatened to form. A few of the others had received letters. She had written two, but received none. One of her duties as lead rider was to hand them out and she did so knowing that it was unlikely she'd be getting one.

I don't have time for pity right now! Captain Lynch will smell it out like a hunting dog. Better go get the section and squad leaders up.

Kayleigh checked her appearance in the mirror one final time and returned to the darkened room. Six to seven riders formed a squad, three squads were a section, and the two sections were the recruit company totaling forty-one recruits in her class. She let a smile cross her face as she approached the first bed.

"Morganstern, time to get up."

"What are you talking about? The sun isn't up yet!"

"Two of the four failures from yesterday's inspection were from your squad. If there are any more today, you'll be getting up everyday at this time, earlier if needed. Do you understand?"

The other girl glared at Kayleigh for a moment before saying, "I understand perfectly, Reese."

"Good. I'm glad we're clear on this." Kayleigh couldn't actually come out and say Morganstern was undermining her and allowing demerits to happen, but it certainly seemed that way.

"Lead rider, your weapon is dull and stowed incorrectly. Mark yourself down for a demerit." Captain Lynch held up the bone Yar knife plucked from her desk drawer.

Kayleigh annotated this on the parchment before stating, "Ma'am, the trainee has not been instructed on how to properly stow her weapon at this time. This material has not been covered in our weapon handling class."

"Is that so?" Captain Lynch looked to Ellen Jacobs.

"Yes, ma'am. We have not covered that material." Ellen nodded furiously.

"Very well. Consider this a warning then, Reese. You need

to show initiative, if you wish to remain lead rider. Your weapons instructor ... all your instructors are there to answer questions. Your job is to ask them. By my next inspection you will have your weapon sharpened and properly stowed. Am I making myself clear?"

"Yes, ma'am." Kayleigh won the battle, but knew the war was already lost.

Captain Lynch nodded and stepped in front of Ellen. "Recruit Jacobs, there is a stain on your tunic right here. Your appearance is the first impression anyone will see. An enemy won't care what you look like, but an ally may be left with a less than favorable opinion of you and, by extension, the rest of the battle maidens. Is that what you want?"

"No, ma'am!"

"Then consider that while you think about the demerit you just earned."

Kayleigh marked it down as Captain Lynch stepped to Ellen's bedding. The woman's hawk-like eyes scanned for the smallest imperfection. "Your bedding is satisfactory, but the only way to be better is to practice. Do you want to be better?"

"Yes, ma'am."

"Good to hear, recruit." In one swift motion, Captain Lynch flipped the mattress out of the wooden frame and dumped it on the other side. Finished, the captain walked to the next recruit and began issuing a demerit for Francine's appearance.

Over the next hour, thirty of the forty-one rider trainees received a demerit. When the "bloodbath" ended, Captain Lynch stepped to the center of the room. "I expect nothing less than the best from all my trainees. Today was not your best. Tonight, you will be tested to see which of the elements you have affinity with. It is a defining moment in your training. Now, you have thirty minutes to clean up this mess and get your breakfast. I suggest you move with a purpose."

With the dismissal, the recruits busied themselves with fixing their bedding, and returning the objects to their desks or drawers. The captain turned to Kayleigh with an emotionless mask. "Lead rider, you would do well to get your fellow recruits into something resembling a company. I suggest you think long and hard on how you are going to achieve this. Your inability to do this has already earned you several hours of extra duty. You only get one day a week off and from the way things are going, you will be spending the majority of it doing extra duty. Dismissed."

Kayleigh handed the inspection form to her commander and watched the woman walk away. In the confines of her mind she gave voice to her anger.

Maybe ten of those thirty demerits were actually warranted! I might not know where to properly stow my knife, but I sure know where I'd like to stick it right now!

The light rain made it difficult for Kayleigh to keep her footing. She sprinted, faster than she would have liked, down the trail, trying to keep pace with the company's best runners. It was a half mile to the first obstacle on the "Trail of Pain," and she focused on breathing in through the nose and out through the mouth.

After the first group of trainees reaches the hand-over-hand bars, they'll be slick and a beast to hold onto. The one constant of our physical training is mud, even on sunny days. I'm surprised that we're not all going to be earth maidens at this rate!

Helena was right beside her. Francine and Ellen were further back. The smallish, red-haired girl from Miros was a very private and intense girl. Getting Helena to speak anything more than three sentences at one time almost required magic. The first time the girl had to carry "the bag" on the wagon trip here, she'd slipped and fell. Kayleigh offered her hand, only to have it batted away.

She wants revenge. It's going to be a long five years before she'll be able to get any. I hope she finds something else to keep her going.

They reached the hand-over-hand bars and Kayleigh dried

her hands as best she could on her tunic before moving across them as quickly as possible. Her arms hurt, but it was nothing compared to the rope ladder a few hundred feet ahead. She seriously doubted that she'd be on a sailing ship anytime in the near future, but climbing up and down a set of rigging was good exercise.

Glancing to her left, beyond Helena's acrobatic efforts, she spotted Majherri in his usual spot. Ellen thought it was a bit creepy that Kayleigh's unicorn was always around, but she knew better. Majherri was cheering her on and encouraging Kayleigh in his own way.

It's nice to have someone that still believes in me!

Now clear of the bars, she used her longer stride to close the gap with the wiry Helena. By the time they reached the twin rope nets, Kayleigh had a few steps. She might not be the fastest runner, but she was one of the best climbers and attacked the net obstacle with a vengeance.

At least all the extra duty is making my arms stronger. It makes this part easier.

Reaching the top of the first net, Kayleigh swung one leg at a time over the wooden support and started on the easy part, the climb down the back. There was a flash from the corner of her eye and instinctively, she reached out. Helena's right hand slipped and she was hanging only by her left arm with her legs kicking to find a purchase on the wet rope, but only serving to tangle her. Kayleigh's hand grabbed Helena's belt and she lifted.

"Get your arm back on the net! I've got you."

Helena's blue eyes raged at Kayleigh, but she complied with the directions and Kayleigh helped get the girl's left leg untangled before continuing down. Once at the bottom, she went up the muddy incline using all four limbs.

"I didn't need your help!" Helena practically spat out the words.

Kayleigh's reply came out broken by her heavy breathing. "Yes … you did. Besides, if you … fell and ended up in the infirmary, … the Captain would find a way to … give me more demerits."

Helena did something Kayleigh had never seen before. She smiled. They approached the next set of nets stretched out over the ground. These they had to crawl under. Hesitating only for a moment before diving into the muck, she used her elbows and knees to worm her way forward.

Of course there's mud. There's always mud.

The two wooden practice swords smacked against each other hard. Kayleigh felt the shock reverberate all the way to her elbow. She brought the sword back to a guard position and awaited her opponent's next blow.

"Is that all you have, Rebekah?" she asked in a whisper. It was the first time she'd been paired up with Morganstern and surprisingly enough, Kayleigh didn't feel bad about having a physical advantage.

"Right side slash! Ready? Go!" Sir Dunlap, one of the few male instructors bellowed. Rebekah put even more effort into her strike and tried to twist it so she'd hit Kayleigh's hand.

The shorter black-haired girl grunted in anger at the impact. Kayleigh knew she shouldn't be doing this, but between the exhaustion today and Morganstern's attitude, she didn't anguish over it much.

"Come on, I barely felt that!"

Captain Lynch did say I needed to get the rest in shape!

"Left side slash! Ready? Go!"

This time Rebekah put all her weight into her swing. Instead of blocking, Kayleigh stepped backwards and allowed the girl to go off balance and topple.

"Halt!" Sir Dunlap ordered. He stalked over to them. "What is going on here?"

"I dodged, sir. The trainee was swinging too hard."

Rebekah started to state her case, but a sharp look from the bearded knight cut her off.

"Get up, girl! Class, let this be a lesson. If you over commit yourself, you may end up in a bad position. On the ground, flopping like a fish out of water is no place to be! Alright, let's switch and let the other side have a chance to attack while the rest of you defend."

Rebekah was furious and Kayleigh thought the day was finally looking up. She made sure to keep her balance.

Their afternoon history lesson was cut short to give the first years enough time to prepare for the selection ceremony. For the second time, they donned the ivory white dress robes.

"I can't wait to find out what element I'm destined for!" Ellen babbled, as they lined up next to their unicorns and observed the dignitaries from the city and the other classes filing into the ceremonial hall.

Tightening her belt, Kayleigh answered, "Are you still hoping for fire to be your element?"

"I don't know. They all have their advantages. I just want this to be over with more than anything else. You're fortunate that you've already figured out your element."

"I suppose," she replied. "I just enter with Majherri. They announce 'fire' and I go sit down. Not exactly a defining moment in my training, but its better than mucking out stables."

They continued talking until Kayleigh spotted Captain Lynch, in full battle regalia exiting the ceremonial hall.

"We're about to start. Good luck, Ellen."

Majherri moved slowly next to her and she got the impression that he was amused at this whole thing, or maybe something else was amusing him. Perhaps it was what could only be the stare from Captain Lynch's unicorn, whose tail swished in anger as the procession started.

They passed by Lieutenant Sheppard, who held her arm out to stop Ellen, allowing only Kayleigh by. The ceremonial hall was kept dark, so that the only real light in the room was the brightly lit dais. An older, dark-skinned woman, also in ceremonial armor, and supported by an elegant cane stood on it. Until now, Kayleigh hadn't seen General Jyslin up close, only in the distance at meal times or when she addressed the entire student body. Bent by age and injury, it was difficult to imagine this woman had once been on of the most skilled warriors in the entire land.

"Kayleigh Reese has already shown an aptitude for fire. We welcome her to the Sisterhood of the Eternal Flame. Let her and her bonded unicorn call upon the fires of justice in defense of the innocent."

She came to attention in front of the General and saluted. The salute was performed by bringing her right hand across her chest and with her palm facing down and only her thumb touching her robes. General Jyslin returned the salute and smiled. Kayleigh executed a proper about face and returned to where Majherri waited for her. They walked the length of the hall to the applause of the crowd. It was a great feeling. At the exit, Captain Lynch stood as impassive as ever. Kayleigh wouldn't let the woman's ire ruin this moment.

"Release your unicorn and go up the stairs and along the back row to join those of your element."

"Yes, ma'am." She patted Majherri on his nose and gestured for him to exit. Once her bonded left, she climbed the steps to the first landing and turned, heading for the area where the rest of the fire maidens sat. Several of the others smiled at her and a few congratulated her quietly. Below, Lieutenant Sheppard released Ellen and her unicorn, Tyrinigen.

Instead of waiting, as Majherri had done, Tyrinigen followed Ellen up to the dais as General Jyslin picked up the first object on the table. It was a stone tablet lined with intricate runes. Ellen was instructed to touch the stone and her unicorn at the same time. There was a fifteen second pause and nothing happened.

Odd, I thought she was going to be Earth for certain. I guess that shows how much I really know about all this.

The second object was a gleaming bronze oil lantern,

burning with a bright blue flame. It was the totem of fire and what Kayleigh would have interacted with. They waited to see if the flame would change colors or grow noticeably brighter. For a second time, nothing happened and Kayleigh felt for Ellen. They'd been told that sometimes the magic doesn't happen at the selection ceremony and that it surfaces later over the first season. A beautiful chalice filled to the brim with water was next and still there was no reaction.

She knew Ellen well enough to spot the panic in her eyes beginning to show as the General grasped a delicate looking hand fan – the air totem. There was an immediate reaction, the room felt as if a cool breeze wafted through the room. But this was because the General was formerly an air maiden. Sadly, her unicorn had died in the final great battle of the Southern Uprising and left her both injured and without a way to power her formidable magic.

Ellen took it and swished it as instructed and a second breeze swept across the audience as expressions of relief and unabashed joy alternated on her friend's face.

The general and the freshly-chosen air maiden exchanged salutes while General Jyslin said, "Ellen Jacobs has been chosen to join the Sisterhood of the Thundering Clouds. Let the actions of her and her mount carry the winds of hope into those in need of salvation." Kayleigh clapped loudly for Ellen as the two followed the same route.

Next came Francine, but she failed to garner any reaction from the artifacts. "Francine Andover still waits for her role in The Academy, but often the longer her magic takes to surface, the more powerful she will become, so take heart young warrior and be assured that it is not a matter of if, but when your day will come."

Kayleigh felt bad for Francine, but suspected that if any had difficulty finding their alignment, it would be her. A second recruit, Marissa, joined Kayleigh as the next fire maiden when the blue flame turned a bright green. A few minutes later, Helena Shaw became the third. It was hard not to get caught up in the giddy atmosphere surrounding the selection. Each time a girl was chosen for an element, everyone in that section of the ceremonial hall would stand and cheer.

When Kayleigh sensed a tremor under the bench she sat on, General Jyslin proclaimed, "Alicia Santiago has been chosen to join the Sisterhood of the Impregnable Mountains. Let those who need shelter from evil find protection in her and her mount's earthshaking power."

That was another surprise, she was certain Alicia was going to be an air maiden. What wasn't a surprise was Rebekah Morganstern touching the cup and the contents began overflowing onto the ground. "Rebekah Morganstern has been chosen to join the Sisterhood of Everlasting Tides. Let her and her mount's magic bring safe harbor to those who are in need of rescue."

As the last candidate was finished, there were thunderous cheers. Five maidens still remained without an element. Ten had joined water, nine for both earth and air, and the remaining eight were aligned with fire. Kayleigh spent the next few minutes mingling with Helena and the others, even noting that some of the recruit's families had made the journey to witness the ceremony. She was nursing a twinge of sadness when a hand brushed the back of her robes.

"Congratulations are still in order, how's the training been so far?"

Kayleigh turned and recognized Rider Annabeth Welsh. Someone *had* actually come and seen her. Her mood instantly brightened.

"It's been everything you promised and then some!"

"That's good to hear. I'm on assignment in the city at least until mating season starts, so you'll see me around, Reese."

"Really?" Kayleigh was excited at the prospect. Though she liked Lieutenant Sheppard well enough, there was still a professional distance, because the earth maiden was an instructor. Only four years separated Rider Welsh from Kayleigh and the friendly young woman treated all the recruits almost as equals on the journey across the continent. Many nights, the fire maiden told stories of what to expect to the wide-eyed trainees.

"I figured I'd stop by and see some of my friends, who are in their final year, and check in on you and the other girls from our caravan. How are your lessons in fire magic going? Well, I hope."

"I'm still as erratic as ever," Kayleigh admitted with a sigh. Of the three lessons she had taken with the second year instructor, twice she could barely generate any flames, and the third time she conjured a four foot long column of fire that impressed everyone present. "I'm working with the second year recruits, but it's a little hard to find time to practice with all the things I have to do as lead rider, and the extra duty."

The brown haired woman looked thoughtful and said, "How much extra duty have you earned?"

"Six hours."

"That's a lot for the first four weeks. Still you get used to it and adjust."

"No, that was just this morning. Since classes started four weeks ago, I've earned thirty-five."

"What? Some people don't earn that many in an entire year!"

Shrugging somewhat helplessly, she answered, "Lead rider rule."

"They don't usually enforce that until ... oh, I get it! She's really got it in for you, doesn't she? You're not giving her any satisfaction are you?"

"Not a chance."

Welsh leaned closer and lowered her voice. "That's just petty. So let me get this straight, you are having a hard time practicing because of all your extra duty and you can't do magic without a trained rider observing."

Kayleigh's smile grew as she understood what Rider Welsh was implying. "That's about right. I've only got half of tomorrow's free day left."

"Do you know that things can get rather boring at the garrison in the city? I should be able to take the afternoon ferry on your free day and if you finish your extra duty in the morning, we'll spend the entire afternoon working on fire magic."

"That sounds great!"

"Then it's settled. I'm going to go mingle a bit more, but I'll see you tomorrow."

Kayleigh nodded and Rider Welsh wandered off. She turned to accept the congratulations of others. Being on Captain Lynch's "bad" side was a problem, but in this case, it actually helped to create an opportunity.

Chapter 13 – Unleashed Fury

It feels odd to have an actual saddle again, after so long. Majherri likened it to an itch he couldn't quite scratch, but he would get used to it. The rains finally stopped and the entire class, both humans and unicorns were gathered at one of the reviewing grounds for a series of demonstrations.

Currently, a stocky male knight mounted on a black charger was moving through the obstacle course attacking the targets with his lance. Pulling back on the reins, the horse reared and smashed powerful hooves into the hay-filled suits of armor.

Enough of this! I am eager to start training with my rider!

Majherri turned toward Tyrinigen. Their riders were friends, but the young male was only slightly less annoying than Abassa, the male who needed his help reconnecting to his rider in the caravan.

"The knight's animal is well trained, but heavy cavalry units won't usually fight against us unless they are supported by infantry and archers. It's the archers and the crossbows you have to worry about. A knight on a warhorse is easily noticed, but a quarrel or a bolt can appear out of nowhere without warning."

It was the first time Majherri had spoken of combat with the younglings and several moved closer to see if he would continue.

"The first thing an enemy is always thinking about is how to separate you from your rider. They are the path through which our magic flows. You must do your best to prevent that from happening."

Most of the other unicorns were now watching him instead of the demonstration. *"That said, you must learn how to function without your rider and that is more than just stabbing with your horn. It is fighting with your hooves, just like the animal out there does. It is recognizing which opponents pose the most immediate threat to you and your rider. Sometimes, you must risk greater injury to protect the human and let her wield the power you share."*

They were looking at his scars and the crack in his horn. He could feel their eyes on him. They were wounds that did not respond to the healing magic of the water maidens.

"Tell us about your battles, Majherri," Paragor asked.

"Perhaps later, the human will ask for one of us to display our prowess in a moment."

On cue, the knight finished the course and brought his horse to a stop in front of the recruits. "That young ladies, is what a knight with a trained warhorse is capable of. But when it comes down to it, a warhorse is just a trained beast and it responds to my commands well enough. Your unicorns are every bit as smart and clever as you are. So while they reset the targets, I'm going to ask one of the unicorns to come up here and show all of us how fast they can finish this course."

"Go ahead, Majherri."

"You've actually fought before."

"Come on; show us all the skills you claim to have."

The rest agreed and urged him to volunteer. *"The exercise doesn't have moving targets. It is more suited to you younglings."*

"So, what you're saying is that you can not do better than any of us," Lycenae challenged.

"As usual, little colt, you are a fool. I was attempting to let one of you demonstrate superiority, but since you insist, let me show you what a real warrior can do."

He paced forward and snorted at the human knight and bobbed his head. Except for the brief battle outside of Miros, Majherri hadn't unleashed his full fury since wandering out of that western desert. Despite it being just a silly demonstration for younglings and the females who ride them, he would give them a taste of what they could one day be.

With the last hay-filled target returned to the upright position the knight shouted for Majherri to go.

Bolting toward the first stop, a set of armor on a barrel that was given legs to create the appearance of a mounted human, he was speed. Majherri used his horn to parry the lance while pushing into a jump with his back legs. Rising from the ground his chest smashed into where the horse's neck would have been. Even if he wasn't wearing any armor, the move and the momentum would have broken the animal's neck and thrown the rider.

He shifted his weight in mid-jump to compensate for the lighter weight of the "non-horse." The moment he landed, he pivoted and launched a devastating kick to the side of the barrel splintering the wood and making it practically explode, but he didn't waste any time appreciating his hoofwork. He accelerated in the direction of a fake bowmen while executing a series of quick turns to prevent the archer from lining up a shot. Most humans would release at either two or three lengths, so Majherri dipped his shoulder which would allow his rider to thrust her shield forward and protect the vulnerable left side of the head.

A blink of an eye later, there was the satisfying tinkle of broken chainmail links falling away from his horn and a gaping hole in the target's midriff. A trio of infantrymen was next, with braced spears.

The targets are only one human deep, I could easily vault them. Their long weapons wouldn't be able to turn that quickly, but I'll fight them as if they were more than one row.

He reared and cycled his front hooves rapidly, smashing the center weapon, and immediately circling right. His horn smacked against the nearest spear and he leapt forward bowling the dummies into each other and moved inside of the effective area the spears could be used in. The front hooves came down with his full weight behind them. The clang of iron shod shoes on metal reverberated in his ears while his forelegs absorbed the shock of the repeated blows.

Normally, I'd be pulling on Kayleigh to set my hooves ablaze at this point, but even without it, there is something to be said for the sheer release of combat.

Majherri galloped into the midst of the final group of fake

warriors and surged like an unbroken pack animal, spinning, bucking and kicking. He was a storm of legs, stabbing horn, and movement, a thunderous explosion of violence that only stopped when there was nothing left standing.

Lathered in sweat, he looked for something else to smash or destroy. Rage pounded in his veins. The symphony of violence ended with him snorting and panting, ears pinned back detailing his anger. The startled looks on the faces of the recruits, the younglings, and even the knight spoke volumes.

Trotting back toward the herd of unicorns, his eyes bore a hole through Lycenae and the others who dared doubt him. Instinctively, they backed away from him and part of Majherri relished the idea that he was feared.

"That," the human male said clearing his throat, "is a large part of the reason why a dozen mounted knights versus a single trained battle maiden is considered an even matchup by most generals."

The flood of anger subsided and he tried to relax. He flinched when a human hand brushed against his coat. He hadn't noticed Kayleigh's approach. He sensed the concern she was feeling through their shared link.

"Its okay, Majherri. I'm here."

Majherri slowly released the tension in his body and let the rage drain away under her touch.

He thanked her as best he could and gave her the message that he wished for solitude.

"Okay, come find me later," his rider responded.

"What did you hope to gain by terrifying the younglings?"

His wanderings took him by a small brook, where he listened to the sound of the moving water. He suspected someone would come looking for him, but Majherri expected it would be Pasha.

Instead, he turned and faced T'rsa. He wasn't pleased and obviously she wasn't either. He came out here to be alone and was in no mood for her stupidity.

"They goaded me into a demonstration, sister."

"Perhaps, but from the stories being told, you went berserk! When I first heard that you participated today, I figured it was to simply be prideful and show off. Instead, you lay waste to a portion of the training field trying to prove that you still have the ability to protect your rider."

He flared both nostrils at her relaying contempt and replied, *"Unlike the others, I require no training or any other assistance from you. Quite the contrary, you could learn many things from me."*

"You lash out like some kind of feral animal, Majherri. I had hoped that with your new rider, there would be some semblance of the brother I once knew. Even with her, you remain broken. I am concerned. You follow your human about, herding her like a newborn."

"Spare me," he snorted. *"You claim to know me, but you know nothing! ... less than nothing!"*

"No, I do not believe I know you anymore, but you will show restraint around the younglings."

"Or what, sister? Your human will continue her vendetta against me through my rider. Shouldn't you be telling her the same thing you are saying to me?"

She flared her nostrils in response and butted her head against him. *"My rider is in charge of her brood and I am in charge of this herd. She has her way and I have mine. You will heed my instructions!"*

He shook his mane in anger and answered, *"Dear sister, you were never my equal, so stop pretending you are my better. Do what you do best, teach the younglings to march in perfect, straight lines, show them how to position themselves during ceremonies, and teach them how to identify the human ranks. Should they want to know what it is like in battle, tell them what little you know, and if they can comprehend that, send them to me, little Misty with your arrogant rider. Now that I have a second rider, I want your orders even less than I wanted your pity when I didn't have one."*

She backed away, but continued to stare at him.

Borrowing a human term he said, *"You are dismissed, T'rsa."*

T'rsa shook her head from side to side. *"There is something very wrong with you, Majherri. Your magic is not right. You can act like things are in balance, but those who knew you before your loss can sense the difference. I will be watching you, brother."*

"Good. You can learn with the rest of them."

She galloped away leaving him every bit as angry as he had been at the end of the demonstration. Majherri returned to his contemplation of the running water and the noises it made. He watched a leaf being carried by the current off into the direction of the great lake surrounding the Sacred Island.

Am I like this water? It travels with purpose. I have a rider and thus a purpose. The water always runs, but is it running to something, or away from something else. Am I running to Kayleigh or from Danella?

Despite his request, the brook provided no answer to his question.

"There you are! I was beginning to worry about you," his rider greeted him with an apple after setting down her pitchfork. She stroked his coat for a moment, and continued, "You're angry about something. I can tell. Do you want some oats to go with that?"

He nodded and didn't bother to hide his ire. Through their connection, he allowed a picture of his sister to flow to his young rider. They were alone in the stable with the exception of a slumbering youngling, who must have exhausted herself. The rest of the herd was out stargazing on such a warm and clear night. And avoiding the herd and the accompanying annoyances was precisely the reason Majherri was here.

Kayleigh crinkled her tiny snout in response. "Well, if T'rsa is anything like her rider, I can see how that would be a problem. You were great out there today. Everyone said so. Even Sir Dunlap said he'd never seen a unicorn move like that before! I'm going to need a great deal of practice at just holding on."

It is ironic. The humans are impressed and my kin are frightened. The ways our two species look at the world are often at odds with each other. Still, it warms my heart that Kayleigh is pleased with my performance.

Majherri munched on the rest of the apple as she filled a wooden bin with oats. Setting the bag down, his rider rested her forehead on his side and seemed to relax while he ate. This lasted for a few minutes and eventually she began speaking at length about the rest of her day. "I found out where I need to store my knife. That empty space we thought was a broom closet and storeroom is really the barrack's arms locker. Since no one in the class but me has a personal weapon in this year, no one mentioned it. She won't be able to get me for that on the next inspection!"

He desperately wanted to congratulate her, but instead he felt skeptical and like everything else, she sensed it as well. Stepping back, Kayleigh stretched and affirmed his opinion. "You're right. She'll probably move on to the next thing she can award demerits for."

"Captain Lynch could easily award you more extra duty for standing there and conversing with Majherri instead of working."

With his greater field of vision, Majherri didn't have to turn very far to see Lieutenant Sheppard. Kayleigh snapped to attention.

"At ease, trainee." Sheppard waved her hand and approached. To Majherri, her movements were not terribly graceful, but filled with purpose. "I came to see you this evening."

"Ma'am?"

"I wanted to make certain you weren't being run into the ground. I've heard what happened on the demonstration field today. Majherri's actions combined with the pressure you've been under to perform lead me to wonder if you're having problems adjusting to life here at The Academy."

"I'm fine, ma'am."

"Rider Welsh came to my quarters the other night and shared her concerns after she had given you a magical lesson. Perchance did you clear this with Captain Lynch?"

Majherri could tell by the reluctance in his rider that she did not want to answer the question.

"Begging the Lieutenant's pardon, but I have been told that if I am not serving extra duty on my free day, the time is mine to use as I see fit."

"Yes, yes and the rules state that a trainee practicing magic must have a trained observer and not a trained instructor. You are operating within the rules, Reese. However, there are rules and there is also protocol. This could easily be construed as an insult to your other instructors."

"The monitored practices for the second and third year trainees occur when my extra hours are scheduled. Due to this, I have been able to attend a few of those sessions. Rider Welsh was kind enough to offer her services."

"Yes she is and she clearly knows that she is also breaching protocol, but Rider Welsh won't be working with the same group of instructors for the next five years. You will and you are getting off to a poor start with some of them. I happen to know you and have a better understanding of your situation than most, so I thought it best to make certain you know the lay of the land. I personally do not take offense and congratulate you on taking initiative when it comes to your education. Others may not be so charitable."

"Yes, ma'am. Thank you for the warning."

The stocky brunette nodded slowly and said, "You're on pace to break the most hours of extra duty served in a single year."

His rider shrugged and said, "At least I keep a tidy stable, Lieutenant."

"Yes, I can see that you've become adept with a pitchfork. I've heard your stable master boasting to his ilk about how nice his building looks as a result. I assume you have extra duty tomorrow evening."

"Yes, ma'am."

"In that case, tomorrow night, you will report to training field one. Under my direction, you will assist in mending the targets that will be used by the fourth year students in the morning for ranged weapon practicals. How good are you with a needle and thread?"

"I am not a seamstress, but I can perform the task."

"Very good. Bring your knife. If you complete the mending quickly enough and time allows, I start instructing you on how to use your weapon."

"Thank you, ma'am." His rider was genuinely grateful.

"Think nothing of it, recruit," the woman said, pausing before smiling and continuing, "Otherwise, your weapon of choice when you leave our care may very well be a pitchfork and that wouldn't look good on the battlefield at all."

Majherri chortled in agreement at the image of Kayleigh, on his back and charging an enemy line, brandishing a stable tool. His rider scowled and folded her arms across her chest before sticking her smallish tongue out at him.

Chapter 14 – Challenges

"You're right. We do spend a lot of time watching demonstrations."

Ellen conceded Kayleigh's point as the two sat in the stands and looked out over the training field. Currently, they were watching the fifth year students maneuvering in formation. But that wasn't the reason for the crowd gathering in the stands. It was the end of the sixth week since the new session had started.

That meant one thing; it was open season on the upper classes' lead riders and the fifth years were already clearing the training field and making their way to the stands.

Kayleigh and the girl who was the second year lead rider still had another six weeks before they could be challenged. It didn't hurt to be prepared for the inevitable.

"So who do you think is going to be your first challenger?" Ellen asked. "I've got a couple coins on Morganstern."

"I don't think so, Ellen. She will probably let somebody else have first crack at me. That way she will see what I can do."

"Well, she was the one to suggest that you resign for the good of the company, last week. Personally, I don't think Captain Lynch will treat us any better just because somebody else becomes lead rider."

"You're probably right. The captain will be just as hard on the next person, if only to prove that she wasn't singling me out. I'm not worried and I certainly don't intend to give Rebekah or the captain the satisfaction of seeing me quit."

The vehemence in Kayleigh's words was surprising and her face flushed slightly. Fortunately, it was still daylight out and no one was likely to notice. It was just one more thing that she couldn't fix or even control. Becoming frustrated wasn't productive and played into Captain Lynch's hands.

Kayleigh spent the previous nine days waiting for any fallout from her private lessons with Rider Welsh. Instead, her next lesson with Annabeth passed without incident. So far, the captain had not treated her any differently than before. But she suspected it was only a matter of time before something happened.

Breaching protocol doesn't qualify as outright insubordination, but Lieutenant Sheppard was right, the other instructors aren't exactly happy with me right now. The odd thing is, a trainee, in their fourth or fifth year, could probably get away with it without offending someone, but since I'm a first year, it's being frowned on.

"Do you ever wonder how old these benches we're sitting on actually are?" Ellen changed the subject and Kayleigh wondered if she knew how uncomfortable the topic was.

"What?"

"Think about it; how many thousands of students have sat right where we are now over the years?"

Kayleigh chuckled and said, "I wonder how many hours of detention they've earned?"

"Don't worry, you'll catch them. I have faith in you. Oh look, here comes the third year lead rider and her challenger!"

These girls were the same age as Kayleigh and she observed them carefully. Both walked with confidence. They had each completed two grueling years here at The Academy.

I wonder if I'll ever look like that.

"I think it's a weapons challenge. They've got their unicorns, but they are headed toward the ring." Ellen babbled smacking her hands on her kneecaps. The two stopped at a weapons rack and selected wooden swords wrapped in thick padding and lightweight shields. Each stopped and said something to their unicorn before entering the circle. A pair of seconds inspected both weapons to be used and nodded, deeming them safe for use. The weapons were dipped in a dye to make their marks noticeable.

A tall, thin blonde, with short hair gracefully stepped to

the center of the ring. Kayleigh recognized Captain Heather Sycroft, the third year commanding officer. She held her hand in the air and waited for the crowd to go silent. "A challenge has been issued. It will be decided in the ring. When it is done, it will not exist outside this ring. We are all comrades in arms."

The two third year maidens moved to opposite sides of the circle. Kayleigh didn't know the name of the challenger, but she had met the brunette named Laurel Whitaker, the third year lead rider. By default, she found herself rooting for the Laurel.

The third year student had helped Kayleigh by giving her tips to make her lead rider duties go more quickly, and she appreciated any help she could get. Laurel was Kayleigh's age and was pleasant enough. Unfortunately, with their busy schedules, Kayleigh hadn't seen her much since those times at the beginning of the year.

With a signal from Captain Sycroft the two warriors circled one another. The challenger made two quick slashing feints with her practice sword and Laurel parried them both. Despite both battle maidens being shorter than Kayleigh, she could see they were much stronger, both due to the training and their partnerships with their bonded unicorns. They were easily as powerful as full grown men.

As the duo exchanged more blows, Kayleigh noticed that the challenger had a longer reach, but Laurel seemed to be quicker and more skilled. The lead rider moved in close and bashed with the shield. The follow-on slash was aimed for the girl's leg and sent the challenger hopping backwards with a painful expression on her face, as the crowd cheered. The contestants returned to their starting positions.

Kayleigh was also cheering, but she couldn't help a dark thought intruding on her mind. *If it had been a real sword, she'd likely have lost her leg.*

Ellen nudged her, "Those girls are so fast! I don't think the challenger is going to win."

"Me either," Kayleigh replied watching Laurel become

more aggressive in her attacks and forcing the other girl to give ground.

The mock battle lasted a scant thirty seconds longer before the challenger was on one knee after being knocked out of the circle by another combination of sword and shield attacks. The dye stain on the challenger's chest indicated a fatal blow. The match was over. Up until that point, Kayleigh had never really considered the shield as anything more than just a means of protection despite what Sir Dunlap had said during their lessons. It was truly an eye opener.

Laurel offered a salute to her vanquished foe and helped her classmate to her feet. Kayleigh wasn't close enough to hear, but she was certain the lead rider said, "Better luck next time."

The applause grew as the contest was officially declared over. Laurel would be the third year lead rider for at least another week and it would be a minimum of one month before that same opponent could issue another challenge.

The captain of the fourth year students came forward holding two blunt jousting lances as Ellen bounced next to Kayleigh. "I love jousting! It's the first thing I thought about when I was chosen. My father would take us all into town every time a tournament was held."

"My mother didn't like them. She never said I couldn't go, but I always felt like I was sneaking around when I went to watch one." Kayleigh replied and stopped to think about what she had just said. It probably explained a lot about her mother's attitudes toward violence.

The two fourth year trainees led their unicorns onto the field dressed in full armor with closed visors. Again, Kayleigh felt a sense of awe watching their smooth movements as they walked to their company commander and received both their lances and their final instructions.

More interesting than the announcement of which girl was the challenger and which was the lead rider was the posturing and body language being exchanged by the pair's unicorns. Kayleigh focused on them and saw the rapid tail swish-

ing, the pawing of the ground, and the snorts. The two unicorns appeared to have something of a rivalry and it looked
like a challenge or a wager of a different sort was occurring.

"I wonder what the unicorns really think of all this?"

"What did you say, Kayleigh?"

She pointed to the two magical creatures and said,
"They're having their own competition."

"You're right! Look over there." Ellen pointed to the ends
of the wooden bleachers they were sitting on. Dozens of unicorns were gathered. None of them were idly grazing, either.

Kayleigh didn't need a reminder that Majherri and the
others were every bit as intelligent as any human, but the proof
was how intently they watched the unicorns and their riders
take position on opposite sides of the hundred foot long
wooden fence. Within the first few seconds, they'd be charging
at full speed. Each rider had two assistants holding additional
lances. Jousting was a best of three passes unless one rider un-
seats the other.

The captain held up two flags, one blue and the other red
to signal both riders to the ready position. Instinctively, Kayleigh held her breath until the flags went down. The unicorns
bolted toward each other as each rider leveled her lance.

Wincing, Kayleigh felt the impact as the blue rider scored
a clear hit on the red rider, but failed to unseat her opponent.
Wood splinters shot into the air, like an angry swarm of in-
sects. The captain waved the blue flag and signaled which way
the point was awarded.

At the end of the fence, each rider took another lance
from their assistant and wheeled around for another pass. The
collision was just as powerful as last time, except the blue rider
was thrown completely from her saddle, and landed in a heap.

Loud cheers greeted the red rider, who pumped her gauntleted fist in the air. The defeated blue rider slapped the
ground in frustration, anger, or injury. Kayleigh held her breath
for a second time. An instructor walked briskly over to the
downed trainee and knelt. Words were exchanged and the in-

structor summoned one of the assistants to help the girl up. From the way the blue rider was protecting her left arm, Kayleigh could tell there was an injury.

"It looks like the fourth years have a new lead rider!" Ellen said while standing and clapping. "That was incredible!"

"Oh, I agree," a voice came from behind them. They both turned to find the gleeful face of Rebekah Morganstern. "Change is inevitable. Isn't it Reese? But don't worry, Kayleigh, you'll be bounced quick enough. I'm glad you're worried about me though."

"Eavesdropping is such a lady-like trait, Rebekah."

The girl rolled her eyes and crossed her arms in defiance before saying, "It's not eavesdropping, if you two are blathering like the village idiots you are. I was just sitting here and being observant, just like my father always said I should be. Might I ask what pearls of wisdom your father imparted upon you, Kayleigh?"

"That's uncalled for!" Ellen gasped.

"I suppose you're right," Rebekah said. "Reality can be so very harsh."

Kayleigh took her time before answering. She drew herself up and said, "We're still early in our training. You haven't really matured very much, Rebekah. I'm sure it will happen, eventually. If you're thinking about replacing me, I've already been recommending you be demoted from squad leader."

Rebekah grinned and replied, "Obviously, the captain pays *so very much attention* to your recommendations. You've probably been trying for weeks."

"You're not worth that much personal attention. Your squad's performance, or lack thereof, is well documented. I don't have to sink to your level of pettiness, Morganstern. I just have to stick to the facts."

"We'll see about that, Reese."

Kayleigh's field of vision expanded from the spiteful thirteen year old over her shoulder and to the group that was following their heated exchange, while the fifth years were setting up for another jousting challenge. It dawned on her just how many ears were listening in.

"I guess we will, Rebekah. But for now, this conversation is over."

"Because you say so?"

"Yes, squad leader. Our personal issues do not belong in a public forum. It shows a lack of discipline on both our parts and if you pursue this matter further, I will place the two of us on report and we'll get to explain ourselves to the captain."

Three hours later, Kayleigh was standing at attention in front of Captain Lynch's desk. "Trainee Reese, reporting as ordered."

The woman left her at attention and continued looking at the documents in front of her. With several quill strokes, she made notes on the parchment. Captain Lynch stood and disappeared into the next room leaving Kayleigh bewildered. The other time she had been summoned to stand in front of her commanding officer, Captain Lynch acknowledged her and immediately began dressing Kayleigh down for her shortcomings as a lead rider. She had expected that.

This silence was even more nerve-wracking. Internally, she fought her panic while remaining as still as possible.

She's going to fire me right now! I just know it! Just keep standing at attention. She obviously knows what she's doing. Don't play her game!

Kayleigh remained still, but allowed her eyes to scan Captain Lynch's office. The desk was old and worn, but it was kept orderly. Behind the wooden chair was a bookshelf. It was mostly empty, with only the books used for instruction pushed to one side. An ornate box, perhaps two feet long, rested atop the book shelve. There was no clue as to its purpose, but it was the first thing she'd seen that gave the room any sense of personality.

She caught her breath at the second thing. It was a small portrait done in oils. The subject was an armored battle maiden on one knee. Her sword was inverted, with the point in the ground and one hand resting on the base of the pommel. The other arm cradled a helmet with a garish feathered plume to the woman's side. Blonde hair cascaded down onto the front left side of the warrior's chest plate. Green eyes and a mischievous smile completed the painting and there was no doubt that she was looking on the likeness of her predecessor, Danella Lynch.

It seemed silly to hold a staring contest with a portrait, but Kayleigh had little else to do at that moment. She passed the next minutes wondering what Danella would think of her and if she would approve. The few things she actually knew about Danella came from either the impressions Majherri imparted to her over their connection or something mentioned in passing by the other instructors.

I should find out more about her, when I have a chance.

As she made this vow, the floorboards creaked and Kayleigh saw Danella's sister returning. The woman slid behind her desk and placed more parchment in an organized pile. Only then did Captain Lynch finally look up at Kayleigh.

"I'm amazed, trainee. You are capable of being silent. After your public airing of matters that should remain inside your barracks, I had my doubts."

"Permission to speak, ma'am?"

"Go ahead, trainee."

"I exercised poor judgment and the moment I realized what was occurring, I stopped and instructed Trainee Morganstern to do the same."

Captain Lynch waited for a moment, eyes boring through Kayleigh's exterior and trying to see what was on the inside. "Yes, while your actions were disrespectful and foolish, you eventually reached that same conclusion. That means you obviously learned a valuable lesson today and there is no need to replace you, since there is little chance this will ever happen again."

Kayleigh released the breath she didn't realize she was holding and replied, "Yes ma'am."

"Now, you have recommended that both Morganstern

and Bucklin be replaced as squad leaders. What is your rationale?"

The questions caught Kayleigh off guard and she stammered her reply, "Well ... well those two squads are producing the most demerits. A change in squad leaders might improve performance."

"Both squads are in second section. Shouldn't you also recommend replacing Hawthorne?" Captain Lynch asked drumming her fingers on the top of the desk.

Kayleigh pondered her answer. Andrea Hawthorne wasn't part of either caravan that had brought the rest of the recruits to The Academy. She was the eldest daughter of General Althea Hawthorne, commander of the southern battalion of battle maidens.

"No, ma'am." Kayleigh answered.

"Explain."

"Uh ... I believe that the problem is at the ground level of the squads and not a reflection of the overall running of the section."

"Very well," Captain Lynch said. "Who do you recommend for replacements?"

"Recruits Shaw and Ashland."

"Your suggestions are noted, lead rider," the woman said filling the names in on the company's Table of Organization. Finished, she handed the parchment to Kayleigh. "After careful consideration, I'm demoting Hawthorne and having her take over Morganstern's squad. If she truly deserves to be a section leader, she can start by straightening out third squad. Shaw takes over for Bucklin. I'm promoting Morganstern to section leader."

"Ma'am?" Kayleigh sputtered.

"Trainee Morganstern will operate under the same constraints as you when it comes to demerits, except she will only receive one hour of extra duty for every five demerits earned by her section. You will continue to accumulate extra duty for every five demerits earned by both sections."

Kayleigh did a poor job hiding her disbelief. She'd be forced to interact in some way with Rebekah every waking hour!

"I see you require further explanation, recruit. You no doubt assume that Morganstern has mismanaged her squad to create more demerits. If she is actually doing this, she will suffer the consequences of her actions alongside of you."

"Oh."

"The two of you will settle your differences and work together or else. Your petty bickering has gone back as far as Helden. Might I ask, what is the source of this feud?"

"It goes back to our parents, ma'am. My mother is an artist."

"It is late, lead rider. Please make this as short as possible."

Kayleigh struggled with her words and shifted uncomfortably. The scandal was very embarrassing. "She was accused of engaging in indiscretions with her clients. Reb ... Trainee Morganstern's father was a client of my mothers for both a painting and a sculpture. When confronted by his wife, Mr. Morganstern's defense was to smear and defame my mother's name throughout the town."

"I see. Since neither of these people is actually here, I suggest the both of you figure out how to get beyond this. I am facilitating this by placing the two of you together. You will learn how to work with each other despite your feelings. If not, you will both be replaced. You are dismissed. Send Morganstern and Hawthorne to my office, immediately."

Chapter 15 – The Prodigal Son

Fortunes fall and fortunes rise, Majherri concluded. *Was it this childish before? Or is it simply that I have become too jaded.*

The unicorn didn't feel the need to follow the standings of the humans, but the others were obsessed with every little change in position and every hour of extra duty assigned. His rider remained on top, despite the injustices done to her. Everything else seemed both trivial and tiresome. Kyrinda, an exceptionally temperamental female, was nearly inconsolable when her rider was demoted and Lycenae's elevated to her rider's previous spot. Her hysterics would likely be remembered by suitors in the future.

Perhaps this is why unicorns shouldn't survive the death of their humans. So they never have to go through this again! Once was more than enough. Besides, this means nothing in actual combat. The humans worry about following orders and working together. A unicorn has but one task ... keep your rider alive.

He stood near the docks watching the food being brought in by burly males. Even when he was first here, the humans planted no food on the Sacred Isle. This land was meant for Majherri's kind. The grass grows year round. Successful matings could only happen on this enchanted ground. In the next few weeks, members from all the battalions would return home and the island would teem with life.

As he continued staring at the humans, a young male, saddled and in riding gear, approached and snorted his greeting. *"Hello father, I trust you are well today."*

"Nyrisso, this is a pleasant surprise. What brings you back to the island little one?" Majherri had fathered three children in the last decade. Nyrisso was the youngest. He had been here with his human last year and was the one that badgered him into eating and drinking after it became apparent that he wasn't going to

succumb to the wasting.

"My rider has been made a battalion courier. I arrived last night and will be leaving as soon as my rider has rested. Imagine my surprise when I learned that my sire not only had a new rider, but was in training! Do you need any suggestions? You have a long road ahead."

He appraised his offspring's reaction. *"Clearly, you are enjoying this far too much."*

"Yes. Yes, I am. You're healthy, alive, and in better spirits then I had hoped to ever see again."

"So, you are a courier. Able to keep up with those ridiculous birds others use?"

"I should be offended that you would even ask, Sire!" Nyrisso exclaimed, pounding his hooves on the ground. His rider was aligned with air magic and that made him an ideal selection to be a courier. The humans used messenger birds for their normal scribbling, but for things they deemed sensitive and important, such as army movements, something more reliable was required.

"Mating season is almost here. Have you located a suitable match?"

"One of my year who also came south. She has deemed me acceptable."

"Acceptable? Your bloodline runs stronger than ever! Perhaps, you need higher standards, I am always willing to offer my advice."

Nyrisso laughed, *"I will always listen to you. Even when others are much more reluctant."*

"I detect the silver tongue of your mother in you, Nyrisso. Fortunately, I see more of myself in you than her. My guess is you had your choice of many in the recent weeks."

"You are correct, but Payorta was the first and my agreement simplifies my chaotic schedule. What of you, Father? Will you take on another mate this season?"

"I have one troublesome female in mind. Time will tell where it leads."

"Troublesome? I am certain there is a story behind that."

"She wants me to pursue her. When I do, she demands I try again. She seeks to break that which will never be broken."

"Perhaps I should be the one offering advice, Sire."

His youngest son has always had an infectious attitude. The female he sired Nyrisso with hadn't been one of his better choices for a potential mate, but nevertheless, he was quite pleased with the result in front of him.

"I must offer thanks youngling. You and a few others forced me to continue living and caring for myself, even when I did not wish to do so. I thank you now for your help, because I was incapable before. Your final seasons on this island were less enjoyable than they should have been because of my crisis. I owe you a debt."

His son went rigid in surprise. *"Father! I do not know what to say."*

"Nor do I, but I think it needed to be stated. My honor demands nothing less. Now, instead of us standing here and looking foolish, perhaps a son will tell his father about the first few months out in the world? Majherri trotted around his son and gave him a close inspection. You've gotten leaner and stronger. Life off the island has certainly treated you well."

As Nyrisso related the events he experienced in the months since they had last seen each other, Majherri found it an amusing turn of events. When his son was younger, the colt would track him down every time he and Danella returned to this island for a full accounting of his adventures. Now, Majherri would be the one waiting for any interesting news.

"I wish I had more to relate, but other than an occasional group of seaborne raiders or an odd ogre sighting, the south is quiet. Honestly, I had expected more. I did learn from another courier recently that the western battalion is still looking into reports of heavy raiders attacking the nomad human tribes."

That piqued Majherri's interest. His last ride as a scout was in that area and the more he thought about his missing memories, the more he was certain that something sinister was lurking out in the western sands.

"Let me know what else you hear during your travels, Nyrisso and always stay aware of your surroundings. Pay no attention to the fools trotting around in heavy armor. The two most dangerous positions in any battalion are the scout and the courier. Ambushes rarely go after an armored

column of riders, but lone unicorns and their riders make tempting targets. Do not be fooled by the quiet you refer to. The south still harbors a great deal of resentment towards the High-King and our riders are easily recognizable symbols of his authority."

His son snorted in agreement. *"I will take your words to heart, Father. Thank you for your wisdom. Unfortunately, I must go. My rider is likely ready and we are due back in the south."*

"I wish I was out there with you."

Nyrisso laughed and replied, *"Was it not you who would visit me here and tell me that my time would eventually come? The seasons will pass, Sire. Your time will come again and perhaps one day we shall fight side by side."*

"I look forward to that day."

"As do I, Father. May the wind be forever at your back."

Majherri wished Nyrisso a safe journey and watched his son gallop off in search of his rider. Humans assigned to courier duty were often the recent graduates with little actual combat experience. The scouts were a different story altogether. The duo of rider and unicorn must be skilled veterans, proven in battle, because they go in search of trouble and were given considerable latitude in how they dealt with matters.

It was that very independence that had attracted Majherri and Danella to the scouts. Ultimately, it was also that thirst for freedom that doomed Danella. Five years from now, he and Kayleigh would go to a battalion. What roll would they be assigned? Would he still be capable of taking those same risks that he had before? Was Kayleigh a good candidate to join the scouts, or was she better suited for another assignment in the battalions?

Too many had already warned him to not try and remake Kayleigh into Danella.

Eyeing the barge separating itself from the dock, the unicorn thought, *That, of course, is easier stated than actually done. Still, the news out of the west is unsettling. I'll have to look for couriers coming in with news from there and ask them what they know. There should also be some old friends to speak with, when they come back to the island to mate.*

Galloping away, in need of a morning run, Majherri knew this was something he'd been missing ... a sense of purpose. His new world started and ended with Kayleigh and there was precious little outside of that.

That needs to change. Others will tell me that I'm intruding where I am not wanted or looking for things that do not exist, but ill winds blow from the west. After all, I owe it to my first rider to learn what happened.

Chapter 16 – The Fifth Stall

"That's it. Hold the flame steady and don't make it bigger if you can help it. Focus. Make it burn brighter. Picture it burning hotter. Slowly change the color. That's it! That's it! Oh, you lost it. Okay, take a deep breath and clear your mind. We'll try it again."

Kayleigh wanted to scream and ask how she was supposed to focus over Annabeth's running commentary, but that would be ungrateful.

The older woman patted her on her shoulder and said, "You've got some of the oddest control problems I've ever seen! Maybe I'm asking too much of you at one time. Let's just stick to a brightly burning yellow flame, but you'll want to put an effort into mastering color change."

Kayleigh was perplexed. "Why?"

"Making fire isn't all about combat. During large scale battles, regular armies use either flags or drums to issue orders to the troops. We generally use fire in different colors to do the same thing. Now, let's get back to work. Conjure the flame and we'll go back to the motion exercises we worked on last time. Let's see how well you do this week."

With her bare hand firmly on Majherri's back, she held out her other, gloved hand and focused on the air surrounding it. There was a sensation of warmth as a streamer of fire emerged, like an animal coming out of its hole. It swirled once over the surface of her palm and then rose into a vertical column, extending a few feet into the air.

"Now reduce the thickness. Imagine it rolled like dough and spread into a flat sheet."

The food imagery was what worked for Rider Welsh. Kayleigh instead drew from art and pictured her mother's pottery wheel. She imagined the flame like a mass of wet clay that needed to be smoothed and flattened. The column shrunk and expanded into a disk shape hovering in the air.

"Better, but keep it vertical and spread it this way," Annabeth said, doing the same, but keeping the disk in front of her like a shield.

In Kayleigh's mind, she lifted her disk of flame up like placing linens on a clothesline. "How does that look?"

"That's it. Now keep it floating right there and reach down with you conjuring hand and pick up the shield."

"Won't the flame go away?"

"Not as long as you fix it there in your mind. The hand is just there to help it come into existence. Watch me take my hand away. See. There's nothing to it. The only thing that will make the magic go away is if you take your hand off your unicorn."

Kayleigh's fire disk flickered, but remained as she slid her right arms through the straps of the round shield and lifted it.

"Alright, here's the fun part. Take the sheet of flame and flatten it against the outside of the metal. Spread it out nice and evenly. Then you'll want to stick the flame right there so that it moves wherever the shield moves. Just like this."

Annabeth raised her arm over her head, as if to protect from an arrow attack. The flames moved in concert with the shield. There was a slight disconnect when Kayleigh attempted to duplicate what she just saw. There was a delay before the flame would catch up to what she was doing.

"Don't worry about that too much. You'll get better with practice, but this same basic concept applies to applying fire to your weapons as well. Eventually, you'll be able to skip the initial steps and just conjure the flat sheet of fire directly around your sword or shield. You're looking a bit tired. Let's take a break."

Letting her flame extinguish, Kayleigh removed her hand from Majherri, who snorted in encouragement and resumed whatever conversation he was having with Rheysurrah. Though Kayleigh had no idea what they were saying, it wasn't laced with the usual antagonism. It was refreshing to see him not making another unicorn angry.

"After mating season is over, I might not have as much time for our lessons, Kayleigh."

"You're not getting into trouble for all this?"

"Nothing like that, but we're going to be short two squads. They're being temporarily assigned to the western battalion and the rest of us are left to pick up the slack."

Majherri's head whipped around so fast that it bumped into Kayleigh. "Hey, watch it!" She exclaimed. Placing her hand on Majherri's mane, she tried to listen to her unicorn.

"He's angry ... no ... he's worried ... about the west."

"Well, I wouldn't worry too much. We're the first place everyone borrows troops from. It's how I ended up on the recruiting trip to begin with. We just got back four riders who were sent up north for the rainy season – they were a team of water and earth maidens trying to help contain the flooding. It happens every year."

Majherri snorted dismissively. It was a sound Kayleigh was intimately familiar with. Rheysurrah responded with several angry noises and aggressive movements.

"Looks like the truce has been broken," Rider Welsh said shaking her head. "Why don't you two unicorns go get a drink from the stream and cool your tempers? I think we're done doing magic for today."

Annabeth waited until both were out of earshot before saying, "That's one obstinate unicorn you've got there. He's got a real gift for stubbornness. It's obvious he doesn't like me."

"I haven't met too many humans or, for that matter, unicorns that he does," Kayleigh said sadly.

"How are you getting along with the other girls in your year?"

"Okay, I guess. Morganstern is one of my section leaders, so there's always some bitterness there. The Captain bumped Hawthorne down to squad leader and since she got a letter from her mother, she has been ice cold to both me and Rebekah."

"General Hawthorne's daughter?"

"The same."

"That's not good. The general has a reputation for being a perfectionist." Welsh stopped and smiled broadly. "I think your captain wants to be her when she grows up. I know, I know. I shouldn't speak about officers that way, but it needed to be said."

Kayleigh couldn't resist returning the smile, but not before glancing for any people eavesdropping. "Still, Hawthorne's squad is improving by leaps and bounds."

"Whether they want to or not, eh?"

"Andrea has a scary side, but she reserves most of her ire for Morganstern, which has actually made my life a little easier. I'm still racking up extra duty, but the two worst squads are coming up to speed and getting a lot less demerits than they used to. If you remember Alicia Santiago, she's the other section leader and she's as orderly as ever."

"I do. She's the type that will make officer in her first five years out in the field. I'll probably still be a rider."

"I think you're great!" Kayleigh offered.

"Yeah, but that's because I'm a rabble-rouser and a troublemaker. I have the distinct impression that we're kindred spirits."

"Not really," Kaleigh said with a sigh. "Trouble goes out of its way to find me."

Rider Welsh chuckled and replied, "Well, if that's the case, embrace it with open arms and use it to your advantage. Of course, there might be a certain stable master you're more interested in embracing."

"It's nothing of the sort!" She protested, but it sounded very weak.

"Oh c'mon Kayleigh, do you think there's a reason they switched him to the first years, where the five year age gap wouldn't make him consider one of you? Problem is, you're not exactly thirteen, are you?"

"I can't believe we're having this conversation!"

Annabeth chortled and said, "I remember when I was here and several of my classmates said that they might look him up after their chastity vow was over."

Kayleigh was preparing a suitable reply, but noticed an object in the distance. "There's a barge coming. It's too early for the evening barge isn't it?"

"You're right. Especially on a 'free' day. I wonder what is going on."

The pair watched the barge get closer. One thing Kayleigh had learned is that this island operated on a predictable pattern. Things happened on a schedule and there was precious little deviation. Before they knew it, they were walking down to the docks as the magically powered barge drew closer.

"Let's hope it's a visitor," Annabeth said just slightly louder than a whisper.

A few of the male dockworkers were scurrying on the short pier. Kayleigh noticed Annabeth with her hands framing her eyes trying to see something. Her neck inched forward and then recoiled as she turned away, muttering something under her breath.

"What is it?"

"The black pennant is flying. It means they're bringing back a riderless unicorn."

"Oh no!"

"I'm afraid she's right." Brian Tomas stepped up next to them. "It's a male. With it being so close to mating season, we're going to try and encourage him to mate."

"Any word who his rider was," Annabeth asked with grave concern.

"I don't know, but I heard the unicorn is from the eastern battalion and it happened a little over a week ago. Recruit Reese, I hate to impose on your free day, but we'll be taking the male to my stables. I only just learned of this when the barge left the dock and haven't had a chance to make a stall ready. Would you be so kind as to prepare the fifth stall for this new arrival? Put a fresh layer of hay down, fill the water trough, and get two blankets out of the storage closet."

"Of course." She would have gladly done anything he asked. Annabeth had the decency to only half-smirk at how quickly Kayleigh answered.

"Thank you. I'll dock it from your extra duty total." He said with half-hearted humor.

Kayleigh scampered off to do as she was told. She worked quickly to ready the stall. Finishing, she waited against the wooden double doors to the stable and watched a small but grim procession grow at the dock and head in her direction. The two mounted riders led the one with the empty saddle and a line of unicorns that had been grazing minutes ago followed behind with their heads hung low. Tears welled in her eyes as the group approached, but Kayleigh made no move to wipe them away. She couldn't take her thoughts away from the fact that a beautiful and majestic creature was being led to his death.

If Majherri survived, maybe this one might as well!

Passing by her, she was able to get a good look at the male. Her fleeting hopes were dashed. His coat had lost its luminescence. The shiny, almost reflective, white was replaced by a dingy white color normally seen in dried bone. The eyes held no spark or energy. They just stared ahead, listless and dull. The rest of the male was thinner than he should be and his stride was awkward and lacked the smooth grace she witnessed every day on the island.

Brian closed the gate behind it and began removing the saddle. The unicorn snorted and raised itself in anger, the first sign of life it had shown. He refused to allow Brian to remove his saddle. After a second time, the stable master relented and draped one of the blankets over the back of the angry unicorn. The saddle formed a strange hump that somehow made the scene even more painful.

It was too much for Kayleigh. She stepped outside the

stable and ran around to the other side, fully intending to cry her eyes out. Instead she stopped, finding Majherri there staring into the window. He was so very still, barely breathing and immobile. Reaching out her hand, she touched him gently. Despite her best intention, he flinched. The negative feelings she was experiencing were nothing like the sadness emanating from her mount. She buried her head in his neck and tried to reassure him. Unicorns don't cry unless in physical pain, so she cried for him.

They stood like that for a minute until Kayleigh heard a shout. She wasn't certain what was wrong.

Huh, what are they saying? When did it get so loud?

She lifted her head and her eyes flew open. They were cocooned in a shell of blue flame. Panicked, she let go of Majherri and the flames faded away. The glass pane of the window was melted and the outer wall was blackened and smoldering. Had they been standing a few feet closer, the structure would likely be engulfed in flames. Curls of smoke rose from the ground where a barren patch was scalded into the dirt. A water maiden rode up. She conjured liquid directly onto the heated wood causing a hiss of steam to be released.

Kayleigh took a step, but was suddenly very lightheaded. Her world spun as she dropped to the ground.

When she came to, she was in the infirmary. Her arms and legs felt like they were made of lead. She reached over to the pitcher of water and poured some into a cup. Her throat was very dry and the water was soothing. A choking cough alerted the others that she was awake.

The bed she was in was comfortable, much more comfortable than her bed in the barracks. Large gaps separated the beds and Kayleigh remembered from the welcoming tour they received that the rider's unicorn was allowed to visit through the wide doors at the other end of the room.

"Quite a little scare you gave us there, lead rider," Brian

Tomas stood from his chair across the room where he was playing a game of chess with Rider Welsh, who also rose. "I know you spend far too much time in my humble stable to begin with, but that is no call to try and burn it to the ground."

"I didn't …"

He smiled brightly and said, "Of course not. If there is any blame to be had, it is mine. I should have had you take Majherri away from there. I was only thinking of the other unicorn. I had thought that the presence of one that had survived the wasting might somehow provide some encouragement. I gave no thought at all to how Majherri would react. I will go get him and bring him through the unicorn entrance. He made his intentions clear that I should come get him the moment you awoke."

"What happened?" Kayleigh said blinking and still trying to focus.

Annabeth sat down next to her and smacked Kayleigh's knee. "Remember those control issues I said you have. I do believe that I have grossly understated them. I don't know if that was a fireshade transformation or even what to call that if it wasn't, but whatever the two of you were doing, it took a lot out of Majherri and even more out of you. The fact you didn't even know what was happening is troubling. You're supposed to be in control and directing the power. Emotions can amplify magic and make it more powerful and that was a serious release of magic. It overwhelmed you."

Kayleigh gulped on her water and choked on some of it. Finally, she was able to croak, "What do we do about it?"

"Right now, you aren't going to be doing anything. Your captain and I had a discussion. … Wait a second, I actually agree with her. You need to work with a better teacher than me. After the festivities for mating season are over, they're going to match you up with a couple of the instructors they have here and see which one you do the best with."

"But I like you," Kayleigh said. It sounded like a childish protest.

"Well thank you. I happen to like you as well. But I'll say this; I've been in a few battles. I had good training here at The Academy and I've worked hard in the battalions. Sure, I've been scared, but I've never been terrified. I've always had my training to fall back on, just like you will, one day. When I saw you, today, I froze. I was terrified. I've never seen anything like it before. That's why you need to work with the best instructors."

"Oh. You'll still come and visit. Won't you?"

"Of course, you couldn't keep me away if you tried."

The healer asked Annabeth to step outside while he examined Kayleigh. She replied that there was a barge waiting to take her and Rheysurrah back to the city and that she had to leave. A pungent draught was forced down Kayleigh's throat and she quickly drank another cup of water, trying to rid her mouth of that taste. He asked her basic questions to check whether she could focus before telling her that she would be kept here overnight, but could return to classes in the morning.

The outside double door to the infirmary opened and Brian gestured for Majherri to enter. Captain Lynch followed on T'rsa and Brian waved before closing the doors behind the Captain.

"Though we don't expect any problems, trainee," Captain Lynch said. "It is a precaution that your contact with your unicorn be either in an open space or monitored by a water maiden. Stables are easily enough repaired or even rebuilt. This infirmary is another matter altogether."

"Yes, ma'am." Kayleigh couldn't help the resentment, but as with all other things involving her captain, there was a sound reasoning behind it. Either way, she didn't care at that moment. What mattered was Majherri. He turned into the aisle and moved next to her, lowering his head for her outstretched hand.

There was relief, gratitude, and even shame swirling through their bond. She closed her eyes and reassured him.

I'm okay. We're okay. They shouldn't have made you watch that other unicorn suffering.

Kayleigh knew bonds don't transmit the words, only feelings, emotions, and images. It's impossible to hide something from Majherri and that worked both ways. Beneath the shame was concern for her health, anger that they'd been separated for hours, and a plea for forgiveness. It was a depth of emotion he did not show after taking her into battle against the Yar. It was a truth both genuine and frightening at the same time. He was scared he hurt her. She did her best to forgive him and more.

After a minute she opened one eye, to make certain the room wasn't burning. There was a sense of sarcastic mirth exchanged through the bond.

"Annabeth thought that was a fireshade. You've done it before. Is she right?"

Majherri shook his head no and confusion and uncertainty coursed through their connection.

"I was hoping you'd know what it was."

Captain Lynch inserted herself into the conversation, "I've already consulted with several fire maidens on the staff. They are discussing possible theories, but have not settled on anything. I assume Rider Welsh explained that your lessons with her were over."

Kayleigh nodded, not trusting the kind of answer she'd give her captain at that particular moment.

"Are you up for additional visitors? I will be taking Majherri back outside for the rest of the evening shortly, but many of your classmates wish to pay their respects."

Majherri obviously didn't like the arrangement and Kayleigh wasn't pleased either, but they both knew that he was going to leave.

"Yes, ma'am. I'll see them."

"Good." Meghan Lynch replied, while backing T'rsa away from them. "I'll give you a few more minutes to say goodnight before the three of us leave. You will need to find me tomorrow and we will schedule time for you to visit with him."

"Thank you." Kayleigh pushed as much false sincerity as she could into those two words.

The amusement on the other end of the bond made her whisper, "Tell me how you really feel, Majherri."

Ten minutes after the captain left with her unicorn, a dozen of her classmates entered. Ellen she expected, but Kayleigh was mildly impressed with the turnout – all six squad leaders, Alicia, Rebekah, Francine, and a few others. After fielding numerous variations of what happened and how she was feeling, her eyes settled on the cold and calculating face of Rebekah Morganstern.

She addressed the short brunette, "You've been dying to say something, Rebekah. Now is as good a time as any."

"It's time you asked the captain to step down as lead rider. You obviously have problems and you need to deal with them. These problems don't involve the company and we would be better off with someone other than you as lead rider."

"Would you be terribly hurt if I said no?"

"Not particularly, I told the rest of them you wouldn't do it. You only think about yourself."

"The rest of them …" Kayleigh trailed off, ignoring the remainder of the comment, and looked at the faces in the room. Ellen looked away, but Alicia met her withering gaze.

The dark skinned section leader said, "It's nothing against you, Kayleigh, but Morganstern's right about one thing. You need to solve the problems with your bond. Remember on the journey here when Francine almost lost her bond? You and Majherri helped her out. That's all we're doing here. You need time to fix things between you and your unicorn. If I'm lead rider and you're ready for it again, all you have to do is say the word and I'll step aside. Lead rider is a big deal, but not nearly as important as your unicorn."

"We don't want to see you get hurt again, Kayleigh. You'll be able to focus on your control without always worrying about the captain." Ellen said, still avoiding eye contact.

Several nodded and offered encouraging smiles. The one plastered on Rebekah's face lacked any real conviction. Kayleigh weighed the possibilities and tried to imagine this as something other than a mutiny. Unfortunately, it felt very much like one.

After all the extra hours and running around trying to help all of them, this is how they treat me! What a bunch of ungrateful ... I shouldn't follow that thought. Yelling at them won't solve anything.

"Give me a few days to think it over. At least let me get out of here, first."

"What? So you can burn something else to the ground?" Morganstern scoffed.

"Trot off! You're just looking for a way to get out of challenging me."

"You're unstable, Reese and unfit to lead. If you had any sense in that whore head of yours, you'd have realized it by now."

Arms grabbed Kayleigh as she bolted upright. Rebekah continued, "That just proves my point. You're nothing but a ..."

"Enough!" A voice screamed. Everyone stopped and looked at the furious visage of Andrea Hawthorne. She shook her head and ground her teeth against each other before continuing, "Reese, you're incapable of leading right now and you weren't all that great to begin with. Morganstern, you're years away from leading anything but yourself to the latrine! I'm tired of both of you."

Her finger thrust out at Rebekah, "I was demoted to clean up your mess! And you got my position! Just so," the digit turned on Kayleigh, "the captain could continue a vendetta against you. Step down, Reese. Step down now!"

Kayleigh crossed her arms in defiance. "Because you'll throw a fit, if I don't? I'm not worried."

"Step down or I'll take you down myself."

"All I asked for was some time to think it over, Hawthorne! Give it a rest."

"Yes," Rebekah said. "Quit pretending that you're your mother, Andrea. It gets tiresome after awhile."

"What's all this shouting?" The healer said reentering. "I heard you all the way down the hallway."

"Good," Andrea said rounding on him. "You're a staff member. Just what I needed. I'm issuing a challenge to my lead rider and going on record as being the first."

"Your challenge is officially noted, Trainee … What is your name?"

"Andrea Hawthorne."

"Trainee Hawthorne. Now, for disrupting my infirmary and causing this ruckus, every single one of you just earned extra duty. You'll all be in here next free day and you won't leave until this place is spotless! I am going to speak to your captain right now and if anyone other than my patient is here when I return, there will be hell to pay!"

All but Rebekah scattered and followed the healer out of the room. She lingered looking like the cat that ate the proverbial canary. Leaning against one of the wooden columns, she let out a self-satisfied chuckle.

"Do you think this is funny?"

"Hilarious is more like it. Now, you can't resign, Reese. The captain can't even fire you until the challenge is held."

"I thought you wanted me to resign. Now you're happy I'll be lead rider for at least a few more weeks."

"Positively ecstatic. I want to see you humiliated – in front of everyone! Even if you win, you'll get fired, sooner or later. My guess is sooner. You're a toxin."

Kayleigh laughed and pointed at Morganstern. "You're pathetic, Rebekah. Do you really want to be lead rider that badly?"

"No. I'm not really even interested in being lead rider, but I won't stand for it being you. You don't deserve it!"

"Why? Because of my mother? Because your father was unfaithful?"

That got under the girl's skin. "You've no right to speak about my father!"

"And you're just a petty little girl clinging to your father's pant leg. My mother's flaws are many, and I know it. But you can't bring yourself to think of him as anything less than perfect. You don't really hate me, Rebekah, you hate him and yourself."

The girl took a step toward Kayleigh's bed and stopped. Her face was red with rage, but somehow Rebekah regained control of her emotions. "You're just trying to keep me here with your lies until the healer gets back. It's not going to work."

She spun and began her retreat. Kayleigh let her words chase after Morganstern. "The only lies here, Rebekah, are the ones that you tell yourself."

Chapter 17 – A Final Breath

"Your rider will be defeated. Andrea has been schooled in the blade since she was old enough to walk." Kyrinda boasted.

Majherri was in an ill mood to begin with and this idiot female wasn't improving things. *"As the challenged rider, Kayleigh has the choice of combat. If she chooses to joust, your Andrea cannot possibly win."*

"They aren't going to let you joust after the incident at the stable two days ago," Lycenae interrupted. *"I heard they're forcing your rider to choose hoof-by-hoof combat."*

"It's hand-to-hand combat, fool. Try to at least learn something from that spineless wretch that sits in your saddle." Majherri was angry. Much of this was his fault and it was being laid at his rider's feet. He hated the knowledge that Kayleigh was suffering due to his actions. Worst of all, it sounded like he would be forbidden from helping her during this first challenge. Again, he sensed the human rules were twisted in order to place Kayleigh at a disadvantage. She'd told him about the challenge during their visit yesterday, but her not being allowed to choose the style of combat wasn't mentioned. He wondered if she knew, or were they going to ambush her with this news as well.

Majherri trotted off, turning his backside on the two of them and flicking his tail in an insulting gesture. Already the first wave of unicorns was arriving for mating season, their rider's tents springing up everywhere he looked. These would mate quickly and after the first few days, leave for the Portal that would carry them back and allow the others to race across the continent before the season ended.

"I can see you are in a foul mood. Should I even bother with conversation, or are you going to circle the island in unpleasantness?"

"Pasha, I'm in no mood for your games this evening."

The female ignored his ire. *"I've been with Gomlius in the sta-*

ble. He's resting now, but he continues to grow weaker. He wishes to speak with you."

"There is nothing I can do for him. Whatever helped me to survive *The Wasting* is not going to help him. He's already progressed further than I ever did."

"That doesn't matter. Go speak with him not for his welfare, but for your own. I believe you can help Gomlius accept his fate and more importantly, he can help you deal with your survival."

Majherri snorted and thrust his snout into the stream. When he looked up, she was still staring at him. *"Oh, you actually wanted an answer. A conversation with a dying unicorn won't serve any purpose. He has no answer for my questions and I have no answer for his. If you're expecting me to attain some new level of awareness, disappointment is on the horizon. I've accepted my survival."*

"I am unconvinced. Why are you mocking me?"

"No, I am just recalling a conversation with my youngest offspring, who visited the island recently."

"You're avoiding this issue, Majherri."

"And you, dear Pasha, are trying to create an issue where none exists."

"Then, perhaps, there is still time to find a different mate. My current choice is infuriating."

"For a change, I agree." He stopped what he was doing and began moving away from her. She'd used that phrase far too often for his liking. Another barge was arriving shortly and he could continue his search for answers with them.

Pasha didn't follow.

After speaking with several of his brethren, he finally tracked a unicorn down. She'd aged some since he last saw her. The muscle tone wasn't quite as defined as it had been almost twenty seasons ago, but he approached just the same. The stars were out, but the moon was obscured by clouds.

"It is good to see you again, Cyemma." His last successful mate was very chatty. News always seemed to find her.

"Who's that? Majherri! This light is a good look for you."

"Ever the comedian. Our son was by recently, he's a courier in the south."

"So, I've heard. What brings you in search of me, this night? Trying to line up a last minute mate? I was pleased to learn you somehow survived, just not that pleased."

"No, that is a path best not traveled again. When I spoke with others, they said you and your rider found a raided caravan in the west. I wanted to know more about it."

"I'm afraid there's not much to tell. Broken and empty wagons, half-covered in sand. No signs of the humans. Their tracks were wiped away by the dust storms. The only thing we could find was the remains of a few animals. You know better than I do how hard it is to keep track of the wandering humans. One week, they'll be camped at an oasis, and then, without warning, they pack up and move. Was it not you who called them defective little ants scuttling across the sand with no sense of civilization?"

Forced to concede her point, he agreed, *"Actually, that was a compliment. The world would be safer if more humans weren't so obsessed with claiming the land as their own. Still, I am concerned about the ominous portents in your area."*

"Oh, we'll get to the bottom of it soon enough. All it takes is for a few scouts to ride with their herds and we'll catch these raiders in the act. If you're looking for real trouble, you'd be better served looking south. I hear some bad things out of that region and they've been too quiet for too long. Some self-important human is bound to start something there just like the last time and the time before that."

Cyemma was making perfect sense, which was why Majherri was certain she was wrong. He could finally bear her company no longer and bid her a good night, hoping that he would not encounter her again during the mating season. The past few nights, he'd stayed clear of his stables preferring the moonlit pastures and star-filled skies, but tonight was a dreary affair and he steeled his nerves and slowly traveled back to the stable.

He started to pass the duo of unicorns from the east standing watch over their fallen friend. It would be so easy to just slip into stall number fourteen and ignore the labored breathing and the occasional whines.

Instead, he cursed Pasha and stopped next to the pair. They looked at him, questions in their eyes.

"I wish to pay my respects. How is he?"

"He sleeps in fits, friend. Who are you?"

"Majherri, born of Thaydra and Korin. If he wakes, I would speak with him in private. Return in the morning. I will stand with him through the night. Should his last breath come, he will not be alone."

They hesitated, but eventually left. Part of Majherri hoped Gomlius would sleep until morning and he could hold his head high and say that he tried.

To say the dying unicorn looked bad was an understatement. Ugly blemishes and bruises marred the skin. They were indications that he was bleeding internally. The water in the trough, laced with water maiden healing tears would only slow the process.

They should have already stopped using them and allowed nature to take its course. Someone still believes he can rally. Delusional fools! They're just trying to get him to mate one last time to strengthen the bloodline. If he was a female, or this wasn't mating season, they wouldn't have even bothered bringing him back.

He didn't know who he was angry with, or even why. He'd given them false hope that this wretch might endure. But he knew it was a terrible waste. With the third week since his rider's death approaching, Gomlius would start to lose his mind. By the end of the fourth week, he'd likely need to be restrained. If he was still alive at the end of the fifth week, a mercy killing would be granted.

The minutes continued to pass. Nearly two hours went by when Gomlius bolted upright, startled, casting his head from side to side.

"Who's there? Is that you Alvia?"

"No. I am Majherri."

"Ah, I was wondering if I was going to meet you. They keep saying your name you know. If I just persevere, I could be like you. That's what

they say. They try to tell me that I'm doing better than expected, but I feel hollow, empty. So I ask you, what is the secret to surviving?"

"I do not know, Gomlius. I have no idea how long I wandered in the western desert. Those memories are denied to me, but when they found me, I was in pain. Probably the same agony you are feeling now. One day it just stopped. The bruises began to fade. My appetite started to return."

"So, do you think I can best this foe?"

"You don't want an answer to that question."

"Yes. Yes I do."

"Then prepare for the worst, Gomlius. Anything else will be a blessed event. Being a miracle survivor isn't as pleasant as it seems. Some company would be welcome."

"Why is that?"

"Our kind shuns me, or fears me, take your pick. At my low points, I feel I've betrayed my first rider. First and rider – those words shouldn't belong together. They sound odd when used that way."

"Ask me how they sound again in a few weeks, if I'm as lucky as you are," Gomlius replied.

"Most of all there is the knowledge that something changed me out in that desert. I've tried to deny it, but my magic isn't right. You saw it yourself. She and I were doing something unnatural. The flow felt wrong, like I was pulling from her. My new rider, she's a sweet, young human. She is pure and desperately unwise in the ways of the world. I fear I could easily hurt her and the thought that I might outlast her as well terrifies me. What if I keep getting new riders only to see them wither and die? What if I can't die at all? Is my gift really a curse and I won't realize it for seasons to come?"

"You sound like you still are waiting for death's final breath."

"I suppose I do, but when I stood where you are, I wanted nothing more than to live and avenge Danella. If you live, we will discuss what comes next. Until then, tell me your story, so that when others speak your name, I can say I know you."

Gomlius forced himself to drink before beginning his life story. Twenty minutes into it, he began to wobble on unsteady legs. Majherri wedged himself into the stall and let the other unicorn balance against his side so the story could continue. At times he repeated parts or paused to recall a name.

When the shakes came for a second time, Majherri bore the extra weight and help the unicorn down to the ground. Instead of going to get a human, Majherri pulled the heavy blanket onto Gomlius with his teeth, taking care to leave the tail exposed so the other could continue his story.

The toll became too much and the ill unicorn drifted off into a restless sleep. Majherri watched every rise and fall of Gomlius' breathing. He counted the seconds between each one and as the hours passed that time continued to grow.

"You can go now." The pair returned with the rising sun.

He shook his head. *"It's almost time. Let us bear witness."*

The humans were heading to their first meal of the day when the breathing stopped. Three pairs of eyes watched, hoping to see movement. Five minutes passed without any movement.

"He is gone, but his story is known. I know of Gomlius born of Pheya and Tyrix. His story lives in me and by the end of this day three others will know it." The female said.

The other male next to him said, *"I too know of Gomlius born of Pheya and Tyrix. His story lives in me and by the end of this day, three others will know it. He will not be forgotten."*

Majherri agreed, *"I also know of Gomlius born of Pheya and Tyrix. His story lives in me and by the end of this day, three others will know it. Stay with his body. I will get the stable master."*

The sun was just climbing into the sky, but it was difficult to bring his head up to meet it. Death had come quickly for Gomlius and it occurred to Majherri that perhaps his tale of life after losing a rider had sent Gomlius racing in the other direction. He was still alone; still the only one to ever survive the loss of a rider.

Chapter 18 – The General's Request

"You're getting more accurate with your knife," Lieutenant Sheppard said.

"Thank you, ma'am." Kayleigh retrieved her knife from the target. She spent nearly as many hours here on the range as she had in with Stable Master Tomas. All this practice had improved both her sewing skills, mending the cloth on the targets, and her own throwing form.

"Don't thank me, you've applied yourself," the stocky brunette said while using a brush coated with a dark dye to draw a rough target on an upright hay bale perched on a slab of stone.

"Now, let's see if you can tap some of the magic stored inside your knife."

"Are you sure that's wise, ma'am?"

"Your unicorn isn't here, correct?"

"No, ma'am."

"Then the only source of magic you have is the tiny amount stored in your personal weapon. One of the reasons, we limit the amount of access you have to Majherri is that we want you to develop better control over the flow of your magic. The captain and I are in agreement on this and we will work with the magic inside your blade. Besides, if you manage to engulf the island in a firestorm with what little you hold in your hand … no amount of training is going to help you. My unicorn is here in the event we need to smother a fire. Let not your young heart be troubled."

Kayleigh laughed at the woman's light-hearted tone. *It was a pity Captain Lynch couldn't be more like her. She's patient and treats everyone with respect.*

Lieutenant Sheppard went to Pasha's saddle and removed the worn, but still deadly looking mace from where it was kept.

"This is my weapon. I didn't get my first kill until I was out in the southern battalions. There was a skirmish with a rebellious duke's forces and I ended up fighting a knight in full plate. I unhorsed him and thought he wouldn't be able to get up because the weight of his kit and moved on to the next opponent. Somehow, the man did get up and pulled me right off of Pasha. He tried to bash my skull in with this, but I used to favor a short dirk back then. To make a long story short, I came out of the battle with this and a few broken ribs. That knight taught me a valuable lesson, which I'll now share with you. Never assume your opponent is finished. It could be the last assumption you ever make."

"I understand."

"Thought you would. Now, I want you to close your eyes and concentrate on your knife. Can you feel the magic in there?"

"Yes."

"Okay, pretend that it's Majherri. Try and pull a tiny bit of magic out of it. Hold it in the throwing position and try to blend it with the blade. Be careful not to burn yourself. Easy. There's not a lot in the knife. Don't use it all up at once!"

Kayleigh opened one of her eyes slightly and saw the knife blade surrounded by a corona of flame. She didn't feel like it was emptying the knife, but she pulled back, allowing the glow around the weapon to subside.

"Ready! Throw!"

As she released the knife, the flame spread over the surface and it was like she was hurling a small fireball at the target. The flame died in midflight.

"Why didn't your weapon stay lit?"

Kayleigh could tell there was a lesson in the answer by the way the woman was asking the question.

"I'm not sure, ma'am."

"You either ran out of stored magical energy, or you let it go out. Go get it."

Kayleigh did as instructed as Lieutenant Sheppard continued, "Do you still feel any magic?"

"Yes." Honestly, it felt the same as when Kayleigh first concentrated on it, but she figured that it would only confuse things if she mentioned that fact.

"That means you've let your concentration lapse. Watch this. I'll make my mace vibrate. It increases the force of my blows. Now, when I set it down, it continues. If I focus, I can keep that going until there's no more magic stored in my weapon. Let's see you try it without adding too much by making you throw it and hit a target. Wrap it in flames and set it down, just like I did."

It was easy to "light" the knife again. She twisted it in her hand and watched the flame dance across the sides of the blade. It flickered when she placed it on the ground, but she kept her attention on it and the flame strengthened.

"Very good. Keep the flame off the tip and put on a glove. I'm going to count backwards from ten. When I reach one, pick it up and bury it into that hay bale. Keep it lit the entire time. Are you ready, trainee?"

"Yes, ma'am," Kayleigh said working the glove onto her hand and listening to the countdown. At one, she grabbed it and hurled it at the target. The miniature fireball struck home and stayed there burning for a moment before the lieutenant tossed a bucket of water on it."

"Good work. Now, let's do it again."

During the next few throws, Lieutenant Sheppard stood near the target and continued dousing the hay with water, while challenging Kayleigh to make the fire stronger. Without warning, her instructor pitched the contents of the bucket at Kayleigh instead of the target. The knife hit, but the fire had disappeared mid-flight. Drenched, Kayleigh gave the lieutenant a sour expression.

Sheppard smiled and affected an air of innocence before saying. "Concentration needs to become second nature, trainee. In real combat, targets rarely stay still and are quite capable of striking back."

"Yes, ma'am," Kayleigh's reply was more a grumble of discontent.

"I think that's enough for tonight. I hear you've been challenged."

Kayleigh nodded. "They won't let me do jousting, so I'll have to choose the weapon challenge. Trainee Hawthorne is much better with the blade."

"The best fighter isn't always the victor," the earth maiden counseled. "The one who executes the best usually is. My advice to you is to do what you can do and do it well. Honestly, I can't even remember who was lead rider for my first three years except for the two week period I held the position, before someone else beat me. It's only as important as you make it, Reese. Do try to remember that."

"I will ma'am," Kayleigh snapped to attention in her wet clothing.

"Dismissed. Go get yourself dried off."

Despite the festive atmosphere, Kayleigh found she wasn't in a celebratory mood. Majherri was being distant after the incident with their magical bond and the death of the riderless unicorn. She could feel his reluctance every time they touched. Added to this was the anger of her classmates. With her stuck in the infirmary, the rest of the company heard the story as framed by the duo of Hawthorne and Morganstern and as a result, most were turning a cold shoulder to her.

Raising her fist, she knocked on the door to Captain Lynch's office.

"Enter."

"Trainee Reese, reporting as ordered." Kayleigh said as she noted that Andrea Hawthorne was present and at attention.

"I'll say this for your benefit as well as Trainee Hawthorne's, since she may be replacing you, I don't like having to send people out looking for my lead rider. I expect you to be accessible, and when summoned, I expect you to arrive promptly."

"I was in the stables, ma'am."

"You are not supposed to have unsupervised contact with your unicorn!"

"Majherri was not in the stables, ma'am. I was assisting the stable master in the upkeep of the building."

The captain didn't look pleased by her explanation. "You have an answer for everything these days, recruit. However, I do not find your answers satisfactory."

Kayleigh paused, trying to decide if she should reply. Though it could probably get worse, she decided to speak her mind anyway. "I am required to answer all questions truthfully, ma'am. I cannot control how you view the answers."

"What was that?"

"I was in the stable. The stable master can verify my presence. I came directly here as soon as I was informed."

That answer and the tone did nothing to improve her relationship with her commanding officer. From the look on the captain's face, it struck a nerve.

"There is a slate board in the barracks. There is chalk next to that board. You can write, can't you? If you so much as leave the common area of the barracks to go to relieve yourself, I want it on that board. Now, enough of this! We're expected in the commandant's office. Follow me."

Kayleigh fell into step next to Andrea Hawthorne. They walked behind Captain Lynch. The younger brown-haired warrior showed no expression. Her face was a mask of complete seriousness.

"Just think Andrea, if you win, this can all be yours."

The captain delivered a scathing look over her shoulder and that stopped any further conversation. Kayleigh decided she'd been insubordinate enough for one day and began to wonder why they were going to see General Jyslin.

This isn't something that happens every day. With Hawthorne here, it's likely about our challenge. What do they want now? Maybe they'll insist that I fight with my hands bound as well! At least Lynch looks as happy as I usually do. Turnabout is fair play.

As the captain raised the door knocker, a voice inside said, "Enter."

They ventured inside and came to attention. Several others were waiting for them.

"At ease, captain, trainees."

"Greetings, mother," Andrea said to the larger than life presence of General Althea Hawthorne. Her defense of the Four Hills Valley from the southern armies was one of the first lectures in their history of warfare class.

The general gave her daughter a brief embrace. "It is good to see you again, Andrea. I've have made a request of the commandant. I know your upcoming challenge is scheduled in four weeks time, after mating season and the festival has ended. Even so, the challenges during the first year are delayed to ensure the participants are physically ready. I can personally vouch for your readiness and the lead rider is almost three years older. I think the question of readiness does not truly apply here."

General Jyslin spoke up, "What General Hawthorne is saying is that she would like to see this challenge in person before she is forced to leave for the southern command. We can schedule it along with the upper classes' challenges and the demonstrations. However, given the unusual nature of this request, I would like for you two young ladies to agree before we announce this."

Hawthorne immediately agreed. To Kayleigh, she looked like an eager puppy wanting to perform a new trick. All eyes settled on Kayleigh.

"It doesn't matter to me either way. Sooner is better than later. I agree." she said.

"You don't seem very enthusiastic, trainee," General Jyslin commented. The silver-haired woman stared through her with penetrating hazel eyes. Kayleigh stiffened under such scrutiny.

"My apologies, ma'am."

"Very well," General Jyslin said and turned her attention to Captain Lynch. "The challenge between Trainees Hawthorne and Reese will be added to the schedule of events. All of you are dismissed, except for Trainee Reese. I would like to speak with you further."

"Do you wish for me to remain?" Meghan Lynch asked.

"No Captain. I'm sure your lead rider can find her way back after I'm through with her. Carry on."

"Yes, ma'am." Lynch saluted and exited. Kayleigh wasn't certain whether this was a good or bad development. As the rest followed out the door, she remained at attention. The commandant's office was spacious and well decorated. A trophy case displayed awards from kingdoms spanning the coasts of the Blessed Continent. One wall was dominated by a stained glass window of a unicorn. She guessed that the setting sun would line up with the window perfectly and create a dazzling effect on the opposite wall.

Behind her desk there was a large oil painting of the mounted and much younger general reviewing her troops. The hair was longer and the skin tone much darker, but there was no doubt who the subject of the painting was.

The general gestured to a chair and said, "At ease. Sit child. I've been meaning to call you up here for a chat since the beginning of the year, but the time was never right."

"Thank you, ma'am."

"Now, how do you like The Academy?"

"It's exciting, ma'am."

"Just what I'd expect you to say child, but if you were that excited and you were fitting in nicely, we wouldn't be having this conversation. Would we?"

Kayleigh fidgeted, trying to look anywhere other than the old woman's eyes, and replied, "I suppose not, ma'am."

"I understand from speaking with your healer after your magical release that your classmates staged a bit of a coup and asked for your resignation. Is that correct?"

"Yes."

"Why did you choose not to resign?"

"I didn't, ma'am. I wanted to sleep on it and not make a snap decision."

General Jyslin nodded slowly and said, "A sensible approach. Now, it's been a few days since and the choice has been rendered moot because of the challenge, but humor and old woman, what would your decision be now? Would you have resigned?"

Kayleigh certainly hadn't expected that! She felt her teeth against her bottom lip as she weighed her answer. Thinking it over, she said, "No. I wouldn't."

That answer seemed to please the general, but she pressed forward. "May I ask why?"

She knew General Jyslin was leading her somewhere. "I haven't done anything that I should be ashamed of, ma'am. My bond with Majherri is unusual at times, but each bond between rider and unicorn is different."

"You are quite correct. Should you be victorious in your challenge, these problems will remain. Suppose your classmates ask a second time. What will you do then?"

"I'll make that decision when the time comes, ma'am. I have to win the challenge first."

"True, there is great wisdom in tackling problems as they arrive and not worrying about what shall be. Still, there is every chance that Captain Lynch will fire you after the challenge. She is, as am I, concerned with the reports from the instructors evaluating you. Your magic presents itself in fits and uncontrolled bursts."

"Yes, ma'am. It does. But since my time with Majherri is now limited and closely watched, it doesn't interfere with how I perform my duties."

"Well said, but what if there is a better candidate among your classmates? What if the captain chooses to replace you? Are you prepared to accept that possibility?"

"That is her decision, ma'am. If one of the others wants to replace me, it's up to them to prove it." Kayleigh answered, nervous and running out of breath. *If this is a polite conversation, I'd hate to see an interrogation.*

"Indeed it does. Our system is often strange, even when viewed through my tired eyes. We take young ladies, special young ladies, from all over. We bring them here, put them together, and immediately tell them that we are all special and that none of us is different from the next. That system serves us rather well in almost all cases, except of course, when someone special stands out from the crowd. That is when we learn how inflexible our system can be, child. Each and every one of you girls here are *my girls*. I want all of my girls to grow to their greatest potential and carry that greatness to all corners of the world. The true measure of my legacy is not on a pillow in that display case. My legacy shows up every year for mating season riding her unicorn. She has many names, achieved many great things, and sits high in her saddle smiling in the face of adversity. I already see a bit of that legacy in you, Kayleigh Reese."

Kayleigh was too dumbfounded to do anything other than nod.

"Well, I should probably dismiss you, but I wanted you to know that I am rooting for you to smile in the face of your hardships. Now, I'm impartial as to who wins, or whether you remain lead rider for your class, or not. But I am rooting for you to achieve you own level of greatness. I wish we had a chance to sit down earlier, but thank you for taking time out of your day to listen to my ramblings. Dismissed."

Kayleigh stood and saluted. She waited until she got into the hallway to wipe the tears forming in the corners of her eyes. For the first time, it felt like someone understood.

Chapter 19 – Mating Games

"You're not seriously worried about your rider? These contests are hardly dangerous."

Majherri shook his head at Pasha. *"I have spoken with several of our kind serving in the west. Alone, none of their stories are worthy of note, but when taken together, they paint a disturbing picture. Someone should speak of this to the Greater Herd."*

"Painting pictures? You're picking up your rider's terms, Majherri. Perhaps you are trying to stare through a group of clouds to see the moon, only to find it is elsewhere. Don't spend all your time looking down and chasing shadows. You might miss the light in front of you."

"Something is amiss in the west. Believe me, don't believe me. That is your choice, Pasha, but do not say that I did not warn you!"

"I am a friend to you, Majherri. As your friend, I say that going before the Greater Herd at this moment would be a mistake – not when your status is questionable."

"Perhaps with your support, they would be willing to listen to me."

The female gave him a scolding look. *"By the stars! You are difficult! I came here to thank you for staying with Gomlius in his time of need, not to be enlisted to help you bypass your sister and address the Greater Herd. How did any of your previous mates keep their sanity intact?"*

He pawed at the ground and replied, *"I stayed with Gomlius of my own accord. It was not done to please you. I am what you see and nothing more. You are young, strong, and beautiful, Pasha. Truly, I am honored to be considered worthy of your interest, but I will not change because you or anyone else wishes it. If you cannot accept that, then perhaps it is time we stopped playing games and found someone else to mate with this season."*

His words stung her and part of him regretted saying them. Yet, the rest of him knew it was necessary. He might have a new rider, but he was still an older unicorn and very set in his ways. Understandably, most unicorns chose to mate with others close to their age groups.

"Damn you, Majherri! You make me so angry. You do the right thing for all the wrong reasons. You pick fights when you don't need to. For what? What does all this get you? Tell me, truthfully, are you happy?"

He paused to consider her question. *"I have things in my life that make me happy. My new rider makes me happy. She is innocent and naïve, but she is my friend and my ally. Her support fortifies me. Occasionally, you make me happy, when you aren't trying to make me prove myself to whatever impossible standards you have in your mind. As for the island, the herd, and the Greater Herd, I am not happy. The atmosphere on this island makes me feel confined. I yearn for the wide open spaces. I was a scout and one of the very best at what I did. You were a lancer, and perhaps therein is the difference. I want to be out there again. My first rider was offered the chance to come here and teach, twice. Both times she refused and turned down the promotion. It was not the life we would choose."*

She tried to interrupt him, but he cut her off. *"The younglings in the herd are foolish well beyond any measure. To them, I am the crazed outcast. Spend some time with the younglings and see the truth of which I speak. As for my sister and the representatives of the Greater Herd on the island, I am no fool. They are content to ignore me and pretend I do not exist, all the while, keeping a careful watch over me. I even heard a rumor recently that my sister objects to my participation in this year's mating season, but hasn't garnered enough support to make her case to the Greater Herd. Is that being truthful enough for you?"*

Pasha was clearly upset. *"I spend more time with the younglings than you think! Many of them look up to you and would gladly befriend you, if given the chance. They see your strength, but you either blindly ignore them, or do your best to destroy their confidence. I am old enough not to be affected by your belligerent tantrums, but the younglings wither under your harsh critiques, so they have learned to avoid you rather than rouse your ire. As for T'rsa, most discount what she says, because it is widely known her rider blames you for the loss of her sister, but it's so easy for you to hide behind your scars, both real and imagined and pretend that every-*

one is out to get you."

"My scars are my own. I've suffered for them and been mocked for them."

Pasha lowered her head. *"I don't want to mock you, but you're impossible to reach."*

"Not from where I stand. I've come more than halfway. When I trot to you, you turn and gallop away, only to tell me that I must again come to you. There's a limit and we have reached it. You need to make a decision."

The female remained skittish. *"You're right. I haven't been fair to you, but I need just a little more time. I promise it won't be much longer."*

Majherri nodded and replied, *"Take what time you need. Just let me know when you are sure."*

He let her trot off. Despite her protests, he knew that many others were listening to the filth his sister spewed. The island was becoming more restrictive with each passing day and he worried that his mood was affecting Kayleigh. Majherri did his best not to let it show during the times they were in contact, but the bond was a horrible place to try and hide feelings.

The sun was setting. On the hill overlooking The Academy, he saw others gathering. With all the visitors, it looked like a sizeable portion of the Greater Herd was coming together. Instantly, he decided to go. If they would call him a fool, so be it.

Approaching the circle, he was challenged by a defiant male. *"You have no business here."*

"The Greater Herd represents all unicorns and the last time I checked, I am a unicorn. I have concerns I would bring to your attention."

A second male, and a much older one, approached. *"So this is the mysterious Majherri. I have heard that you stood with my son during his final moments."*

"If you are Tyrix, then you have heard correctly." Majherri showed respect for male. His rider was one of the human generals and his status was elevated because of that.

"Your name is often mentioned when the Greater Herd meets. Yet this is the first time you have graced us with your presence. What matter do you bring before us?"

T'rsa reared angrily. *"As the head of his herd, I have not given him permission to address this gathering."*

Majherri stiffened and replied, *"Apparently, I have no business here. If I did, I would say that I am troubled by stories coming out of the west. Caravans going missing, poisoned wells, and other tales that have been recently related to me. My first rider is not the only rider that has been lost in the west over the recent seasons. With our eyes ever looking southward, it may be prudent to glance to the west every now and again."*

"I do not support this speculation."

Tyrix nodded. *"Your objection is noted T'rsa. Majherri, I thank you for bringing this matter to our attention. Losses in the west have been unusually high in recent times, but it is also true that the nomadic humans are prone to violent conflicts over the scarce resources. You know all too well how hostile the living conditions are there. Rest assured I will speak with the leaders of the western herds when they come here, or as other opportunities present themselves."*

Majherri didn't detect any real sincerity in his words. He knew enough to realize that he was being placated. *"Thank you for hearing my words. Safe journeys to all of you."*

"The Greater Herd exists to serve all of our kind, Majherri. Safe journey to you as well."

His message delivered, Majherri turned and left. *They will ignore me. That much I am certain of. I can only hope that all this is just foolishness on my part. If I could leave and go find proof, I would. For now, I can only watch the seasons pass me by from the shores of this island prison.*

Chapter 20 – Of Fighting and Frustration

The days leading up to the challenge passed like the clouds in the sky. The history class was given a series of lectures by the legends that put down the southern uprising. The fourth and fifth years received personal lessons from all eight of the finalists in the High-King's annual jousting tournament.

With the day of the challenge at hand and the bleachers of the reviewing stands already filled to capacity, Kayleigh lined up her recruit company into a tight marching formation, six abreast and on foot. The column was surrounded by two squads of battle maidens. The mounted air maiden in front of her, looked over her shoulder and nodded at Kayleigh.

"Company! Forward march!" This was one part a parade, combined with a trust building exercise, and a demonstration of why even a small group of battle maidens could wreak havoc upon a group of defenders.

The air maidens on the flanks worked together and created an overlapping dome of hardened air. Kayleigh swallowed involuntarily, as fifty of the High-King's Royal Archers stepped up on the pair of elevated platforms they marched between. They took aim at the students, but their best shots bounced harmlessly off of the overlapping disks of hardened air with the sound of hail on a rooftop.

Just ahead, a ditch ten feet wide had been created. It was filled with water and on top of that water was a layer of oil. A single archer sent a flaming arrow into the water and a plume of flames threatened to halt the march. Four fire maidens parted the wall of flame almost effortlessly as a pair of water maidens solidified the water into a hard surface. Kayleigh did her best not to pause before stepping onto the water. She did not sink. It was if someone had hidden a bridge just below the surface.

Racing by her, a trio of earth maidens galloped up to the side of the "city wall" and then rode sideways along the length of it, scurrying like spiders on woodwork. The ground shook, but it was nothing compared to what was happening to the stone wall. It separated and collapsed into a pile of rubble creating a rough, but very passable gap.

On the other side of the wall, was a group of nobles, who symbolically raised the white flag indicating the surrender of the fake city to the thundering cheers of the crowds in the stands.

It was an emphatic demonstration of how easily a trained group of battle maidens could approach a city unimpeded by that city's defenses and break through the walls in just over a minute, all without the use of catapult, ballista, or battering ram. Kayleigh's company could easily have been armored knights now racing through the enemy city and overwhelming the ill-prepared defenders.

"Company halt! Right face!" Kayleigh stepped forward and marched quickly to the middle of the column, executing a turn before snapping to attention and saluting General Jyslin, who returned her salute.

"Company fall out by the rows!" Kayleigh called out and led the single file line over to where seating was waiting for them. They took their places as the other classes performed their demonstrations. Kayleigh cheered, but did her best to keep her muscles from getting stiff. They didn't have much practice sitting in armor and there was still her contest with Andrea Hawthorne to be decided.

As the fifth years were performing, Captain Lynch appeared from nowhere. "Reese, Hawthorne. On your feet by me."

Kayleigh stood as the captain said, "You've selected your seconds?"

"Yes, ma'am."

"Seconds, stand and join us." Ellen stood up. Things were somewhat cool between them since the night in the infirmary.

Kayleigh had listened to her apologies and accepted them, knowing it would be insane to alienate one of the few people who were genuinely nice to her. Even so, there were still enough hurt feelings to spare between the two girls.

Surprisingly, Morganstern also stood. Hawthorne liked Morganstern about as much as she liked Kayleigh. The girl had a penchant for turning up where she wasn't wanted. Andrea might be doing this as a strategy, or she could see Rebekah asking to be her second. Either way, she was going to battle Andrea Hawthorne. She wouldn't let Rebekah get under her skin during the challenge.

Majherri and Kyrinda made their way to the outside of the circle. Kayleigh stepped up and selected a padded sword and medium shield from the weapons rack. She handed it to Ellen, who went to meet Rebekah in front of the captain, so the weapons could be inspected.

Meanwhile, Kayleigh went to Majherri and stroked his mane. She took off her helmet and rested her forehead against his side, searching for his strength and encouragement.

She was not disappointed. He was proud of her and urged her to victory.

"Thank you," she whispered, replacing her helmet and turning to face the circle. Ellen offered the practice sword to her and pointed to the barrel of dye. Kayleigh inserted the sword into the red dye and allowed the liquid to seep into the padding. She was the red champion and Andrea the blue. The marks on their armor would be easy to spot in the crowded stands. She practiced with the weight of the weapon and shield while Captain Lynch explained the rules to the audience and the reason two first years were allowed to participate in a challenge before it was normally permitted.

Odd, she didn't mention the real reason was that Andrea's mother requested it.

Lynch commanded them into the circle. "The victor is the first one to score either three clean hits to the arms or legs, or one clean 'kill' shot to the torso or helmet. May your training serve you well. I will now step outside the ring. You will turn to each other, salute with sword across your shield. When I say begin, you will do battle."

Seconds later, Kayleigh's nerves were on edge and she stared into Andrea's neutral expression. She almost missed the command to begin, lost in the sea of rising noise, but was alerted by Andrea's sudden movements.

Sliding to the right, Kayleigh used her shield to blunt the force of the thrust. Andrea used her smaller size to keep herself lower to the ground and use leverage. It worked, forcing Kayleigh backwards. She barely evaded a swipe aimed at her shin plates.

Hawthorne had the initiative and continued to press it. Her aggressiveness made Kayleigh scamper around the edges of the circle while her opponent prowled the center and dared her to attack.

Almost thirty seconds of this went by before Kayleigh realized something very important. *I haven't even tried to swing my sword other than to block her attacks.*

Kayleigh tried an overhand slash, which was blocked all-too-easily and found herself immediately on the defensive. Just as she thought she was going to get away, there was a resounding smack on her left shoulder where her shield didn't protect. It was like a gong rang inside her skull.

"Point blue! Contestants back to your ready lines."

Kayleigh had to walk back to the other side of the circle, passing Hawthorne. Her eyes fell on Morganstern's gleeful expression and Kayleigh's frustration built.

"Begin!"

Andrea was back on the attack, relentlessly wearing down Kayleigh's guard. The weeks of training she possessed paled next to the years of lessons Hawthorne had been given. Kayleigh's sole advantages were her height and reach. Calling on the instincts Sir Dunlap drilled into her; Kayleigh swiped her sword back and forth in varying patterns trying to keep the smaller, but faster girl away.

This will wear me down and she knows it!

Still, it bought her valuable time to beat back her own nerves. Hawthorne blocked her sword, but was unable to get inside Kayleigh's guard. Trying to exaggerate her fatigue, Kayleigh tried to lure her opponent into attacking, but Andrea didn't rise to the bait for another ten seconds and by that time, Kayleigh wasn't faking the fatigue anymore. The wooden practice swords smacked against each other and Kayleigh threw her weight and strength into a shield bash, which managed to knock Andrea backwards.

She was feeling proud of herself for doing something right up until Captain Lynch spoke, "Point Blue! Second Point! Contestants back to your ready line."

Stunned, Kayleigh examined her armor. Somehow, Andrea had managed a blow to Kayleigh's right leg that she never felt. The ground was getting a little slick. She was getting angry and it seemed like Andrea was just toying with her. Walking back to her starting position, she caught the hint of a smirk on Hawthorne's face. She avoided looking at Morganstern.

Kayleigh grabbed on to that anger and allowed it to fuel her. Her panting breaths became something of a growl. *I'm being too timid! I'm letting her control the entire fight!*

Begin!"

Kayleigh exploded forward. She threw her strength and weight into each swing. Andrea countered and tried to attack, but she plowed forward repeating the same overhand slash. Hawthorne tried to block, but the blows came in too strong. It drove the smaller girl back. Kayleigh's assault was as subtle as using an ax to chop wood.

Andrea stabbed, attempting to score her final hit, but Kayleigh spun awkwardly away using the edge of her shield to block the attack. Finishing her spin, she brought the wooden sword full circle and cracked it against the side of Hawthorne's helmet.

Her opponent staggered and fell to the ground. The practice sword in Kayleigh's hand was still held together by the padded wrappings, but it was in two pieces.

"Winner Red!" Lynch shouted, but was pushing by her to get to Hawthorne's side. The captain slid down next to the girl and helped to get the dented helmet off Hawthorne's head. The cheers and the noise came to an abrupt halt as an uneasy silence fell across the training grounds.

Kayleigh listened as the captain asked her opponent basic questions. Hawthorne's answers were slow and her eyes were unfocused.

The captain summoned another to help get Andrea to the infirmary while saying the girl had a concussion. Kayleigh looked over at Ellen, who looked equally as horrified. Uncertain of what to do, Kayleigh walked back toward Majherri. She dropped her shield and shook the gauntlet off of her left hand. Her mind was a whirlwind. She needed Majherri to ground her.

Through the swirling emotions, she heard a voice. "What were you trying to do, Reese? Kill her?"

Kayleigh's hand grasped onto Majherri's neck. Her grip was akin to someone who had fallen off a fishing boat grasping for a lifeline and her unicorn winced. She sensed the safe harbor ahead, through the bond and fought to reach her sanctuary.

"Aren't you going to say anything, you stupid cow? You should never have been allowed here in the first place!" Morganstern continued.

"Leave me alone, Rebekah," she grunted with her body shaking.

"Hah, you'll be lucky if Andrea's mother doesn't call for your arrest!"

"Shut up!"

The storm inside her threatened to break free. Kayleigh's head was pounding and her blood was beginning to boil. In the distance, she heard Captain Lynch shouting something, but she was past the point of understanding. Rebekah's taunts blended with the roar in her mind. She had to get rid of the noise. Morganstern was right next to her and Kayleigh reached out to push her away. Her still gauntleted right hand lashed out and exploded into flames.

The roar in her mind was replaced with the whoosh of all-too-real flames. The jet of fire hurled Rebekah away.

She dropped to one knee and there were screams from the audience. Kayleigh was still trying to process what just happened, when the armored form of Meghan Lynch slammed into her back and drove her into the ground. Her connection with Majherri was severed as the woman's greater strength and weight pinned Kayleigh to the ground. Kayleigh struggled and for a second time blacked out.

Some time later, there was an awful smell that startled her out of the darkness. Kayleigh came around, woozy and rapidly blinking her eyes. The sheets and mattress at her feet were damp with water and she was no longer in her armor.

In front of her was the face of Captain Lynch and that face looked less than pleased.

She was in the infirmary ... again. Bits of memory reassembled into coherent thought and she slowly remembered what happened.

"Are they going to be okay?" Kayleigh asked. Her throat was dry and the words came out painfully.

General Jyslin cut off the captain. "Trainee Hawthorne has a concussion and some bruising. Trainee Morganstern's burns are being treated. There will most likely be a lasting scar, but she will live. Unfortunately, we now need to deal with the repercussions."

"I'll readily admit to being biased, Naomi, but she's far too dangerous to be around first year trainees. We should have never allowed this challenge to proceed," General Hawthorne said folding her arms and looking ready to attack her at any moment.

"In hindsight, it certainly looks that way, Althea. For the record, Captain Lynch, you were the closest trained observer.

What did you witness?"

The captain, red-faced with fury, never took her eyes off Kayleigh. "As the challenge progressed, it was clear that Trainee Hawthorne was the more skilled contestant. After losing the second point, Trainee Reese became erratic and unfocused. Her attack was borne of fury and overwhelmed Hawthorne. From the force of the final blow and the dent in Hawthorne's helm, there is no question in my mind that the blow was delivered with the intent to kill. As I tended to the injured challenger, the trainee went to her unicorn. She has been previously instructed not to touch Majherri without direct supervision. In violation of those directives, she made contact. Trainee Morganstern was reacting to what she considered an assault on her classmate began demanding an answer from Trainee Reese. I recognized the danger of the situation and called out for Morganstern to stand down and get away from Reese and for Reese to step away from her unicorn. Both my orders were disregarded and Reese conjured a life-threatening fireball injuring Trainee Morganstern."

Silence fell and the only sound was the scratching noise of quill on parchment as the scribe performed her task.

"To your knowledge, Captain, has the trainee been instructed on how to produce a fireball?"

"No General, she has not. However, this is not the first time she has been observed performing feats beyond what she has been trained for."

"Do you believe Trainee Reese was responsible for her actions at the time?"

"No."

General Hawthorne asked, "Do you believe that Trainee Reese constitutes a threat to the rest of the trainees under your care?"

"Yes, I do." Those three words were a dagger through Kayleigh's heart.

The two generals exchanged a meaningful look. Kayleigh could see there was a battle of wills taking place. General Hawthorne spoke, "I'll take her into the field, Naomi. She's too dangerous to be around children, even the upper classes. We can't drum her out, her bond is obviously too deep. It'd kill her unicorn. My warriors can get her up to speed without endangering trainees. I don't think The Academy was meant for a girl like her."

"That's one option, Althea. I'll take it under advisement, but your task is to protect the southern kingdoms and mine is to train our future riders. I'd like to speak with my other captains before rendering a decision."

"Begging the General's pardon," Captain Lynch said, "but I don't think it's the girl's problem. I believe it's something wrong with her unicorn. Trainee Reese hasn't displayed any real outbursts of violence before now. Tradition allows for the unicorns to be present at the weapons challenges. I should have insisted that Majherri not be present. My theory is that the berserker level strength she displayed was drawn across the bond even though they were not in physical contact. There have been recorded instances where that has happened before."

"Not with trainees." Hawthorne said.

"True, ma'am. But there is no denying that their bond is stronger than most."

"Put yourself in my place, Captain," General Jyslin said. "What would you do?"

The captain paused for a moment and composed her words. "I'd exile Majherri, ma'am. I actually believe he'd survive the separation. Give the girl the choice to go with him or return to her home. The trainee's behavior is a symptom. The unicorn is the root cause."

"No!" Kayleigh screamed.

"Silence!" Captain Lynch shot back.

The general intervened, saying, "Unfortunately, that is a second option. I like it even less than the first, but we must consider all paths before us. For the moment Trainee Reese, you are relieved of your lead rider position. I cannot in good faith allow you to remain with the first year class, but I am not ready to give up on you at this juncture and see you leave this island. Until a decision is rendered, you are not to leave this infirmary. Your meals will be brought here to you. Is that clear?"

"Yes, ma'am."

They filed out. General Hawthorne stopped to kiss her daughter on the forehead. Standing up, her eyes narrowed and she stared Kayleigh down before turning and leaving.

Kayleigh pulled her legs off the wet section of the mattress and up to her chest protectively. Suddenly, exile with Majherri seemed like the better option over going with General Hawthorne.

Andrea was propped up by her elbows and looking at her. "Are you okay, Reese?"

"Not really. How about you? I guess we both lost."

"You could say that. Right at the end, you were just moving too fast. I couldn't keep up."

"I'm sorry, Andrea. I lost control. They're right. I am too dangerous."

"Well, it probably doesn't mean a blessed thing, but I wasn't completely in control the night I challenged you. I shouldn't have done it. I got a letter from my mother. She'd heard that I was demoted to squad leader and … well you've met her. She doesn't take bad news well. I let Morganstern get to me. She's a vile one to say the least."

Kayleigh nodded and motioned to Rebekah's bed.

"They gave her a sleeping draught. We could be screaming in her ear and she still wouldn't wake up. She'll be like that until tomorrow."

"Let me guess, she volunteered to be your second."

"The night I issued the challenge, practically begged me to be ringside. I agreed because I knew it would upset you and give me a greater advantage. My actions were less than honorable and I bear some responsibility for the grave consequences you are faced with."

Kayleigh sighed, saying, "It still doesn't excuse what I did to you, or her for that matter."

"No, but my hands aren't exactly clean either. If Captain Lynch requests that I take over as lead rider, I will refuse until I feel that I've earned that position."

Kayleigh shrugged. It didn't really matter to her. She wasn't a first year anymore. "You should take the job, Andrea. You'd do well at it. It sounds like you learned something useful from all this. It's more than I can say."

"Don't sell yourself short, Kayleigh. Why don't we talk about something else? The healer said I need to stay awake and gave me a draught that has me all jittery."

So, the two of them began sharing stories. The healer brought two food trays and checked on Rebekah's bandages. They ate and continued talking until the door opened and Captain Heather Sycroft entered.

"Trainee Reese."

"Yes, ma'am."

"Your belongings are being moved to the third year barracks. As of now, I am your commanding officer. General Jyslin still believes in you and so do I. However, you will be watched closely. You will not be allowed to practice either jousting or melee combat against another trainee. You will always be paired with a trained warrior or instructor. Your time in contact with your unicorn will continue to be watched closely."

Kayleigh nodded, she didn't really have any other option, as Captain Sycroft continued, "There is also a two year gap in your education. Until that gap is closed and I am satisfied with your progress, you will not be allowed to hold any position within my company. You will have two extra hours of duty each night and on your free day. They will not be spent in the stables and barns, but with myself or another available instructor to help you catch up. I expect nothing short of your best effort, every single day. Can you accept those terms?"

"Yes, ma'am."

"Then welcome to your third year of training, Trainee Reese. I will go speak with the healer and get you released for duty and we'll take you to where you belong."

Chapter 21 – Shunned

His rider was becoming increasingly miserable. Majherri knew this, even though she tried her best to be upbeat.

With the first year humans, she ran at the front of their herd during their physical exercises. Now, Kayleigh struggled not to come in last place against trainees who had spent two more years bonding and becoming more powerful as a result. His heart filled with despair, watching her gasping for breath and straining with effort to keep up.

To add further humiliation, she was prevented from working with him except for short periods of time, where the constant presence of instructors reduced her to near uselessness. So afraid of causing another problem, she would recoil against all but the flimsiest tendril of power.

She jousted, but even that was an empty effort. Her opponent was always an instructor and victory was measured in whether or not Kayleigh could stay in the saddle.

Like an underfed youngling, her growth was being stunted and he was virtually helpless. Before, she was so used to T'rsa's rider's anger that she would rise to the challenges. She stepped up and was a leader. They forced her to fight the challenge early, for their own benefit! Yet she was the one punished. Kayleigh was the one with a crushed spirit, looking more and more like a meek follower with each passing day. Worst of all, they forced her to beg the forgiveness from the Morganstern girl. So eager to punish his rider were they, that the behavior of that insipid little girl was completely forgotten.

To say this gross injustice being perpetrated on his rider was unacceptable was an understatement. The worst part of all this was Majherri couldn't make Kayleigh see what was happening to her. Each time he broached the subject across their bond; she would fume and break contact, refusing to address the matters and instead burying her head in the sand like a flightless bird.

Of course, Majherri had problems of his own. He was on his way to meet her right now. Over by the rocky shore, there was a female staring out over the lake. Pasha continued to delay their mating after the events of the festival and the end of the mating season was approaching. Finally, she had sent word to him to meet her here tonight. He understood. She wanted this done in privacy and his status in the Greater Herd was questionable at the moment. The stars were reflected in the smooth waters. It took only a few more paces for him to recognize that this was not the female he was looking for.

Puzzled he approached. *"Greetings sister, you'll forgive my confusion, but I was expecting to meet Pasha here."*

"She's not coming, brother."

"May I ask why?"

"She came to her senses and decided to seek a different mate."

"What?"

T'rsa snorted. *"Your magic is out of control and that could possibly carry over to any offspring you produce. It is far too great a risk. Your rider almost killed those two females!"*

"I sense the hand of your rider in this, T'rsa. The same one who would exile me, with or preferably without, my rider."

"Yes brother, blame anyone other than yourself. That is your way isn't it?"

He was angry, but to give in to that anger would only play into her words. *"Instead of telling me herself, Pasha sends you. Perhaps I overestimated the strength of her character."*

"No, I came because there is every possibility you will become violent."

"And you thought you could stop me? Or were you hoping the three sets of eyes in the woods could get here in time to save you? You've become consumed by your rider's delusions, T'rsa and are a waste of my time. Since you've turned Pasha away from me, I will seek out another."

"Dear brother, you will likely find a dearth of eager partners. You still walk the sacred land, but to the rest of us, you are already exiled.

With so many of the Greater Herd here, the news spreads quickly."

"Very clever, sister. Suddenly, Pasha coming to her senses appears to be more a case of Pasha surrendering to your threats. I assume any that would mate with me would suffer this same punishment?"

"Assume what you will, brother. It matters little to me."

"One thing you forgot in your rush to do your rider's bidding, T'rsa, perhaps my ability to survive beyond the death of a human rider is meant to be spread to the Greater Herd. If you are concerned that my supposed lack of control could spread, you must consider the other side."

T'rsa was beginning to display her own lack of control. She reared angrily. *"You are an affront to the harmony we live in! You are tainted by chaos and madness. No, I would not like to see this spread to the Greater Herd. My brother did not return from the wasteland – a cursed shell bearing his likeness did!"*

He turned away from her rage. Majherri suspected that if he stayed longer, it would lead to actual fighting. Part of him wondered how many he could take before they brought him down, but he buried those thoughts. Dead, he couldn't help his rider. They would be able to simply cast her out then. She'd given up everything to come with him and he would gladly do the same for her.

Majherri knew what must be done.

"Your riding is improving, trainee." The new captain said to his rider as they navigated the terrain. The air was cool. Soon, the city on the other side of the island would receive the first snows of winter, though none would touch the forever green pastures of the Sacred Island.

"Thank you, ma'am."

Majherri hadn't bothered to make any conversation with the male that Captain Sycroft was riding. He hadn't spoken to another of his kind since that night with his sister and that was three weeks ago. T'rsa's and the herd council's declaration had spread quickly and he was truly an outcast. He'd even given up on investigating the events in the west. The only creature that wanted his help was in his saddle.

"Have you decided on a topic for your history of warfare class?"

"Yes, ma'am. I was thinking of doing it on the significance of the Portal system and the impact on past conflicts."

"It is a good choice, recruit. Have you ever been through a portal before?"

"No, ma'am. I've seen wagons come out at the exit points before, but my trip here was the first time to Talcosa."

"It is a disorienting experience, but you'll see it firsthand in eight weeks. I've decided to let you go on your first patrol with the rest of your class."

Kayleigh brightened and Majherri felt her relief. "Thank you, ma'am."

"Don't thank me, recruit. You've earned it through hard work. You'll be going to the east with Lieutenant Townsend's group. Now, onto your paper, the Portals are one of my favorite subjects. Tell me, what have you learned so far? What do you believe is their primary purpose?"

"When the twelve portals were first created by High-Queen Nolan, she had just won the war of the seven kingdoms. She developed the portals as a means of rapidly deploying forces to suppress any further uprisings."

"Good so far. Why not make them allow travel in both directions?"

"It would open Talcosa up to invasion from multiple locations."

The captain smiled, "Correct. Continue."

"Two of the gates have been destroyed. One was in Henchill two hundred and ten years ago and the other nineteen years ago in the southern city of Coedrif, at the start of the southern uprising. Henchill was raised in retaliation. Coedrif was spared because their royal family abdicated and went to exile after the defeat of Count Darius."

"Why do the kingdoms allow the remaining ones to stay?"

"Other than the threat of destruction … I guess there's

too much money involved. Raw materials pour into Talcosa and the finished products go through the Portals. It also allows travelers to shorten the length of their journey." Kayleigh answered bringing Majherri to a halt near the stream. He stuck his head into the water and tried blocking out the conversation.

"That is the heart of the matter. The kingdoms need the money and fear the power. Why haven't more been built?"

"High-Queen Nolan took the secret of their construction to her grave."

"… and the graves of the five men and women who helped her make them."

He felt Kayleigh's surprise, "Really?"

"Yes, but most people have forgotten about that. Their names might be found in some of the rare history books in our library. Now as soon as our unicorns are watered, let's head back. Since we've covered some of the lessons, let's talk about how you're fitting in to the company. How are the rest of my girls treating you?"

"Laurel is very nice. She's gone out of her way to be helpful. Julia and Amanda are friendly. The members of the squad encourage me, even when my performance puts them behind in the rankings."

Majherri could feel Kayleigh trying to be sincere. Her lie didn't fool him, but it seemed acceptable to the Captain. Other than Laurel, the rest had barely made an effort and that was due to the fact that she was still lead rider for that year.

Captain Sycroft urged her unicorn to start back. "That's good, Reese. Given the situation, you've made substantial progress. I hope to see that progress continue. I've seen a few first years approach you during mealtime."

Kayleigh nodded. Majherri knew that the one called Ellen and even her challenger, Andrea had sat with her occasionally.

Majherri concentrated on speed during the return trip, pushing the other male to try and keep up with him. It minimized the amount of conversation the two females could make and helped to reduce his rider's discomfort.

Back at the stables, Majherri waited while Kayleigh removed the saddle and stowed her gear. With the captain watching from the entrance, his rider used a bucket of water and some rags to wipe the dirt off his coat. The third year stable master, an older man named Gregory, struck up a conversation with Captain Sycroft.

His rider missed the first year stable master, Brian Tomas. That much was clear. Aside from the physical attraction, the male was much more friendly and approachable. The new one showed none of the interest in the human females' lives and was devoid of humor or any other traits either Majherri or is rider found interesting.

Kayleigh placed her head next to his and whispered into his ear. "I did it. They're going to allow us to go through the Portal. That first night, we'll just get up and ride wherever the path takes us. They don't want either of us here. I tried so hard to fit in with all these girls, but nothing worked, and what the unicorns have done to you is wrong. Soon, we'll put this all behind us, I promise."

Majherri snorted his agreement. He was the one to first put forth this idea of just leaving. Kayleigh thought it over for three days before deciding to go along with it. The herd didn't want him and what loyalty he had for it had dwindled to nothing. His rider found this life more restricting than her previous existence as her mother's assistant.

There was no joy left for either of them on this island. For Majherri, it was just a hollow and empty existence. His rider's day was filled with work that began before the sun rose and ended hours after the sun set.

Naturally, the solution was to leave, but that meant convincing the humans that Kayleigh was sufficiently prepared to go on her first training patrol.

They had originally said that she wouldn't be allowed to go. This meant that they would have had to wait until the fourth year patrol, or the break between fourth and fifth year, when the trainees could leave the island without requesting permission. So, Kayleigh worked harder than ever to impress her new captain. He was proud of her.

Initially she had told him that they should just go to the General and state their case. Majherri didn't want to leave on someone else's terms. Perhaps this was selfish, but he knew the General's style well enough to realize that the woman would not allow Kayleigh to leave with him.

"I'd better get going, Majherri. Captain Sycroft looks like she's getting impatient. Just eight more weeks until the patrol and then we can put this all behind us."

He sent feelings of reassurance through their link. Freedom, true freedom was coming soon and both their lives would have meaning again. Majherri was certain, deep in his core, he no longer belonged here.

Chapter 22 – A Time for Leaving

"Wake up, Kayleigh. Nothing like a night out under the stars! You're up for guard duty, Reese. We're counting on you to be able to pull your weight. Are you sure you're up for it?" Laurel Whitaker asked. The still-reigning third year lead rider had an angular face and a slightly upturned nose. Despite her harsh features, the girl was good-natured and diligent. Everyone, including Kayleigh, liked being around her, except when it was very late at night and the air was quite cold.

There was still some residual light from the campfire, Kayleigh frowned. This was just a rehearsal for the actual patrol in two weeks. Whitaker had this "treat every exercise as if it were real" mentality. That was probably the only thing about the lead rider that Kayleigh didn't care for.

"I'm ready. Anything happen?" They had been warned to expect various surprise "attacks" during the remaining three days and two nights.

Laurel shook her head. "No, everything's quiet. I thought I spotted some movement earlier and scented it, but it turned out to be a rabbit."

"Scented it?"

The lead rider rolled her eyes and said, "You know, used my powers and changed the direction of the wind for a moment. Air maidens can enhance the smells. It's what makes us great ambushers and hard to sneak up on – not as good as an earth maiden listening to the ground, mind you, but still good nonetheless."

Kayleigh was so involved with trying to understand her powers that she hadn't learned all the things the riders aligned to the other elements could do. Sadly, it was part of the second year curriculum that she'd missed. All she could manage was, "Oh."

"It's okay. Part of this is to learn how to work as a team.

Just stay alert and keep an eye out."

"Don't worry, I might not be the best, but Majherri has more experience than our instructors and their unicorns combined. They'll have to work pretty hard if they want to get by us."

"I know," the other girl said and leaned in closer. "My guess is that they don't want to risk another incident with you and Majherri, so I think you'll be fine, but even so, stay sharp and look alive."

Kayleigh nodded. Laurel had been forthright with her ever since she arrived in the third year barracks. Her unicorn, like all the rest, didn't like Majherri and by extension Laurel didn't trust Majherri either, but she was honest about it and that said a good deal about the air maiden's character.

Climbing out of the warmth of her bedroll, Kayleigh stood and stretched. She opted to only strap on her chest plate and not the rest of her armor. It was left near the fire to prevent it from becoming too cold during the night. Grabbing her helmet, she walked over to Majherri.

The chaperone, a rider on loan from the King's battalion and here to monitor the trainees, immediately stopped her. "I was given special instructions to closely monitor your interaction with your unicorn, trainee. What do you intend to do?"

"I was going to use heatsight and survey the area. After that, I was going to familiarize myself and my mount with the terrain directly around the campsite doing five counterclockwise rotations followed by two clockwise rotations to vary my movements. Periodically, I will stop and briefly use heatsight again to see if there is anyone approaching."

The woman nodded. "Proceed. Use no other magic than heatsight. If you feel anything out of the ordinary, you are to break contact with your unicorn immediately."

Kayleing agreed while thinking, *Air Maidens aren't the only ones with nifty tricks up there sleeves!* She touched Majherri's side and his eyes immediately opened. He had been on the ground and asleep. The other unicorns slept standing up with their legs locked in position and treated this as if they were in the field.

She knew Majherri couldn't care less.

Concentrating, she drew on his magic while closing her eyes and bringing it up into her. Unlike the first year classes, there was an entire class devoted to each element's magic. This was one of the first things she'd been able to master, although it still made her head ache if she did it more than twenty seconds at a time. When her eyes opened, the whole world was tinged with red. She could see the heat given off by everything.

Looking beyond the group of unicorns and sleeping riders, Kayleigh stared into the distance, seeing some small creatures, but no signs of any other humans. She was troubled by the rocks on a nearby hill, because someone could be hiding amongst them.

With no threats immediately visible, she saddled and mounted Majherri. He sent an image of them bolting and running through the night. It made her smile. Though she was ready to be done with this place, Majherri was ready within days after mating season, but then again, Kayleigh was still learning things. Majherri's days were filled with boredom.

He bucked against her slightly, noticing that she was feeling sorry for him. That obviously offended him.

"Sorry, Majherri. I figured we'd go counterclockwise around the camp and then change directions for two times."

Indifferently, he set off as she requested and she let him set the pace. The pair moved along the edges of the camp, by the path, which they were pretending was a major road between two cities. She spent her time thinking about the places where this year had gone horribly wrong. The lowest point had been when she was ushered into Captain Sycroft's office and stared at Rebekah Morganstern's face knowing full well that the burn mark would mar the girl's otherwise perfect complexion. The base of the scar was hidden by her tunic, but it began on her left shoulder and ran up the girl's neck and onto her cheek.

"You think I'd actually forgive you? I'm only here under

direct order." It wasn't the only direct order the girl had received. Rebekah had been spreading her filthy lies about Kayleigh with impunity, until, and the irony wasn't lost on Kayleigh, Captain Lynch ordered her to stop.

"No, Rebekah. I do not. But I apologize nonetheless. I accept my role in your injury and will use that as a lesson that I must learn to control my power."

The girl stood and walked up to Kayleigh, until they were only a foot apart. "If you had any honor, you'd leave and never come back. I am through with you, Reese. I've already made certain my father knows you attacked me. That harlot mother of yours will be run out of Helden the very day he reads that letter." She stopped and tried to sound as menacing as a thirteen year old could and said, "Unless they choose to do otherwise."

Kayleigh shook her head and prevented her from passing with a grab to the shoulder. "You ignorant girl! Still counting on your precious father to do something for you! Maybe he should be here riding your unicorn. My shame was an accident. What you have done is deliberate. Not that it matters, but she already left Helden. I tried sending letters, but I received a letter back from an elder explaining she left a long time ago."

The irony was Kayleigh had every intention of leaving. Rebekah would no doubt feel vindicated by this, but Kayleigh no longer cared. Majherri sensed her anger and sent her an image of the two of them riding free and alone.

Clearing her mind of that awful encounter, Kayleigh focused on her patrol. After one hour had passed, she spotted something approaching along the path. It was a wagon. She stopped and used heatsight again, trying to determine if the wagon driver had any other companions.

Deciding that there were none, she dismounted and shook Laurel.

"What is it?" the lead rider asked quickly waking.

"There's a wagon approaching. Do you want me to challenge or let it pass?"

"Go ahead and challenge. I'll be your back up."

Kayleigh climbed back into Majherri's saddle as Whitaker stood and went to her unicorn. Kayleigh used her heatsight again and looked at the rocks that concerned her earlier. There was no movement except for the sound of the wagon drawing closer.

She positioned Majherri in the center of the path and made a small flame shoot up from her index finger. "Halt, who goes there?"

The driver brought his wagon to a stop and raised his hood. It was Brian Tomas playing the part. He said, "Just a humble traveler going from one city to the next, warrior."

"Why are you traveling without light?"

"My apologies, but there are rumors of bandits plaguing these parts, my cart and the wares inside are all I have. Obviously, you've heard these rumors as well, otherwise you and your comrades wouldn't be here."

"True, very true, kind merchant." Kayleigh tried to remember things she was supposed to ask him, but sometimes his smile had a way of making her forget. "What news to you have of the road you have already traveled?"

Majherri bucked slightly to get her attention. An image of her using heatsight sprung to her mind. She did as he recommended and scanned around as Brian continued to speak. Noticing that he rambled and was not trying to be terribly quiet, Kayleigh quickly discerned that he was trying to distract her, she looked at the rocks and saw several figures making there way down the hill.

It was then that she realized that she and Laurel hadn't agreed on a "danger" signal, that wasn't blatantly obvious. Kayleigh placed her left hand behind her helmet and tried to make her hand glow.

"My goodness! You're a fire maiden! I've always thought that fire maidens are the most fascinating of all. Can you tell me what it is like being able to control fire like that? Can you make it change into different types of pretty colors?" He asked loudly. If Laurel could hear, it eliminated the next thing she was going to use.

That's just evil!

"Well, I'm still learning how to do color changes, but I could try. Is there a particular color you'd like to see?" Kayleigh turned Majherri sideways to mask what she was doing.

"How about blue, like your eyes?"

Oh, he's flirting with me! Now he's being cruel.

She laughed loudly and used the noise to pull her sword part of the way out of the scabbard. If Laurel missed this, she'd have to be an idiot. A quick check of the raiders showed they were already halfway to the camp.

Glancing over her shoulder, she saw that Laurel was in motion and breathed a sigh of relief. Turning back to Brian, she noticed two things, his dazzling smile and the crossbow he had slipped out from under a concealed cloak. The tip was replaced with a bag soaked in dye. The bolt clanged off her chest plate and she winced at the impact. Disgusted with being duped, she smacked her thigh.

"So what did you do wrong, Kayleigh?"

She liked that he didn't call her trainee or Reese. "My partner and I didn't agree on a danger sign. I was too busy watching the raiders and trying to signal her that I took my eyes off of you. You were the closest threat to me."

He took a sign that said 'dead' out and handed it to her. She hung it around her head as he casually reloaded his crossbow and continued, "You were at least able to warn your patrol, so your death is not in vain. Still, you can't help too much, if you're dead. Just remember that, because you do have some of the prettiest blue eyes I've ever seen and that would be a terrible waste. Now, if you'll excuse me, I have to participate in the rest of the ambush."

He leapt off the wagon and ran toward the encampment, where the rest of her squad was getting out of their bedrolls and forming a defensive perimeter. Kayleigh was flabbergasted by what he had just said. Majherri was somewhat indifferent about the whole episode, but there was a hint of amusement underneath.

"That's about enough out of you!" She growled and turned to watch the rest of the ambush play out.

By the time it was over, two other trainees were also declared "dead," and they received a stern lecture about how to properly challenge parties approaching the camp.

"Well, my guard duty is over," Kayleigh said, handing the "dead" sign back to Brian.

"Get some rest," he replied. "You'll probably need it tomorrow."

"That's reassuring."

"Well, I'd love to stay and chat, but I've got to head down the road. There's another squad camping there. I wonder how pretty the eyes of their guard are."

Angry, she turned away from his teasing. *Just like the boys in Helden and Laurent, he was toying with me. When will I ever learn?*

Brian paused and Kayleigh could tell that he wanted to say something. Eventually, he said, "Goodnight, Miss Reese."

She grunted her reply.

"Do you really think you're going to need all that? It's only two weeks." Ellen Jacobs asked in the foyer to the third year barracks. The first year girl stopped by to wish Kayleigh a safe journey and that made her feel a twinge of guilt.

"Remember how I didn't have much coming here?" Kayleigh answered Ellen easily. "I just don't want to end up having to beg for things like last time."

It was a convenient lie and it made perfect sense. She had no intention of coming back for anything.

"So, are you excited to be going out on your first patrol?"

She smiled at one of her few friends on the island. "Yes, I think a change of scenery is what's needed."

"I wish I was going as well. Do you need a hand with anything?"

"Thank you, but no, Ellen."

"Okay, well I've got to get going to my class. Sorry that I won't be able to see you off. Come to think of it, you'd better hurry up."

"I'm all done. I just have to post some correspondence."

"I could do that for you," the younger girl offered.

Kayleigh shook her head. It would seem odd if Ellen saw them and found the one meant for her. "I'll take care of it. Better get going, wouldn't want Captain Lynch to give you any more demerits on my account. Tell the others I said goodbye."

Ellen promised she would and gave her a hug before running off. Kayleigh removed the five letters she'd written over the past few nights. They were addressed to Annabeth, Ellen, General Jyslin, Captain Sycroft and Lieutenant Sheppard. Kayleigh felt the need to explain her actions to them. They had given her a chance and tried to make this work. She didn't want them to blame themselves. A sixth letter had been started, to Brian, but after thirty minutes she crumpled it and tossed it into the fire.

Kayleigh shouldered her bags and crossed the foyer to Captain Sycroft's office. Sliding the letters under the door, knowing that by the time they were found, Kayleigh and Majherri would already be through the portal and it would be inactive for a full day.

Walking toward the dock, she tried to take the essence of the island in. More than likely, this would be the last time she'd ever see it. Kayleigh etched the surroundings in her memory. Perhaps one day, she would paint it and think about what might have been. Her coin purse jingled with the small amount of money she'd earned to this point. Though there wasn't much, Majherri assured her that between a unicorn and a partly-trained fire maiden they could find something that would provide a living.

If she went back to her artist roots, she could use her

powers to help her sculpt with metal. She enjoyed a brief fantasy of her becoming a famous sculptor. Wherever her mother was, she'd appreciate the bittersweet irony. She had given up on her mother's dream that Kayleigh would follow her only to pursue the dream of becoming a battle maiden. Now, she was considering her future as an artist again.

Part of her felt empty and without direction, like a rudderless ship at the mercy of the winds and the tides. She needed to be brave and take her next step.

Majherri was waiting for her down by the docks. The barge was making its way back from taking the first group to Talcosa. The girls in her section were laughing and excited, so ready to prove their worth. It was ironic, because they were all going to the either the north or the east, which were hardly areas teeming with trouble.

Placing her hand on the side of Majherri's head, she felt his excitement and that stiffened her resolve and eased her doubts. He was telling her everything was going to be okay.

You're right. It's time to go. Our place isn't here, anymore.

When the barge docked, she led Majherri on with barely a second thought. Kayleigh recalled the moment roughly six months before when this island held so much promise. She'd been cheated – like Lynch's promise that she would treat Kayleigh fairly! There was a small tear in her eye as she turned her back on the sacred island and looked ahead to Talcosa. Even the trip across the lake was hollow and lacking. Before, the High-King had been their captain. There was pomp and ceremony. This time, there was a bored looking minor wizard, doing his job, and nothing more.

"It looks larger than ever," she whispered to Majherri. *We might not even have to go through the Portal. We could almost get lost in that city alone!*

Majherri didn't like that idea. She could tell he wanted to go somewhere far away.

It was the middle of the day as they made their way through the massive city. Their destination was on the other side of the Great Market. Unlike the market, whose open spaces were crammed with people. There was a forbidding sense of order on the approach to the Portal. Once per day, and only for fifteen minutes at a time, the Portal would align with one of its ten counterparts across the world and a connection would open. The line of carts and wagons waiting for that destination would rush forward to get as many through in that window as possible. Those that missed the opportunity would be forced to wait in Talcosa for another day. For merchants that meant lost profits, and armies might miss out on valuable resupplies and reinforcements. It was not a place to waste time.

The structure itself was unimpressive. It looked like the frame of a building that was never completed, except metal etched with runes replaced wood. A black mist filled the box-like structure as people and wagons moved through it. Kayleigh was reminded of an anthill, with people disappearing into the mist. During her travels, she'd seen the opposite – people, wagons and horses emerging from the mists when they were in the eastern kingdom of Derab. That was where their destination and it was a relief to Kayleigh. She had only been nine when they traveled through that land, but she did recall enough of it to help them plan their escape.

Being emissaries of the High-King had certain privileges. One of them was bypassing the lines of people waiting for a particular destination. They rode to the front of the line for Derab.

"Why the serious look?" A voice asked next to her. Kayleigh looked to her left and saw a familiar face.

"Annabeth? What are you doing here?" The rider had a full kit on Rheysurrah.

"Didn't I say that riders from my battalion are always getting loaned out?"

"Yes," Kayleigh replied, trying to mask her nervousness.

"Well, there's a gaggle of third years heading out for their first patrol and General Jyslin requested a few extra bodies on this trip. The rest is history. What's the matter Reese, surprised to see me?"

How are we going to sneak away now? "No, it's not that, Annabeth. I just didn't expect to see you here ... and I'm a little worried about my first time going through the Portal."

"There's nothing to it, Kayleigh. You might feel a little disoriented, but it passes quickly." Annabeth said while pointing to where the mist cleared and the soldiers were changing the sign to their destination.

"This is where we go. Follow me!"

Still worried, Kayleigh felt Majherri's reassurances and followed Annabeth into the dark mist.

Chapter 23 – A Fighting Start

Majherri lost count of how many times he'd been through the mists. The experience was always the same, a sudden rush of wind and the sensation of rapidly falling. The secret was just to keep moving. He always found it amusing when the humans screamed, but this time he was doing his best to keep his agitated rider calm.

Unfortunately, the moment they entered, something went wrong. Everything began to vibrate, humans were shouting something. Majherri had never heard of something like this happening before.

The winds rose to almost tornado like intensity. He fought his way forward and told Kayleigh through their bond to hold on. Her arms wrapped around him as the falling sensation began, only this time the falling was like crashing down a hillside.

The screams of the others, both unicorn and human worried him. They jostled next to another unicorn. That one's rider was trying to hold on with one arm and fight the winds blowing against the shield on the other. It threatened to pull her right out of the saddle. Kayleigh reached over and grabbed the other female's waist to help steady all of them.

The deceleration was ferocious. Majherri dropped to the ground, as his rider was thrown clear. The landing was awkward and painful. Breath rushed out of him like he'd been hit by an ogre's club, but then he realized it was the other female rider they'd been next to.

He winced, blinking in both pain as the mist swirled and went from darkness, to a fiery red before starting to dissipate.

It's never done that before! I must get up ... must get to Kayleigh!

As the vapors disappeared, he saw darkness. The eastern city of Derab would still be light. This was not Derab. Momentarily forgetting Kayleigh, he struggled to recognize where they were by the surrounding structure. There was the slightest hint of light on the horizon. It filtered in through the holes in the wall. That's what troubled him. Every Portal, except two in the north, was either in a large market area or behind fortress walls. None, except for the broken Portals were located in ruins and these ruins were recent.

From the position of the sun, we're in the west! How is that possible? Is this Salif? No! The hills to the north! We must be in … Mon Alder. The westernmost portal city is in ruins! When? How?

"Sound off! Everyone on your feet! Call out if you're injured?" A voice barked the command. It belonged to Lieutenant Sandra Townsend, a tall woman with long auburn hair. She was the History of Warfare and Air Magic instructor for the third year riders. The woman used her right hand to cradle her left shoulder. Her face betrayed the amount of pain she was in.

Majherri moved his head back and forth. He counted nine unicorns and as many riders. *Where are the rest?* Beyond the Portal frame, there was wreckage strewn everywhere – wagons, tossed like a human child's playthings. He sniffed deeply, but failed to find the stench of death and decay. The fact that the smells were missing was even more troubling. Sensing movement, Majherri scanned the debris searching out the source.

"Trainee Reese, no injuries … just shaken up." The sound of his rider's voice brought him out of his stupor. Her touch brought concern as she quickly checked on his physical condition. His side was bruised and her leg moving against him in the saddle would probably bother him if they were going faster than a trot. He practically screamed for her to get on.

Other voices shouted out, reporting their condition, but the Lieutenant shouted them down. "We need light and a defensive perimeter! Something's moving out there!"

The trainees scrambled to comply. Another fire maiden, the Welsh woman sent a burst of fire into the air. After a second, Kayleigh followed suit and the area was partially illuminated.

Majherri tensed, identifying a hostile shape moving toward them. Kayleigh saw it as well. It was a desert creature, but it was impossibly large. Its claws clacked together with audible noises. The tail waved over the monster's head. Scorpions were always a problem in the steppes of the west, but at most, even multiple stings would only make a unicorn ill for a day.

Of course that was for a normal scorpion, the kind that could be crushed under his hooves with barely a second thought. That wouldn't work for a scorpion nearly the same size as himself! It was black, almost obsidian, and blended in with the predawn darkness. Only the forward motion and the quivering tail gave it dimension.

"Sacred Mother preserve us! There's more! Over there!" A human screamed.

Majherri wanted to look, but he couldn't. The abomination was too close. He fought down his own fear and Kayleigh's. *Do something, girl! Now!*

Her arm extended, slowly, almost as if he was willing her too inch-by-inch. The thing moved closer and he began forcing magic into her as he backed away, trying to give her some extra room.

The flames formed on her finger tips. She was scared and resisting. *Unleash it, or we die!*

His plea touched something in her and whatever dam had been there burst. Majherri's power flowed through her. Kayleigh's fear was a tangible presence and that with that fear came a tidal wave of energy.

Flames washed over the creature's protective carapace. Claws rose to shield it from the heat. Majherri focused on the motion of the other claw and the tail, watching for every shift and calculating when to avoid a strike. The over-sized claw snapped out and he move left. The tail shot forward a split-second later. There was no room left to maneuver, so he reared, blocking with his hooves. The strike slammed against the metal shoe and dislodged it sending a jolt of pain surging up his right foreleg.

Magic swirled around him and his hooves exploded in flame as both he and his rider responded as one. Enraged, he brought his front hooves smashing down on the claw. The heated shell cracked … and crumbled. Confused, he wondered if it was alive or a construct, but he didn't put much thought to it. Whatever it was, it was a threat, an enemy to be destroyed!

Majherri pivoted to the right giving his rider a shot at the damaged side and his rider sent a continuous spray of fire onto the shell. The center mass, where the "brain" should be, blackened the extreme temperature. It floundered as he pounced for the second time. The monster's body vibrated and broke under the impact. Like the claw, it crumbled and sand ran like blood from an open gash. Majherri decided that it was a golem as it sagged to the ground.

His rider didn't stop. She sprayed her flame without really aiming it. He sensed her terror and tried to redirect it against the next one. A trio of trainees, two earth maidens and one water combined their powers to sink the second creature into the sand, where it struggled to move.

"They're just statues!" Kayleigh screamed. "Made of stone!"

That clued the two earth aligned warriors to start directing their magic directly at the monster. It began disintegrating as they ripped it to shreds.

With two down and more approaching, Lieutenant Townsend conjured a wind slowing the advancing things and moving the debris back to give them more room. "Hicks, Anderson, make us a hole in the nearest wall! Reese, Welsh keep burning everything in sight.

The broken wagons became a bonfire as his rider and the other sprayed their flames into the debris.

"I see movement in the towers!" Laurel Whitaker yelled. Majherri saw men pouring out of the two intact towers and onto the catwalks carrying bows. They were wrapped in dark cloaks and bore little resemblance to the regular guardsmen.

With the unexpected arrival, they were caught unaware. Majherri need only look at the flaming remains left behind by the previous ambushes to know what awaited the next regular Portal travelers.

Towsend's wind gusts pushed the heat and smoke into the faces of the archers, buying time for the earth maidens to break an exit point in the wall. Majherri sent a warning through their link, drawing Kayleigh's attention to another one of the golem-like creatures closing with them. The flaming jet from her hands ceased and he felt more of their magic flowing across the bond. Momentary weakness invaded as a flame snaked around the knife she'd drawn. Kayleigh leveled it and a second later the flame gathered into a white hot fireball that leapt from her blade and slammed in the beast. The monster's shell darkened and the front legs fused. Already, Kayleigh was creating a second fireball using the tip of her dagger as a focal point.

Majherri was suitably impressed. Even Danella, couldn't conjure fireballs that quickly. Kayleigh's lack of control was an asset in this battle.

The archers were firing blindly into the maelstrom of fire and smoke. One bit into his flank and he cried out.

"Where's that blessed hole!"

"Almost there, Lieutenant. One minute!"

"Work faster! Whitaker! Protect Reese. Temple, you Protect Welsh. I'll try and shield the rest of us."

The third year lead rider and her unicorn bolted next to him and he felt the air near them solidify. He maneuvered behind the small area of protection provided by the air maiden while his rider's second fireball stopped the scorpion in its tracks. Kayleigh looked for the next target, when she didn't find one, she pointed her sword in the direction of the tower area. She hesitated and he knew she was thinking about the difference between an enchanted rock monster and an actual living being. What he did next was distasteful, but he let her feel some of the pain from the arrow in his side.

With that sudden reminder that the opposing side wasn't

engaging in questions of moral values, Kayleigh began tossing random fireballs and forcing the enemies to seek cover.

"The hole's big enough!" An earth maiden trainee bellowed.

"Get through! Fall back! Welsh take point on the other side. Lead us out of the city."

Most were already through the gap created in the wall. Lieutenant Townsend's protective dome rose over Whitaker's as the older woman said, "Whitaker get out. Reese and I will bring up the rear. Go! Go!"

Majherri always appreciated the human officers in the battalions. Only the best rose to command and Townsend was no shrinking violet. Her unicorn had three arrow injuries and the human sported one sticking out of her thigh along with another in the shoulder.

"Reese! Turn off the flames and go! I'm right behind you."

The flow of magic through their bond ceased and a sudden wave of exhaustion passed through them both, but their combined adrenaline pushed it away as he bolted through the rough arch created in the wall and onto what was once the streets of a populated city.

A few arrows from the ruined fortress walls chased them into the darkness, but Majherri sped up. He knew this city well. Danella had been stationed here for their final three seasons. *We're heading the wrong way!*

He reared and snorted! Drawing the attention of the other unicorns, before bolting.

"Reese! Get back here with the patrol!"

"It's Majherri, ma'am! He knows the quickest way out!" His rider shouted. "It's this way!"

"Alright then, everyone follow Reese. Ride hard and stay low."

Through the streets, filled with rubble, but devoid of life, Majherri guided himself by memory and instinct. Seeing some campfires near the oasis cluster this city was founded on, he pivoted and skirted that area while hearing the shouts from the people around them. Some came running with bows or spears, but the unicorns were moving too fast. He caught a glimpse of the royal palace. It was a ruined shell. This once proud city wasn't captured. It had been razed.

The only thing slowing his frantic run was the damaged hoof on his foreleg. The breached walls of the city drew near. He searched for the gap that would lead them to freedom.

There! There it is! He leapt another rubble pile and skidded on the stones of the street. Breaking free into the desert he breathed in the cool morning air, knowing that with the rising sun, it wouldn't last.

Townsend and her unicorn caught up with him. The superior speed of an air maiden and his shoeless hoof made it easy for them. The lieutenant pointed to a cluster of rocks with some mangy scrub brush surrounding it. "We'll stop at the rocks and tend our wounds."

Minutes later, the humans were dismounting and Majherri could tell the fear was setting in. The fact the trainees held up for that long was a credit to the instructors at The Academy. They obeyed the orders of their superior and did their job during the crisis. The aftermath might prove more difficult.

Other than the bruises from being thrown off of me at arrival, Kayleigh seems ... no wait, her hand is badly burnt again. She just doesn't know it yet.

The weight on his back was less than when they left Talcosa. Some of the equipment Majherri carried had been lost in the battle. He wondered if they still had enough to leave and, more importantly, if leaving was still an option.

Chapter 24 – Wasteland of a God

"Hold your hand out. These tears are going to sting a little. You might have overdone it this time. This will probably leave a permanent mark."

Kayleigh winced as the drops of water hit the reddened and swollen skin on her hand. "I guess this is where you tell me that I still need to learn how to control my fire, isn't it?"

Annabeth gave a morbid chuckle and said, "Reese, if that's what you're like with hardly any control, I really want to see the day you do master your abilities. If I threw as many fireballs as you did back there, I'd be crawling under that rock over there to sleep it off!"

The older rider placed a hand on Kayleigh's shoulder and continued, "Control or not, you did what you needed to do to survive and we're not of this yet. If we get attacked again, you just keep doing the same thing. Okay?"

Nodding vigorously, Kayleigh said, "Okay."

"Here, put some salve over the palm and wrap a bandage around it," Welsh said while turning to inspect Majherri's arrow wound. "It's not too deep. You steady him, while I pull it out. Good thing for us that these aren't barbed tips, otherwise we'd have to cut them out and that's never fun."

"What happened? Why are we here? I've never heard of the Portal doing something like that." Kayleigh's words echoed those of the other recruits milling around and tending to the injuries. Majherri's snort told her that she was doing little to calm him down while Welsh removed the projectile from his side.

"Listen up," Townsend called for attention. "There's no use dwelling on why this happened. Accept it and move on. We're in the desert. That means we'll need water. Edwards, you're our only water maiden. How much can you conjure?"

The girl meekly answered, "Only a few gallons at a time, but I've never tried it in a desert before."

"Doesn't matter. You'll be doing it now. Pull moisture from the air or try the area around the roots of those plants. We'll need all you can summon. Akers, stone shape a trough or just make a depression in that rock so we can water the mounts. All of you riders will drink from your water flasks, but the unicorns need to stay hydrated or we're going to be in trouble. Whitaker, don't take your eyes off those ruins for a second. If they come after us, we'll need to hit the trail quickly. Let's get to it."

Using the same magic that helped break a hole through the wall, one of the earth maidens bored a hole into a rock as the water maiden placed one hand on her unicorn and held the other one over the crudely created area. A small distortion appeared near the girl's palm and fell, like a thin stream into the hole. The amount Edwards conjured didn't look promising with nine unicorns needing water.

"Rider Welsh, you ever serve in these kingdoms?"

"No, ma'am."

"Me neither. Alright ladies, I've only got maps for the kingdoms we're supposed to patrol. We're going to have to move using the trails and visual landmarks. Unfortunately, there's an army out there, somewhere – the same army that just destroyed this city. They may already be attacking the towns and cities east of us. We may run smack into their rear elements at some point. I know you're worried, but you've all trained for this. Right now, we're better off together. If we're forced to split up, you all need to focus on surviving and making your way east. The news about this has to get back to Talcosa."

Kayleigh walked around to the other side of Majherri and rifled through the sheaf of parchments in the saddlebag. "Ma'am, I've got a map of the area."

"That's a lucky break. Bring it here, Reese. You'll have to hold it for me."

She opened it and allowed the injured lieutenant to look at it while hoping the woman would be too preoccupied with their current dilemma to ask why Kayleigh had a map of the western kingdoms, along with all the other areas of the blessed continent. Her thoughts flitted back to the letters she'd left.

I can't think of them now. I'll worry about them later.

"Okay, any of you ladies from this part of the world."

Kayleigh watched as everyone shook their heads. The rider who had grown up closest to where they were was from a city over three weeks journey away. Kayleigh said, "Majherri gave me the impression that he knows this area pretty well. He was out here with his last rider for several seasons."

"I'll keep that in mind, Reese. How's that water coming?"

Edwards was kneeling next to some of the bushes, the ground trying to pull more water out of the soil. "I've got a little over two gallons, ma'am, but that's about all this place has to offer. If we're not riding all out, I can fill the flasks while we ride."

"It'll have to do. Give your unicorns some water and then get saddled up."

"We're almost ready, Lieutenant. I just need to patch your wounds and fix up your unicorn."

"Okay, Welsh. While we're riding, I need to know how much we have. Water is critical, but eventually food is going to become a problem. Each trainee was issued a vial of healing tears. Find out how much we have left. Edwards, can you make healing tears? ... That's okay trainee, I didn't expect that you could."

Kayleigh was amazed that the officer kept asking questions and giving orders while Annabeth was pulling the arrow out of her shoulder. A short time ago, she'd wanted nothing more than the confidence and swagger of a third year student.

She started to lead Majherri over to get some of the water, but he shook his head and basically told her that the others would already have drank it all.

"There's a group of riders leaving the city!" Laurel said

with a hint of fear in her voice.

"How many, Whitaker?"

"Two dozen, maybe more."

Kayleigh could see the woman weighing the options. Majherri was ready for another fight, but expected he wouldn't get a chance.

He was right. "We ride east. We're too close to their reinforcements. If they try to follow, we'll find a good spot for an ambush and take them. Reese, take point. Your unicorn should know the way to Jaruciax and he's our best scout. That's the direction we're heading in. Keep your eyes open for the enemy and remember – any spot that looks good for an ambush could already have one set up and waiting for us. Finish up that water and move with a purpose, ladies!"

Kayleigh took a sip from her water flask and poured some into her hand, letting Majherri lap it from her uninjured palm. When he finished, she climbed up into the saddle and patted his neck. He responded with the image of them running free and alone.

Leaning down to his ear, she whispered, "After we get to safety. Let's get to Jaruciax first." He could sense her doubts and indecision, but chose to leave the matter alone.

Riding on the island was usually a pleasant affair. The worst experiences involved mud and downpours. Even then, that was a mixed blessing, keeping the unicorns and the riders cool. The desert steppes were an unforgiving mix of vicious heat and wind driven sand. Kayleigh kept her chest piece, but the helmet was replaced with a towel wrapped around her head.

They halted midway through the morning and sought what little shelter was available and hastily improved by the trio of earth maidens manipulating the rock. Her services wouldn't be needed until nightfall, when the desert rapidly cooled, giving up its heat. Even then, it was doubtful, because they'd be riding after the sun sets. With her Yar knife, she drew lines in the hot sand and watched the overworked Amanda Edwards struggling to summon more water.

"How are you holding up, Kayleigh? Is your hand okay?" Annabeth sat down next to her.

"It's very tender, but the vial of healing tears worked wonders. I feel like I should be doing something right now."

"We all do our part, when called on. There's not a lot for either of us to do at the moment, but if we run into part of that rearguard, you'll have more than enough to keep you busy. So, stay sharp and be ready. Good thing you had a map for this kingdom."

"Just lucky I brought one."

"Yes it is. I saw you had lots of other maps too. I saw you lost your bedroll and some other bags at the battle. Hope it wasn't anything that will be too difficult to replace."

"Everyone said I was over packing," Kayleigh answered cautiously.

"It's you and me, Kayleigh." Annabeth said quietly. "You had a heavy jacket rolled into your bedroll. Something you wouldn't need anywhere except in the far north this time of year. You were over packing for just a few weeks off the island, but I have a theory. Would you like to hear it?"

Kayleigh looked the older woman in the eyes and said, "Please. Let's not do this now." Her blue dress was also rolled up in that bedroll. It was the last connection she had with her mother. She couldn't think of that now.

"Okay, but if you're really considering what I think you are, all I ask is that you give me the chance to talk you out of it. Alright?"

"So, what do we have to be on guard for in the desert … other than this army?" Kayleigh nodded and quickly tried to change the subject.

"Aside from the usual assortment of snakes, spiders, and everything else, I guess sand trolls are probably the largest and most dangerous thing around. Ogres and giants are a rarity in these parts. The trolls bury themselves near trails or by an oasis during the day and come out after the sun sets – very tough to spot from what I hear, though they get sand everywhere."

Kayleigh rolled her eyes at the joke and said, "Sounds like a charming place. It is amazing people live out here."

She nodded watching the unicorns cluster around where Amanda was making water. The reddish-brown haired girl was doing her best to meet there needs. Her eyes drifted over to Majherri, who was separate from the group. He was inspecting a few of the desert plants.

Lowering his head, he used his horn to stab into one of them and thrashed his head back and forth. The top of the plant fell to the ground. Majherri turned and looked at his brethren, giving them a look of contempt, before sticking his snout down over the exposed body of the plant and licking.

Annabeth stood and motioned for her to do the same. They walked over to Majherri. Welsh crouched and picked up the prickly top of the plant the unicorn had skewered. Using her two fingers, she scooped out some of the pulp and put it into her mouth.

"It's actually kind of sweet. Smart unicorn, you've got there Reese," she said offering the piece of plant to Kayleigh.

"Yes he is," she replied. Kayleigh used her knife to peel the skin and barbs off of the plant to make it more accessible for Majherri as the others waiting in the water line started to make their way over.

"That reminds me of a conversation where you said he was worried about what was happening in the west. Obviously, I owe him an apology. Rhey gave me the impression that all the other unicorns ignore Majherri. Considering we're out here and nobody else seems to know about a Portal city being destroyed or an army moving right under everyone's noses, I'm woman enough to know when to say I should have listened, not that it would've done any good."

Majherri stopped gnawing on the pulp of the plant long enough to acknowledge Annabeth.

Kayleigh peeled a few more plants for the other unicorns and cut another in pieces for the riders to chew while Lieutenant Townsend called Annabeth over to talk strategy and ordered the others to rest and stay out of the sun. She got under the improvised shelter which was noticeably cooler, but still unbearably hot, and passed out the pieces of the plant. Some of the girls may have actually been asleep, but for most, it was an exercise in futility.

"I'm worried about the lieutenant," Laurel whispered pointing to where Rider Welsh helped their leader drink from her canteen. "Her one arm is broken and the other arm took an arrow in the shoulder. She can barely move it let alone fight."

"Why are you telling me this, Laurel?"

"The day the reassigned you to our year, the captain summoned me and the section leaders into her office. She told us to keep a close eye on you because you are that powerful … powerful enough to even make General Jyslin concerned. We were ordered not to speak of this with you, but given the situation, you need to know. I saw this firsthand at the Portal. If we get into another fight, we're going to need you."

She flushed, both from the heat and a bit of embarrassment. "I'll do everything I can, Laurel. I might be as powerful as you say, but I don't really know how to use it. Do you have any ideas where those rock scorpions came from?"

The other air maiden, Marcia Temple, crawled up next to them. "My guess is the army is being led by a sorceress or a sorcerer and their acolytes. Whoever it is, they are strong enough to leave those things behind and not really care about them. I'm scared to think of what that army might have with it, if those aren't the frontline troops. My great aunt is an enchantress and no slouch either. It would take her months to create those golems. So the other side has been preparing for years. This might be the start of another great war."

"Let's hope not," Laurel said.

"We should try and get some rest. Something tells me that things won't get any easier from here on out."

The other two girls agreed and Kayleigh closed her eyes

and tried to pretend that it was like falling asleep on Helden's beach at the height of summer. When that didn't work, she waited for exhaustion to catch up with her.

Fortunately, it didn't take long.

The difference between day and night in the desert is … well the difference between day and night!

Kayleigh chuckled at her internal joke. In the driving sun, the desolation was everywhere you looked, an ever present, all encompassing landscape where little existed. In the darkness, the view was narrower and more focused. With the stars in the sky, she could see fairly well, but she found herself staring at the area that was visible around her. She was looking for any change, or even a hint of change as they moved along, even though there was none.

Every few minutes, she used her heatsight. Though the desert sands releasing the trapped heat interfered with vision beyond a very short range, she was able to see some shapes on the landscape surrounding her. The trailing unicorns behind her stood out remarkably well. That worried her, because she was "on point" and responsible to spot any ambush ahead.

Sure! Put the girl who's been doing this for a few months right up front. At least, I have you, Majherri to fall back on and you're in a better mood. The wide open spaces call out to you, don't they?

Majherri agreed with her. There was too much to do right at the moment for the usual feelings of worry that often traversed their bond. It was a refreshing change to not feel the bottled up anger and frustration that vexed both of them to no end.

Shapes were moving toward them. Majherri spotted them as well and Kayleigh raised her hand to alert the group of riders behind her. Within thirty seconds, the lieutenant was next to her, covering the ground at a speed only an air maiden could achieve.

"Small party of travelers, ma'am – two wagons and five,

maybe six riders. What are your orders?"

Townsend signaled for Welsh and Whitaker to come up and join them. Kayleigh sensed the tension building during the wait. When the other two riders arrived, Townsend continued, "Welsh and I will approach and get what information from them we can and if possible barter for some of their water. If hostilities break out, we can outflank them and reform a mile down the road. Whitaker, you're in charge, any questions?"

"No, ma'am."

The two made their way ahead to the wagon as the other trainees rode up. The group watched and waited as the lieutenant and Annabeth conversed with the nomads.

"Is it wrong to admit that I'm nervous?" Amanda Edwards said to no one in particular.

"Just be ready if we need to move," Laurel said trying to sound official and calm everyone's nerves.

Kayleigh swallowed and waited for something … anything to happen. She felt Majherri's anticipation. It didn't matter whether they were going to fight, run, or just talk.

Long seconds dragged into minutes and things were going well. She started to relax, as Annabeth began moving around the side with one of the nomads. That's when the monsters burst out of the wagons. The first one's arm smashed into Welsh and knocked her from Rheysurrah's saddle. She'd never seen them before, but Majherri assured her that the grotesque creatures were sand trolls.

They stood nearly nine feet, with long, thin arms that stretched down to their knees. Their faces were covered with rubbery leather-like skin.

Kayleigh froze in horror, but Majherri was already speeding to the fight with the cries of Laurel Whitaker calling for her to stop. Flames spattered across the sand as they released their combined magic. Drawing her dagger, Kayleigh sent a fireball at the one terrorizing Annabeth.

The dismounted warrior brandished her flaming sword defensively and was trying to get back to Rheysurrah, but the trolls and one of the riders circled about the pair and prevented that reunion. The injured lieutenant was allowing her mount to join the fray and engaged four of the mounted riders at once.

Kayleigh knew her fireballs wouldn't be enough of a distraction. She had to do what Annabeth asked her to do, throw all notions of control to the wind and just let the magic she shared with Majherri do what must be done. She started pulling on her end of the bond, seeking all the magic her unicorn had to offer.

Welsh sliced one of the troll's hands off, but the other troll dashed her to the ground. This made Kayleigh's fury build. The flame grew, almost becoming a third partner in the bond between her and Majherri. It swirled around them and coalesced into a wave of energy surrounding them. For a brief second, it collapsed back on itself, and almost disappeared. Kayleigh shook with the effort of pushing more magic into the wave and screamed when everything broke loose.

Pushing herself high in the saddle, Kayleigh sensed the elation on the other side of the bond. This was fireshade – warrior and unicorn combined into a speeding mass of flame from which there was no escape. Majherri accelerated, faster than she'd ever ridden him, despite the damaged hoof.

Annabeth's attackers forgot the fire maiden in front of them and spun to face the new threat. Impossibly long arms reached out to strike as Majherri left the ground and bowled into the sand troll. The energy of the fireshade exploded on impact and the dark desert night was momentarily driven back by the light of a miniature sun.

The troll trying to stop them did not survive the impact and the other was tossed aside like a plaything. Both wagons were upended. Kayleigh gasped for breath and could do nothing more than stay in Majherri's saddle. She saw his hooves lifted and some of the ground clung to them like webs of a spider as the sand was converted into molten glass.

The lieutenant had seen what was coming and gotten clear. Her mount was engaged with one of the few remaining human warriors. Rider Welsh was rolling on the ground extinguishing the flames on her clothes. A warrior with his rags burning charged at Annabeth with his spear. Kayleigh scrounged for any magic, but was too weak. She opened her mouth to shout a warning, but the words died on her lips. It wasn't necessary. Laurel dashed by on her mount and delivered a killing strike with her sword.

The other trainees arrived seconds later and the two nomads still able to flee did so. The badly injured troll was crawling into the desert, likely trying to bury itself in the sands and heal. Back on her feet, Welsh would have none of that. Flame sprung to life on her blade and she finished it by cleaving the creatures head off.

The older fire maiden stepped away from the monster's body and walked over to Kayleigh. Midway there, Rheysurrah came alongside her and she vaulted into the saddle. "You don't follow orders very well do you, Reese?"

Kayleigh looked sheepishly at Welsh's singed garments and hair. Rheysurrah's mane had also lost much of its luster. "Sorry about the burns."

"They're nothing. I'll take them over being dead any day. But you've got to promise me something."

"What's that?"

"When you do figure out how your magic works, you've got to teach me how to do the fireshade. Is that a deal?"

"Okay."

The others were surrounding the lieutenant as she interrogated the remaining nomad.

Welsh turned to Laurel Whitaker and said, "I also am grateful to you. Was that your first kill?"

"Yes, ma'am."

"Well, you're blooded now. It's time to look him over and take a weapon from him. Take a moment and choose wisely, it should be something that you will become accustomed to using as a primary weapon. The spear might not be sturdy enough, but the scimitar at his side looks promising."

"What?"

"Is something wrong, Kayleigh?"

"I didn't choose this knife, Lynch told me to take it!" Kayleigh tried to remember what other weapons the Yar had, but he must have had something more threatening than a small throwing dagger. Once again, she felt cheated.

"Oh, somehow nothing you say anymore about that woman surprises me. I recommend you ask her for an explanation in front of the General when we get back. Now, let's get back to Laurel. What do you think? An air maiden could throw that spear an incredible distance, but what do you do after that?"

Laurel nodded, "I'll go with the scimitar."

"That's what I'd do in your place as well."

Kayleigh sulked, already trying to picture Meghan Lynch's excuses. No doubt she'd make up something that sounded perfectly acceptable to everyone else. They went to Lieutenant Townsend. The woman was crouched in front of the injured nomad, who was leaning back against the bottom of the overturned wagon.

"Look at his eyes," Amanda said. "Don't they look strange? Is he under some kind of a spell?"

Annabeth thrust her hand forward and touched Rheysurrah with the other, her conjured flame lit the area. The nomad shrunk back from it, but everyone could see that there was no white in his eyes, just large oval pools of black.

The lieutenant didn't care about his unusual eyes. Instead, she said, "I'm getting tired of asking you the same question. Why did you attack us?"

"You intrude on the Master's domain."

"You've already said that. Who is this master? What were you doing with those trolls? Where is your army now?"

"The Master is our god! You walk upon his land. He … he will …" the man broke off in a fit of coughing before spitting up blood. He winced in pain. "I go to him now, but I know he will come for you and your heart will beat for him, or you ... you will suffer ... a thousand days of torture."

Two more fits of coughing came and went before the nomad ceased breathing. Weary, the lieutenant stood and looked at them. "See if they have any usable water and food. Unhook the horses and let them go. Move quickly, ladies, we are running out of nighttime and the sooner we can leave this desert, the better."

"What about the things he said, ma'am?"

"Never trust the words of a fanatic, Edwards – a dying one even more so. It's cause for concern, but we can assume much of what he was saying was a lie. My guess is this god of theirs is nothing more than a powerful wizard. Look at his eyes now ... back to normal."

Kayleigh looked at Annabeth and she shrugged, "I've never heard of a compulsion strong enough to turn a troll into a thrall. Then again, I know precious little about this species of trolls."

It took only a few minutes to find what little the nomads had to offer. The small amount of food and water found was added to their meager supplies. Townsend stared at Kayleigh and said, "I assume your unicorn disregarded my orders."

"Yes, ma'am."

"Both of you did a good job, but you dragged the rest of the trainees along with you. I can accept that Majherri and, by extension you, aren't going to listen to me. That said, be mindful of the others. I will make it clear to the others that if you decide to go solo again, they are to leave you on your own. Anyone who can do what you just did doesn't need a bunch of trainees in the blast area. Are we clear on this?"

"Yes, ma'am."

"How are you feeling?"

"Drained and exhausted."

"Alright, I'll put Welsh on point. You deserve a break, but we can't afford to stop now. Anything within a few miles probably saw your explosion and might decide to investigate. We need to be moving."

Chapter 25 – Destiny's Touch

His rider was more exhausted than she let on. She sagged in the saddle as their trek in the cold night continued. Kayleigh had done something extraordinary. Let them try to deny both of them status! His showered her with pride and comforted the tired girl.

The other unicorns moved alongside and some of them actually acknowledged him. That was what power could do.

"Do you all still consider me an exile? What will you say about me when you return to the Sacred Island?"

Strangely, he no longer felt the desire to run away. Perhaps it was Kayleigh and her doubts, asserting their way over the bond. He wasn't certain, but at this moment, he wanted to see their faces. Though they were well behind enemy lines, Majherri felt the touch of destiny. This time he would emerge from the desert in victory.

Hours went by and the group moved on. As the sun began to rise, Kayleigh was barely awake. In contrast, Majherri felt strangely alive. He wasn't tired at all and still felt full of power.

Welsh helped Kayleigh from the saddle as the humans and the other unicorns retreated to what little shade and shelter the desert provided. He did not. He would not. When they left here, he would be vindicated. Those who had wronged him would hang their heads in shame and beg for his forgiveness.

Perhaps I should insist that T'rsa not be allowed to participate in the next mating season.

Majherri circled in the sand as these thoughts went through his mind. He searched for a few plants to slake his thirst. Wandering far, he felt something in the distance calling out to him. It was a whisper in the corner of his mind … so very familiar. His destiny was out there in the sands, pleading for him to come to it.

"Majherri, are you well?"

"Rheysurrah? Oh yes, I have never been better. Why the sudden interest, you foolish creature?"

"Foolish? You are the one walking away from the encampment. I had to gallop to get to you. Come back and get in the shade. You're delirious."

"No! For the first time in a long time I can see clearly. I warned you! I told you something was wrong in the west! Did you listen? Of course not?"

The idiot blocked his way. *"Fine Majherri, you can gloat all you wish when we get out of the desert. Right now, you need to come back to camp."*

Majherri was barely listening to Rheysurrah. His words meant nothing … less than nothing. *"Go away, you stupid child. Your words grow tiresome. Leave my presence and go crawling to that wretched bovine who calls herself my sister."*

The fool continued to stand there, blocking his path, so Majherri trotted around him.

"Your rider is back there, Majherri. She needs you. Slow down. Will you stop!"

"Never, you jealous little males and envious females are always trying to stop me! Look at your weakling of a rider! She is a sad excuse for a fire maiden, but what else should she expect with a thin-blooded unicorn like you."

The youngling continued to demand he stop. He had no intention of stopping, ever again. He would be corralled no longer. Rules were for the weak, but he was no weakling.

"For the last time, Majherri, stop!" Rheysurrah butted into him.

"Stop? Stop? Never again!" Majherri spun and kicked the interloper. *"I've heard enough from you!"*

For a moment, Rheysurrah lowered his horn like he would attack. Majherri had no such hesitation. It was long past time he settled this score. The other was immediately defensive. Their horns smacked against each other as each fought for leverage. The weakling danced away and would not reengage.

"Majherri! We should not do this. You need help. I'll retrieve your rider."

"Coward! Stay and fight me. Isn't this what you want? To prove yourself to my sister?"

"If I thought you were sane Majherri, I'd gladly fight you, but this is wrong."

"Bah! I've wasted enough time on you. Cross me again and I will kill you. Nothing will get in my way."

Majherri watched Rheysurrah gallop back to the camp – probably to spread more lies. It was nothing to concern himself with. The whisper was getting louder. It reminded him that there was a reason for everything and offered encouragement. It told him that he had journeyed so far and was so close to the end. The voice begged him to travel faster.

He paused by some plants and ate. It hurt when he bit on some of the stickers. He was careless, but this was a waste of time and he only needed enough to get him to where the voice told him he needed to go.

The sun beat down on him and threatened to make him delirious, but he increased his speed. There would be no further interruptions. It was just him and the sand flying out from under his hooves.

Cresting another large dune, he saw a group of riders and a trio of wagons waiting below. Men skulked around in the shadows provided by a group of rocks. The rational part of his mind warned him to the danger, but he was certain that they meant him no harm. He wanted to laugh and scream to the sky. His heart filled with joy and sorrow. The warriors watched him, but one figure waved them aside and moved toward him. The cloaked human walked with confidence and wide-open arms.

His pace quickened until he was almost in a full gallop. He spotted the bullwhip hanging from the belt and almost collapsed. His footing became uncertain. The world began to spin around him. Confusion seeped into every facet of his being, but there was a calming hand in his soul. It was like a firm grasp on his reins. The serenity centered him. Doubts began to vanish and they were replaced with assurance and calm. Nothing but the figure mattered. His entire world shrunk down to the space separating them.

The outstretched hands were female. They peeled back the hood and his heart hammered away. The hair was sun-bleached and the smile on the woman's face beamed at him. It was a look he swore he would never see again.

This doesn't make sense! It isn't possible.

The woman regarded him and was at his side stroking his mane. He did not flinch at the contact. She fished around in her pack and produced a peach, Majherri's favorite fruit. He greedily bit into it, savoring the trickle of the juices down his throat.

She laughed at him and said, "Hello, boy. It's been a long time and I've missed you."

Chapter 26 – The Whip and the Knife

"Reese … Reese! Get up!" Someone was shaking her awake.

Kayleigh struggled to focus. She had been in a deep sleep and fought to figure out where she was.

It came back to her in a rush – the desert and the danger. "What is it? Are we in trouble?"

"We're not sure. Majherri ran off. He was behaving strangely. How do you feel? Whatever was happening to him may also be affecting you."

"I don't feel anything," she replied.

"That's good."

"No Annabeth, I don't feel Majherri – at all! It's like the bond isn't there!"

She was panicking and her friend knew it. "Easy there, Kayleigh. On your feet, we'll sort this out, but first let's make certain that you're okay."

The others crowded around and it felt like everyone was pressing in on her. The lieutenant ordered everyone back. "Close your eyes and clear your mind, Reese. Search for your unicorn. If he's still alive you should be able to feel it."

Taking deep, calming breaths, Kayleigh tried to block everything out except for Majherri. "I don't feel him. Wait! It's faint and in that direction!"

Annabeth nodded and said, "That's the way Rhey said he ran off in. Lieutenant, I'll take Reese and go get her unicorn."

Townsend shook her head, "I'll be able to ride faster, even with the extra weight of another rider, and you're the best fighter we have. You stay with the rest of the riders. If we're not back by sundown, break camp and keep heading east."

"Yes, ma'am." Rider Welsh answered. She didn't look like she cared for the orders, but acknowledged them just the same.

"Good. Reese, take only what you need – the less weight, the better. Leave the rest here, we can retrieve it later. Your unicorn has a good ninety minute lead on us, but Osalon and I know how to cover ground in a hurry."

Kayleigh grabbed only a few items; her sword, the Yar knife, her helm, and the two canteens of water. "I'm ready."

"Alright, help me get up into the saddle and let's get going."

Annabeth helped Kayleigh get the injured warrior into Osalon's saddle and Kayleigh clambered up behind the woman.

"Good hunting," Rider Welsh called out as the sped into the desert heat.

For Kayleigh, it was a strange experience riding with the air maiden and her mount. She felt like an intruder. Concentrating, she searched for Majherri, but the presence of a bond right next to her was interfering. Oddly, she could actually feel the bond between Sandra Townsend and Osalon.

"Whatever you're doing, Reese, stop it. It's making Osalon and me uncomfortable. He's considering throwing you."

"Yes, ma'am. I was just trying to find Majherri again, but the bond between the two of you is all I can locate."

The woman looked over her shoulder and back at Kayleigh. "You can sense the bond between another rider and her unicorn?"

Kayleigh shrugged, "Yes. Sorry it's the first time I've ever doubled-up with another rider."

"I've never heard of that happening before, Reese. Make certain to tell this to Captain Sycroft when we return to The Academy. What about when you tend to the unbounded younglings? Do you feel anything with those unicorns?"

"A little. The younglings are like a rope or a string that's frayed on one side. With you and Osalon, the frayed ends of each string are joined and form a knot. It's just like my bond with Majherri. I thought all of us could do this."

"No. We can't, Reese."

"Oh," Kayleigh felt embarrassed. It never occurred to her to ask anyone else if they could feel the younglings. "Do you have any idea what this means?"

"No. We don't really teach classes in the bond beyond the meditation techniques to help strengthen your connection to your unicorn. The bond itself has always been considered a private matter, between the two involved. That you can actually sense my connection to Osalon is significant."

"I guess that explains why the younglings always acted so skittish around me. After awhile, they just stopped giving me that task, which is why I ended up in the stables all the time."

"The more I speak to you, Trainee Reese, the odder you become. Do you have any idea why Majherri would want to run off? Welsh said her unicorn tried to stop him, but Majherri attacked him."

Kayleigh bit her lower lip and turned to look across the dunes, seeing the distortions of the heat rising off the sand. *Did Majherri decide to just leave on his own, abandoning me?*

"What are you thinking, Reese?"

She weighed her options. Just saying nothing was probably the best course, but the lieutenant was risking her life. *She deserves an answer.*

"Ma'am, this is going to sound horrible, but before we went through the portal, Majherri and I weren't planning to come back. It's why I had maps of the world and so many supplies. Things just weren't working for us at The Academy."

Osalon stopped in his tracks and moved his head sideways so he could look at her. His rider was equally as incredulous.

"Reese? Are you serious?"

"Well that was the plan, until we ended up in the wrong spot with a bunch of monsters and crazy people trying to kill us."

"You should have talked to someone."

"Ma'am it wouldn't have done any good. The other unicorns had all but banished Majherri. Their council or whatever you call it, refused to allow him to participate in mating season. Go ahead and ask Osalon, I'm sure he knows. Majherri was miserable. I was hardly able to spend any time with him without an instructor around, and I was considered too dangerous to work with anyone but an instructor. The other trainees are always telling me how lucky I am to get pummeled during weapons instruction or continuously knocked out of my saddle during jousts. It's funny, but I didn't see it that way. Laurel all but admitted that she and the section leaders were ordered to be nice and spy on me."

"Reese, listen to me. This insane trip does prove that you are too dangerous to work with anyone but trained instructors. Leaving the island without learning how to control your fire would place the villages you visit in danger. Your journey has been hard and will no doubt continue to be so, but you must fortify yourself and your unicorn. You've been a model student in my classes, but you never once asked for help or advice. Every trainee has problems. Your problems happen to be more than the usual homesickness. I can't speak for how the unicorns treat Majherri, but running away is never the answer."

"I know, ma'am and I'm certain Majherri knows. With a war about to erupt, I don't think he still wants to go out on our own. He's a fighter, but I won't be sure until I'm with him again."

"Understood. First we find him and then we get out of here. After that, we'll have time for a long and serious discussion. Come on, Osalon. Let's get moving."

Majherri's tracks were easy enough to follow, though they were very erratic. Kayleigh was troubled by this and one other thing – the distant thread connecting her with Majherri didn't seem to be getting stronger. *Are we getting any closer? Is he running away without me?*

They stopped only to give Osalon a chance to rest and drink some of their water. Kayleigh worried how much they would have left for Majherri whenever they caught up with him. Walking around, she probed once more across the bond. She sensed that he was happy. *He knows that I'm coming!*

Hurrying, she helped the lieutenant back into the saddle. The afternoon sun showed no mercy, but Lieutenant Townsend's air magic helped drive back the incessant heat.

It was nearly sunset when they found him. He was standing by a cluster of rocks.

"Go get him. We've got a long ride to catch up to the rest."

Kayleigh nodded and dismounted. Majherri watched her approach. His head tilted from side to side, almost as if he was looking at her for the first time.

"What's wrong, Majherri?" He was backing away from her. She felt a sudden flicker of danger and confusion through the bond. He backed around the side of the rocks and she sprinted to follow him. Rounding the turn she saw nomads waiting on the sides of the rocks. A weighted net came down on top of her and she struggled in its grasp, crying out for help.

Landing helplessly on the ground she stared up at an approaching figure. A female voice said, "So, this is the little girl that would dare to steal from me."

The woman threw back her hood and Kayleigh gasped. "Danella Lynch?" It was the same woman from the painting, except the lively green eyes were completely replaced with the same dark black she saw yesterday in that fanatical nomad.

It was the last words from her mouth before something hit her on her helmet and she lost consciousness.

It was night time when Kayleigh came to. She wasn't in the net anymore, but her hands were bound and the rope was tied around one of the larger rocks. Her dented helmet was on the ground next to her. She looked around and saw that most of the nomads were gone, only six remained along with a sand troll. There was no sign of Lieutenant Townsend and Osalon. Majherri locked eyes with her and neighed loudly.

"Ah, did you have a nice nap? I was beginning to worry about you and debating the punishment for stealing my unicorn."

"I didn't steal him. We have a bond."

"No, I have a bond with him. How else could I pull him

through the Portal to me? I don't know what that thing you have with him is, but I wanted you awake, so I could break it before I kill you. After all, I wouldn't want Majherri to suffer any backlash when you die."

"Where's the lieutenant?" Kayleigh spat out her question and rose to her knees. There was precious little moisture in her mouth.

"Oh her, you'd be better served worrying about what is about to happen to you. She surrendered, like a good little soldier, rather than watch me gut you. She and her unicorn are already on her way to meet the Master. He will take very good care of our new recruit, but you … you don't get to serve the Master, little thief. I get to punish you."

"You're under some kind of spell. You don't have to do this, Danella."

"First you steal from me and then you address me like you're a friend. I'm going to enjoy this. Majherri, come here!"

The unicorn approached. Kayleigh felt a distant sense of confusion. *Fight her, Majherri! Don't let her control you! Break free! You can do it!*

He shook for a moment and Danella looked at him and grabbed the unicorn's mane. The woman's face twisted in rage. "No, there will be no little insurrection from you. He obeys me … now and forever! Now, I have an irritant that needs to be removed."

Danella's hands moved up to the spirals of Majherri's horn. In the dim light, the cracked horn glowed and Kayleigh felt like a vice was crushing the suddenly fragile tether between her and Majherri. She fought with all her mind to keep the bond from unraveling, but piece by piece, Danella was prying it apart.

"No!" Kayleigh's screams mixed with those of Majherri as the bond snapped. Falling to the ground, she pounded on the sand and howled in pain. Majherri had also collapsed and even Danella appeared shaken as two of the nomad warriors steadied her.

The crazed woman practically hissed at her and unfurled the bullwhip, her personal weapon. A second later, it burst into flames and crackled on the sand. "That was the last pain you will ever cause me. Now, it's your turn to suffer!"

The fiery whip snapped across Kayleigh's arm and stung. She screamed and rolled to the ground as Danella brought her weapon back for a second strike. Kayleigh partially blocked that next blow with the length of rope that kept her a prisoner of the rock. The rope smoldered and she was able to break free. She wasn't certain how this would help her, but it felt like a small victory.

"Oh, so very clever you are thief! You'll make a fine dinner for the scavengers, but first you will dance for me!"

Kayleigh scanned around for anything that could be used as a weapon, while trying to avoid Danella's strikes. Her knife was missing. She spotted it stuffed into the sash of one of the nomads, but the flaming whip coiled around her leg and ripped her to the ground.

"Yes! Yes! Burn and bleed, girl! Scream louder! I want to hear it!"

Thrashing in agony, Kayleigh rolled free of the whip. She thrust her bound hands out to that knife and tried to will it to her. It was an act of desperation. There was no conceivable way this would work.

But it did.

The knife erupted in flames and the man screamed. It fell to the ground, drizzling like a liquid and pooled in the sand next to the injured man. That flame race across the desert floor and slithered into her hand reforming into a solid blade and parted the rope around her wrist. She pushed up from the ground and stood with the throwing dagger in front of her in a guard position and wondered how many fireballs she could hurl before the magic stored in the knife was expended.

Danella craned her neck and studied Kayleigh, "My, oh my, what an impressive little trickster you are. A knife in the hands of a toddler – should I be frightened? No, I think not."

"I will kill you," Kayleigh stated, trying to sound as dangerous as possible. She circled on her injured legs to maintain her distance from the whip and searched for a plan.

The fire maiden stepped into her next whiplash. Kayleigh slipped the knife into a throwing motion and released it, willing to take the blow if she could injure Danella.

Her target twisted and dodged, making the whip go wide. The flaming dagger clattered off a rock and landed on the sand. One of the nomads reached for it, but for the second time Kayleigh changed it into a puddle of fiery liquid and it returned to her hand.

"I grow weary of this little game, girl," Danella said slipping behind Majherri, never taking those soulless eyes off of Kayleigh. The whip's flames vanished, only to be replaced by fireballs from Danella's out stretched hands.

Kayleigh rolled out of the way, but was burnt by the heat of the blast. The nomads howled in laughter and the sand troll pounded its chest. With practiced ease, Danella slid into Majherri's saddle and strapped a shield to her other arm. The whip lit again and Kayleigh readied for her next throw.

"I think it's time we end this, girl. I have a long ride ahead and I need to be on my way."

Kayleigh's dagger flew true, but Danella intercepted it. The woman shook the flaming liquid off the shield, careful to avoid any splattering on Majherri. "Your parlor trick is losing some luster. Do you have anything else? Let me show you something I can do!"

The whip bit into Kayleigh's left arm for the second time. The flame disappeared, but something happened and the edge of the whip came alive and leapt around her neck. It tightened and began strangling her. Instinctively, Kayleigh struck at the whip with her knife, but it didn't slice easily.

"I could drag you behind Majherri for a few miles and see how long you last. I could simply strangle you. You'll be dead long before you could cut through. But I like this one best of all. Watch and learn, trainee!"

Fire started at Danella's hand and started crawling down the length of the whip.

Kayleigh was sure she was going to die, but she refused to end it all like this. The magical whip wasn't splitting, so she reared back and threw her dagger one last time, pleading, begging, and willing it through that shield.

The flaming knife spattered against the shield and Kayleigh could see the maniacal eyes of Danella mocking her final attempt, but those eyes opened wide as the flames danced over and around the shield, reforming into a knife and burying itself in the mesh of Danella's chain armor.

The fire died just short of Kayleigh's face and the whip grew slack as Majherri reared. The force jerked Kayleigh to the ground, and she frantically removed the whip from her neck.

"How?" Danella croaked tugging at the dagger and tossing it to the ground. Kayleigh didn't know either. *That's a water maiden skill! How did I do that?*

There was no time for contemplation. She could tell Danella's injury was severe. One more throw could finish her. Once again, she willed the knife back to her hand.

Majherri must have known it as well, because he danced away from her next throw and bolted into the night. Her heart broke watching the unicorn's retreating form. He was lost to her!

Summoning the knife back to her hand, she faced the six nomads and the troll. They were going to swarm her all at once. She reached for the energy in the knife and found it was still unchanged. The magic inside was still at the same level as when she started this battle.

There was no time for questions – no time to search for a rational explanation. She called on the magic and it responded. The flames licked up her legs and surrounded her in a vortex of power. She became engulfed in the fire and one with it – a living statue of magical flame.

"Let's finish this!" Kayleigh screamed and charged into battle.

Chapter 27 – The Heart of Darkness

Galloping into the night, the world made no sense to Majherri. He didn't know what to think. Danella was alive – at least for the moment. And Kayleigh? He was torn from her ... by Danella. He was angry, hurt, but compelled to obey his first rider. Majherri could only stand there helplessly while Danella toyed with Kayleigh. But Kayleigh somehow won.

Onward through the darkness, he was guided by Danella's weak words. They needed to catch up to the wagon transporting the air maiden prisoner. She passed out when cauterizing her wound. The intense wave of pain shot through the link and spurred him on.

Behind him, he saw a light break through the night. He skidded to a stop and look back seeing the glow.

Kayleigh? It must be her! I should go back and make sure she is ... no I can't. That path is gone and I can't return. Danella needs me.

His decision made, he galloped on, still trying to accept Danella Lynch's return. *But how was it that I bonded with Kayleigh? How could she produce magic? I am no longer the unicorn that survived the death of my first rider and received a second one. I somehow had a second rider.*

He tried to reconcile Danella's actions. It didn't seem right for her to try and kill Kayleigh. The girl had done nothing to hurt her. She'd saved him from wallowing in self-pity. When he sensed her approach, Danella told him to wait for her. He thought it was to say goodbye. He was a fool.

What has happened to you, fair Danella? Why has your heart darkened?

She spoke of a master and that was troubling. Danella was a free and independent spirit. It didn't sound right and his rider was only half-conscious. No answers were forthcoming and his life was once again tied to his first rider, but he wondered where her life and loyalty belonged.

Who are these people who she owes allegiance to now? They are starting a war with the High-King. What do they hope to gain?

He accelerated, cursing his damaged hoof and following the tracks in the sand. It took a full hour to reach the wagons, the riders, and the other captive unicorn. Men held pungent herbs to her face to wake her. Vile tasting draughts were forced down Danella's throat. Majherri sensed rage and hatred directed at Kayleigh Reese before she passed out.

When she woke, Danella ordered two horsemen to turn around and make certain she was dead. He didn't like that order and told her as much.

"It's for the best, Majherri. I'm your rider and she isn't." Her honey-sweet voice dispelled most of his worries. If he wasn't so suddenly calm, he'd be concerned over how easily Danella could alter his mood. After using a second vial of healing tears on her wound, she brought him alongside the wagon containing the bound lieutenant. Her angry unicorn, Osalon, was attached by chain to the rear of the wagon.

"Lieutenant Townsend," his rider said, "Lead Senior Scout Danella Lynch at your service."

"I suppose ordering you to release me won't work, Lynch. May I ask what has happened to you, sister warrior?"

"I have been liberated."

"What does that mean?"

Danella wagged one of her fingers at the air maiden and said, "It is difficult to explain, so I won't even try. You'll see when your time comes."

"It's not too late, sister. Come back to us," Townsend implored.

"Look at you there, observing, calculating how you are going to make your escape. You appear to be cut from the same cloth as my sister, Meghan. I do look forward to that reunion."

"What of Reese? You swore she would be released. I see your betrayal runs so deep that lying has become second nature. Is that a benefit of you *liberation?*"

"It was no lie. The little thief was released from this life, or she soon will be."

"Your actions dishonor not only yourself, but they shame all of us as well."

Majherri could feel Danella's indignation. "Is that so? Well, I'll have to ask you to bear my share of this shame you speak of. I, for one, can't be bothered. You seem to be a likeable enough person, for an officer. Perhaps once you have pledged yourself to the Master's great cause, we will become comrades again."

"I'd rather die first."

"Pity, but then again you don't have a choice."

"I may be bound in these ropes, Lynch, but we both know who the real prisoner is, don't we? Do tell me of this Master – does he have a name?"

"Yes, but we are forbidden to speak his name with those who are not faithful to the cause."

"And what is the cause you speak of?"

"Nothing less than the salvation of the Blessed Continent, Lieutenant."

"You'll need more than just a handful of misguided tribesman, Lynch."

"The Master will provide. He always has."

"*Traitor! You've doomed my rider!*" Osalon exclaimed from the chain linking him to the wagon. The two females continued their conversation, but Majherri turned his attention to the shackled unicorn.

"*I did as I was commanded, by my rider.*"

"*The other girl is your rider.*"

"*No. That was a false bond. This is my rider. She is taking yours to meet her master.*"

"*Sandra will be no thrall! She is not weak, like the female riding you!*"

"*I would not be so certain, prideful male.*"

"*You disgust me, Majherri. You and your rider have betrayed us all!"*

Majherri felt a pang of guilt, but it was immediately replaced with anger. *"You and the rest of the Greater Herd turned their backsides on me! Did you vote to sanction any female that dared mate with me this past season?"*

"Your sister made a compelling case. It was the right thing to do."

"I'll wager she did. So, you admit that you were against me, but now try to shame me when I am obeying my rider. Whatever has changed her, it is impossible for me to refuse. I am compelled, but when you betrayed me, you acted with free will. Which of us should truly feel shame, Osalon?"

"Your rider appears to be lacking in free will also, Majherri. Should you not be trying to free her? Do you wish to see that happen to my rider as well?"

Majherri stiffened. *"I do not know what my rider needs. I've only just been reunited with her. If I can free her, I will. Though I wish you and your rider no harm, I'll not feel pity for what happens to you."*

"Your words leave a bitter taste in my mouth, Majherri. Our conversation is done."

"As you wish, Osalon."

Two days later, the caravan reached the Syetha oasis. During his prior days in the desert wastes, he and Danella had stopped here many times. Instead of the small collection of tents he recalled seeing here, there were hundreds, spilling out onto the sands. From the large numbers of women and children present, Majherri knew this was the rearguard and part of their supply lines.

Carts laden with clay jugs, filled with water moved eastward under the protection of mounted warriors. It was still roughly two days to Jaruciax, which Majherri realized was under siege. Danella was thinking about the siege as well and he felt her eagerness for battle.

Leaning down to his ear, she said, "Finally, I can prove myself worthy to the Master and it is all thanks to you. I called and you came back to me!"

Dominating one side of the oasis was a massive tent – one part bazaar and another part headquarters. That was their destination. It was the hub of all activity and Majherri prepared to face the person his returned rider called "Master."

Still feeling the sting of Kayleigh's dagger, Danella dismounted and led him inside the huge, fabric structure. A throne carved from a single piece of volcanic glass filled the center of the space. At the base of the throne was a small stone table with an empty circle-shaped inset. There were pillows there, positioned for a human to kneel in front of the table. The heady smell of incense permeated the room and made it difficult for Majherri to breath.

An acolyte, with a shaven head and arcane markings covering his face looked up from a scrying glass. "I alerted the Master that you would arrive yesterday. He is on his way back from the frontlines and will be amongst us shortly."

"Can you view the site of the ambush? I wish to know if my enemy is dead." Danella said.

"The release of magic in that area interferes with my perceptive skills, lady warrior. I will check again soon, but my priority is monitoring Jaruciax and ensuring that reinforcements are not coming to the city."

Majherri could tell that Danella was not satisfied with his answer, but she gave the impression that the sand sorcerer was closer to the Master than she was. "Thank you, noble sorcerer."

He nodded and bent back over his scrying glass, resuming his guttural chant.

Observing the proceedings, Majherri was impressed by the organization of this army. Whoever the Master was, he inspired those who toiled for him. Many had the blackened orbs for eyes, like his rider, but an equal amount did not. The sand sorcerer called out troop movements and two officers moved figurines around on the map.

"The west wall appears only lightly defended. I estimate only two companies of archers at this time. They continue to evacuate across the river, but there are only two barges in service. Given the size of the barges, it will take weeks to complete the evacuation. I will check the settlements to the south." He spun the ball set in the metal stand and watched as the images changed. "Yes, two days south along the river, I see three barges. One contains soldiers and the other two supplies. They are making their way north to the city. Deploy troops to kill the reinforcements and capture the supplies intact."

In reply to the wizard's words, one of the officers scribbled on a slip of paper and attached it to a messenger bird's leg and took the animal outside.

The man sprinted back in and exclaimed, "The Master comes!"

Most went to one knee as the officers held the two large flaps wide open. Majherri's view was blocked by the support poles for the tent. Something large enough to shake the ground landed and roared. In his heart, Majherri felt a twinge of fear. *This Master rides a flying beast! There are so few left in all the world.*

The creature lowered its body and crawled through the opening. It was massive, easily three times Majherri's size. The body and face were that of a lion, the mane was black and devoid of color. The eyes glowed with a vile red light as the rustlings of its black leathery wings folded to the side. The tail resembled that of the enchanted rock scorpions, except there was a glaze apparent on the tail barb indicating a lethal poison. The creature's walk was one of confidence. It declared itself to be the supreme force in this tent and dared anyone, animal or human to challenge it.

He has a manticore! There hasn't been a sighting of one since before I was born!

A large saddle, suitable for riding an elephant, was on the monster's back. There was a man in that saddle. Like the nomads, he was wrapped in cloth, except his was light brown mixed with a dark leather chest piece. Only his left eye was visible and it reflected that same red light.

"Greetings my faithful. It is good to be among you." The

wizard had a deep baritone voice. "The fight at Jaruciax goes well and we will soon control the city. It is as much your achievement as mine. Once we wrest the control of the river from that petty spell spinner, who masquerades as a king, we can use it to spread our holy message into the southern kingdoms and see our movement thrive."

There were tears in Danella's eyes and Majherri recoiled from the adulation he sensed from her. His hopes of helping his rider break free of this control sank. The man ascended his throne and was immediately brought platters of fruit by scantily clad women and listened to reports from his sorcerer and officers. He lounged, crossing one leg over the other knee and propping his chin up with a hand. He gave off the impression of a coiled snake, ready to strike at a moment's notice. The manticore curled up next to the throne as five platters laden with meat were set in front of it. Raising its head, it whimpered to the man, waiting for his permission. With a nod, the request was granted and the beast lurch forward and savagely attacked the meal.

Majherri listened. He wanted to know every detail. A scout's currency was information and he committed everything said to memory. He wasn't certain how he could use the information, but he needed to know as much as he could discover. Once again, he was shocked at the size and scope of this shadow army emerging like a frightening mirage from the desert heat.

After several others gave their reports, the Master turned to his rider and said, "Danella, my pretty, what have you there? Is that your unicorn?"

"Yes, Milord. With the help of Sorcerer Amir and the rituals you taught me, I was able to call to him when he entered the Portal. Reclaiming him from that peasant girl was no small challenge. She proved more resourceful than I thought."

"So she is dead, Danella?" The hypnotic quality of his voice sent a shiver through his rider. Majherri felt Danella's reaction to it.

"I am awaiting Amir's word, Master. I was injured and did not witness her death first hand."

He flicked his hand in irritation. "This displeases me. For your sake, I hope you have something else that does please me."

Fear and humiliation swirled inside his rider. "I understand, Master. But I have brought you another battle maiden and her unicorn to join our ranks. She is one of our officers and an air maiden. Once she has been liberated, she will be a valuable asset."

"Now that is good news, Danella. Your transgression is forgiven. Bring me my new warrior. Let us set her on the path to righteousness!"

Townsend was dragged in and over to the stone table. She cried out in pain as her arms were strapped down. The Master stood and descended the stairs. His acolyte, the man named Amir, hefted a large chest and opened it for his liege. A metal object, steaming with a thick, oily smoke was removed. It resembled a large incense burner. Glowing glyphs danced along the rusted surface and a rhythmic thumping sound was loud enough that he could hear it. Whatever was inside scared Majherri in ways the manticore couldn't approach. It was blind terror … and something he had felt before!

The device was placed into the circular inset on the table and two soldiers forced Townsend's head over it. The woman screamed and choked on the vapors.

"Easy, boy," Danella tried to calm him, but he wanted to leave the tent and was pulling her.

"Calm down, now! Be still!" He felt her force of will, backed by whatever magic she now possessed, overpower him through their bond. His resistance crumbled and could only stand there and observe the thrashing air maiden.

It went on for a few minutes before the wizard said, "Enough for today. You will eventually surrender to my control. I look forward to breaking you."

"Never!" Townsend spat bile at his feet.

"Such a brave woman – I salute your spirit, but you are delusional. Would you care to know what this is?" The Master asked gesturing to the object on the table. "It is the still beating heart of a nether-beast. The magic will corrupt you, just as it did Danella and the other seven of your sister warriors that fight alongside my army at this very moment. Soon, you will beg to join my cause. Guards, take her away. She needs to recover her strength before her next treatment."

Even Danella's willpower couldn't stop Majherri from rearing. This wizard had done the unthinkable and opened a rift to the nether realms!

The Master stopped and looked at Majherri. The eyes probed his soul. "Ah, you don't like it, Majherri. Bring him closer."

Danella commanded and his hooves grudgingly responded to her orders. The putrid smell made him nauseous. He looked into the metal container and saw the heart of darkness. The color was such a deep red that it was almost black. The thumping grew louder until it seemed like it was penetrating his body. Even so, Majherri's eyes were drawn to a tiny sliver of white piercing the infernal organ. The area around that piece of bone dripped ichor that hissed and pooled in the bottom of the cistern. Majherri quivered, both in rage and terror, as the flood of memories rushed back to him – the battle, the beast that wouldn't die, even with his horn piercing its chest. That tiny piece of bone … it would fit perfectly where the crack in his horn was.

His angry words slithered past the pounding in Majherri's ears. "Were it not for Danella's loyalty, you would already be killed, unicorn. Fortunately the beast has two more hearts, but the wound you inflicted forced me to send it back through the rift, where it recovers and waits for the stars to align. Your great victory was only a minor delay. Soon, I will call that beast back to me and the world will know that Count Darius has risen again. You'd best prove yourself worthy, Majherri. When my nether-beast returns, it will be hungry."

A line of humans were paraded in, all to kneel before the heart of darkness. Some succumbed almost immediately, while others fought against the control. Majherri wanted nothing more than to destroy that abomination, but Danella's control made it impossible.

The sand sorcerer motioned for his rider and she approached the scrying glass. Majherri tried to look around her, but couldn't. He did hear the man's cryptic words.

"Lady warrior, you may have a problem."

Chapter 28 – Loss Heartbreak and Forged Resolve

She woke to the relentless heat of the morning sun. Devastation surrounded her. The rocks bore horrible scorch marks and other than the patch of sand under her body, the nearby dessert had been turned into a sheet of glass. Her hand was sore from clutching the dagger for so long.

Kayleigh's clothes were in tatters and her dented and discarded helmet was partially melted. Choking back the bile in her throat, she looked at the bodies of the sand troll and the nomad warriors. Her explosion had taken them all out.

Forcing herself up, she staggered across the destruction. The weight of her steps cracked the glass sheet she'd created. She looked for anything salvageable, especially water canteens. There were a few weapons, but no water.

"All this!" She exclaimed to the heavens above. "All this and I'm still going to die in this cursed desert!"

The burning sun seemed not to care about her fate.

It felt foolish to continue speaking to the desert, but she did anyway. "I did fire magic, without my unicorn! I think I even did some water magic … hey, wait just a minute! If I did that, maybe I can do another water trick."

She cupped her hands together like she had seen Amanda Edwards do before and concentrated. Nothing happened for a moment, but then it felt as if the air was hotter and drier than before. This was offset by the dampness on her palms. Skeptically, she opened one eye and saw her hand was half-full with liquid. It was ambrosia to her parched mouth.

Walking twenty paces, she repeated her actions and was rewarded with a second handful of water. Her immediate problem was solved, but it once again raised questions about how she was able to do any magic, let alone water magic, without a unicorn. She searched for traces of the bond she shared with

Majherri. There was only her end, broken and frayed.

"Maybe I was really supposed to be a water maiden and it was only Danella's interference? Wouldn't Captain Lynch be shocked? No, that still doesn't fit. I can still do fire magic and it still doesn't explain where the magic is coming from. The only people who can do magic on their own, without a familiar to draw on are … no, that doesn't make sense. I couldn't be! Could I? Am I a sorceress? Does that mean I'm really not a battle maiden after all?"

The sun, the sand, and the bodies of the slain did not answer her questions. Kayleigh knew that whatever she was, this wasn't the place to ponder it. She needed to get moving and looked at her two choices.

She summoned another handful of water and drank it. *In that direction is Danella, Majherri, this Master person, and a large army. Maybe I could disguise myself and follow the tracks and try to free Majherri and the lieutenant. What are the odds I'll survive? Not very good.*

Frowning, she looked back over her shoulder. Behind me are seven trainees and a friend. Their only crime was being in the Portal when Danella summoned Majherri to her. I should rejoin them and see them safely out of this desert. If I really am a sorceress, I'll need to learn how to use my powers before I face Danella again.

"I'm sorry, Majherri. Saving you will have to wait. Now, all I need is a way to travel faster."

The desert answered as two horseback riders appeared on a nearby dune. They raised spears and raced toward her.

Next time, I'll be a bit more specific in my request! But they do have horses.

Kayleigh reflected on the changes in her over the last months and, more importantly, the last few days. If this were still Helden, she'd be running in terror and looking for a place to hide. Now, she was already wondering what supplies these riders had.

A burst of flame from her outstretched hand made both horses rear. One rider was thrown and she hurled her dagger at the second nomad. The blade struck true and the warrior fell to the ground.

The first nomad grabbed his spear and jumped to his feat as Kayleigh reformed the flaming blade in her hand. She looked into his eyes and saw they were normal, not pools of darkness. They were also full of fear. He was just a normal man, maybe even a boy.

She knew she could kill him, but she didn't have to. Kayleigh needed to make certain she was still capable of mercy. Making the fire around her knife larger she said, "There's been enough killing. If you get back up on that horse and ride away, you can live. Otherwise, you will die."

The nomad warrior lowered his spear and nodded. He backed away and grabbed for the reins of his horse.

"Wise decision. Assuming you tell them that I am still alive, tell Danella Lynch to start looking over her shoulder. I *will* find her one day and I *will* take Majherri back from her."

"I will deliver your message," he said quietly.

"Why do you fight for this Master?"

"He promises our people a better place in this world. He will lead us out of the desert and to a fertile land."

Her studies of leaders at The Academy came to mind. This was usually the hollow promise of someone who had no intention of keeping it. Yet people still fall prey to that lie. "You realize someone is probably already living in that fertile land?"

"You say my people do not deserve a better life, witch!" The rider growled his reply.

"A better life is earned. It can not be taken." Kayleigh quoted General Jyslin and wasn't sure how to react to being called a witch. If her suspicions were correct, she would have to get used to people calling her that.

The horseman turned and rode away as Kayleigh ensured the other rider was dead and tried to approach the remaining horse. The next ten minutes proved laughable as she attempted to get the reins. The horse was a female and finally let her near when Kayleigh summoned some water for it.

Swinging herself into the saddle, she saw water skins and a sack of dried meat and fruit. Uncertain of what the source of the meat was, she selected some of the fruit and put it in her mouth. The brown horse just stood there. She'd forgotten that a horse wasn't an intelligent unicorn.

"Oh right. Sorry, I've never really ridden a horse before. Alright, how do I make you go forward?"

Using her new abilities, she was able to make good time and keep both her and the horse she'd named "Brownie" watered. As expected, the trainees and Annabeth were nowhere in sight when she reached the previous campsite. Her clothes and other items were still there and Kayleigh could change out of the tattered rags she wore. Resting the horse, she waited for nightfall.

As the sun set, Kayleigh followed the tracks of the party. They were probably a full day ahead of her and she really wasn't able to fall asleep. Although, she was able to keep the horse watered, and that meant she should be able to gain ground on them.

She tried talking to the horse. It was lonely without the emotions of a bond and no other human company. Riding through the night, Kayleigh felt small and insignificant in the vast wasteland. As the sun came up, she prepared to stop, but noticed birds circling a few miles ahead. Fear replenished her fatigue as she kicked the beast into a gallop.

Please don't let it be them! Please don't let it be them!

She chanted that mantra as she covered the distance. Worst case scenarios ran through her mind like wild fire.

In the flatland in front of her, were the bodies of a dozen nomads. That wasn't the sight that sent a chill through her. What did was the lone unicorn standing over an unmoving body. Tears were forming and she didn't even know who it was yet.

With a heavy heart, she rode into the battle scene. The unicorn wasn't well and lowered its horn in a defensive manner as she approached.

The knot in Kayleigh's throat grew when she recognized the male unicorn. It was Rheysurrah. She dismounted and fell to her knees.

The tears lasted for minutes. The blame would last much longer. From the look in Rheysurrah's eyes, he blamed her as well. Kayleigh rose and walked to the body of her friend. The logical part of her mind reconstructed the battle scene. From the few bedrolls strewn over the ground, they were attacked while camping. Annabeth would have ordered the girls to run while she held them off. A glance at the tracks leading away showed that Annabeth had been successful, but paid the ultimate price.

She leaned down and closed the woman's eyes. "I'm so sorry, Rheysurrah. Maybe if I'd been here, this wouldn't have happened. This was all one horrible trap. Majherri's first rider never died. She's a thrall of this master person and they did something to make the Portal bring us here to the west. She snapped my bond with Majherri and took him with her. I could feel him fighting it, but she was too powerful. They captured Lieutenant Townsend and her unicorn. Did the rest of the trainees get away?"

The unicorn nodded.

At least Annabeth didn't die in vain.

"We can take her someplace better. I don't want to leave her or you out here in this forsaken place. I'll clean her up and tie her to you. Is that what you want?"

Again, Rheysurrah nodded. He seemed indifferent to her, which was a change from the earlier harsh gaze.

She removed the arrows from Annabeth's body and hoisted her onto Rheysurrah's saddle. It was difficult for her to do by herself and the effort left her panting. Clasping her hands together, she summoned water. Rheysurrah looked at her intently.

"That's the other thing I figured out. I don't really think I'm a battle maiden. I think I'm a sorceress. I might even be able to do some earth and air magic, but I never really spent much time watching them. Would you like some water?"

He moved closer. As his face brushed against her hands, she could sense his broken bond. It was a frayed rope dangling and slowly unraveling. In her mind, she could feel the strands. An idea came to her, but before she could do anything, he backed away.

"Rheysurrah! I might be able to save you. Danella said my bond with Majherri wasn't a real bond and she broke it. I might be able to make a bond with you."

The unicorn did not like the idea. When she stepped forward, he lowered his horn.

"So dying is the better option then? What would Annabeth say? What would she want you to do?"

He pawed the ground with his hoof and warned her to come no closer.

"Do you want to avenge her? I do! Do you want to make sure those trainees make it out of the desert alive? I do! Don't you want to know if you fathered a colt or a filly with T'rsa?"

Her argument seemed to have an effect on him. He raised his head and took a less threatening stance.

"I won't try it unless you agree, but I still have to secure her body. So let me approach. We need to start moving. You can decide along the way. It might not even work, but I'd like to try. You shouldn't have to die if you don't want to. I may even be able to learn how to cleanly break the bond at some point and you could go and find another rider."

Rheysurrah moved closer and allowed her to tie Annabeth's body across his saddle. She scrounged for supplies from the dead nomads and used some of the dried fruit to feed and water the wary unicorn.

Climbing into the saddle of Brownie, she led the unicorn in search of the other girls. The sun continued to lash out at them and Rheysurrah tired quickly. Kayleigh didn't realize that he'd stopped and had to turn back and ride for a quarter of a mile.

"Do you need some more water or food?"

He shook his head.

"We can break here, but that won't help us catch up to the others."

He shook his head and backed away a few more paces.

"What? You're just giving up! Do you really want to die in this desert, when you could still fight? My friend wasn't a quitter and I don't think you are either!"

He snorted.

"I loved her too. She was one of the few people that believed in me, treated me with respect, and helped me when others stood by and did nothing. You might think you're betraying her, but if I don't try to save you, I'm betraying her friendship and all the times she came to my aid. War is already here and I don't know if I'll ever get a chance to bond with Majherri again. I know I'll be able to try and forge a bond with another unicorn to spare it from the wasting. I'd rather save you. Will you please let me try?"

The unicorn stared into the sand for a full minute. He lifted his head and walked to her.

All she could say through her tears was, "Thank you."

Placing her hands on either side of his head, she closed her eyes and saw each side of the frayed ropes that symbolized their broken bonds. In her mind, she brought the ropes together and began the process of tying the frayed strands into one. A tingling feeling, like when a limb falls asleep spread over her body. She could feel Rheysurrah shudder also. The sensation spread and built as more strands came together. At some point, it was no longer her doing it, but the bond was taking on a life of its own. It was a beautiful and precious thing to behold. The last of the strands knotted and the finished product surged with energy sending both of them reeling.

Kayleigh opened her eyes. She looked a Rheysurrah and could feel his surprise. Standing, she brushed her clothes off and walked over to him. She ran her fingers through his mane and he did not rebel against her touch. The bond was successful. Her new unicorn would live.

When the sand started to give way to solid ground, they found a hill. Using Annabeth's sword, Kayleigh cut through the scrub brush and pushed it into a pile. She tied a rope to Rheysurrah and he pulled portions of downed trees into a pile. With the greatest of care, Kayleigh positioned Rider Welsh's body on the funeral pyre and said her goodbyes. Walking back a few paces, Kayleigh gave Rheysurrah the privacy to say his own farewells. She tended to the horse and waited.

A few minutes passed and her unicorn lifted his head and neighed loudly. Kayleigh walked back to him leading "Brownie" and tied the horse to the unicorn's saddle. Touching Rheysurrah's mane, she drew the magic connecting them and used that magical fire to light the wood.

As she stared into that cleansing flame, Kayleigh knew she was forever changed. She'd been weak and unprepared. Majherri was captured by the traitor Danella and Annabeth had perished. The other recruits were running scared and could be in grave danger.

"Never again!" she cried to the sky above. Her anger drove back her fear. The world didn't need another frightened trainee. It needed a warrior. Strife had come to the Blessed Continent and her powers would be needed – whether she could master them or not.

Mounting Rheysurrah, Kayleigh looked eastward, toward the slumbering kingdoms who were unaware of the danger facing them. She leaned forward and whispered in her unicorn's ear.

"Let's ride, Rheysurrah!"

About the author:

Jim Bernheimer is the author of the acclaimed thriller *Dead Eye: Pennies for the Ferryman*, and the short fiction anthology *Horror, Humor, and Heroes*. He lives in Chesapeake, Virginia with his wife Kim and two daughters, Laura and Marissa. Somehow, they put up with his foolishness. By day he is a Network Admin and runs his own computer consulting firm. Amazingly enough he also finds time to write.

Visit his website at
www.jimbernheimer.com